PROMISED

AN URBAN FANTASY

BOUND BY SHADOWS
BOOK THREE

ANN GIMPEL

CONTENTS

PROMISED

BOUND BY SHADOWS, BOOK THREE

Urban Fantasy

By

Ann Gimpel

Tumble off reality's edge into a cruel world where only the perfect are valued.

Copyright Page

BOOK DESCRIPTION, PROMISED

Magic runs strong in me, but power isn't enough.

Actually, these days nothing is enough. I've done a fine job alienating everyone who ever cared about me, from the witches in my Coven to the man I love to my wolfie familiar. Mother's familiar left, winging a path to Faery. My wolf made it abundantly clear he'd have gone with her except the familiar bond doesn't allow that level of latitude.

He howled up a storm about being stuck with me, and then quit talking.

Meanwhile, the babe growing within me is equally silent. He misses Damien's soothing voice, mandolin, and Fae love. I'm under a geas to return my son to Faery the second he's born. Ha! They'll have to find me first. No power words in the universe will make me relinquish my boy.

Hecate still rattles around in my mind. I'm done with her. If I hadn't allowed her in, I'd still be in Faery with Damien's arms around me.

Woulda. Coulda. Shoulda. Talk is cheap.

Pregnant. Nowhere to call home. No money. Nothing but my magic. Somehow, it will have to carry us through.

BOOKS IN THE BOUND BY SHADOWS SERIES

Scarred, Book One
Cursed, Book Two
Promised, Book Three

AUTHOR'S NOTE

When I finished Grigori, last of the Circle of Assassin books, I surveyed my newsletter subscribers to determine what to write next. I may have gone overboard this last Black Friday, but I now have covers for three very different series. Covers are always an author's rate-limiting step, so I stock up when I can.

The consensus amongst my newsletter group was they wanted the misfit witch series. A reaper series, Urban Sisters, came in second. A dystopian series, Shattered Worlds, was a distant third. Gosh, wonder if I'll ever get around to writing that one.

I love plotting out brand new series. Who will the characters be? Where will it take place? Will the world be open (e.g. humans know about magic) or closed? Will there be portals?

So many directions.

Books one and two are done. Onward to *Promised*, book three of Bound by Shadows. Whole lot of loose ends to tie up.

CHAPTER I
MORGAN

I left Faery in a huff because I was too humiliated to endure the expression on Damien's face a moment longer. Betrayal had twisted his features into harsh planes that shattered my world. My temper has never been my friend, and I was devastated—and mortified—he'd uncovered my secret.

To avoid lashing out and accusing him of snooping where he had no business, I took off. Not that I had any moral high ground, none at all. I was at fault. No apology in the world would make up for this particular fall from grace.

Keeping Hecate's visits to my psyche under wraps was unrealistic; thinking I could was stupid. It wasn't that I never planned to reveal her presence, but I needed more time. Damien had nearly died because of a plot spawned by witches and the Greek gods.

Except he's convinced Hecate was behind it.

I didn't know anymore. About much of anything. She

swore she was innocent, but she's scarcely an uninterested party in this game. She's locked behind iron shielding on a border world.

I'm her only hope of escape. At least, that's her story.

"You sure fucked that up," Zeke snarled, not bothering with mind speech. His words were garbled, but after all the centuries we've spent together, I don't have trouble understanding him. He's a huge white wolf and my bonded familiar.

"How could you?" Sita squawked and came as close as she ever has to jamming her beak into me. A large hawk with russet plumage, she'd been Mother's familiar.

We weren't far from the veils separating Earth from Faery, mostly because I had no idea where to go. Part of me hoped Damien would come after me, but a bigger part knew he never would. I'd wounded him beyond forgiveness. All he wanted was to rip our child from my womb and get on with his life.

Could I make my familiars understand my side of the equation? Both of them were glaring at me. It was worth a shot, but animals place loyalty above all else. From their perspective, mine should have favored Damien. Instead, I'd snuck behind his back to visit Hecate.

"I felt torn," I began. "She formed me from her own essence."

"So?" Sita clacked her beak. "Not as if you didn't have a perfectly good mother."

Ouch. I winced. Mother was dead. Because of me. So far, Sita had avoided casting blame. I girded myself for a barrage of accusations.

Tears threatened to spill over. I truly was cursed. The witch who'd thrown it in my face spoke true.

"You should have told Damien." Zeke's howl was full of reproach.

"I was hunting for the right time—"

"The only time was right after she showed up," Sita cawed. "I'm done. Your mother would be appalled by your behavior."

"Done? What do you mean?" My voice shook.

"I'm going back to Damien." Screeching like a mad thing, she wheeled and flew toward the veils. They parted to allow her passage, something they'd never done for me unless a Fae unlocked them.

"I'd go too, if I could." Zeke turned his back on me, hackles fully displayed.

"I won't hold you," I said stiffly. If I was going to lose everything, I may as well get it over with.

"Unlike you"—he was still snarling—*"I value honor above my own desires."*

Aw crap. Could he have lobbed his blow any harder? I already felt like the lowest of the low.

"What's the point if we can't work together?" My words were ragged because my throat housed an enormous lump.

"I will do what I must, but nothing more. Stop talking. You disgust me."

I sank into a crouch, hands folded over my belly, but the usually chatty babe was silent as well. They all hated me, but I deserved it.

"You handled that splendidly, my dear." Hecate was back, sounding positively jovial. So delighted, perhaps she'd

dropped the idea to spy on my dreams into Damien's head.

"Go away," I moaned.

"You don't mean that. We're finally rid of that pesky Fae. Now we can get down to the real work."

"Which is?" I inquired acidly.

"I can't believe you even asked that," Zeke growled.

Come to think of it, neither could I.

"I'm confused," I told the witch goddess. "Until I see a clear path forward, I'm not doing anything for you."

"Confused about what?" Compulsion, warm as heated mead, swirled through my mind.

"Everything. Who you are. Whose side you're on. Whether you were responsible for Damien's accident." I was on a roll, so I kept on going. "I don't know you—at all. You plotted with Mother to create me, and then you were gone."

"You know I was held against my will." More compulsion, slithery and inviting.

I wound a ward around my mind.

"I don't know anything. Surely, there was a window between my making and your imprisonment. Yet, you did nothing. Leave me alone. I know where you are if I change my mind."

"I'm the only one who can mitigate the geas, so we can keep your son."

"We?" I yelped. "What in the fuck do you have to do with him?"

"Why I'd planned on raising him with you. Male witches have untapped power. Nearly as potent as your own. Speaking of which—"

I snugged up the weave of my ward and blocked her. It would hold for a while, but not forever.

"No need to put on an act on my account." Zeke still faced away from me.

"I'm not putting on an act," I protested. "She's how I got into this mess, and—"

"No. You're how you got into it," Zeke spoke over me.

Out of the mouths of wolves.

"We can debate this later. I'm going to find a place to hole up for a few days."

"Did you take the Fae money?"

He was referring to a sack containing money, ID, and credit cards the Fae had given me before one of my sojourns. I shook my head. "Of course not. What do you take me for?"

He shrugged his furry shoulders. *"Not sure who you are. Still figuring it out."*

His words cut deep. Trust is a funny thing. Until it's gone, you assume it has resilience when it's actually as fragile as butterfly wings.

Zeke fell silent. I played options through my mind. The boardinghouse where I'd met Damien was out. I'd killed five witches there, and the local Paranormal Detective Agency was keeping a close eye on the place. Maybe the cabin in the southern Cascades where we'd gone right after that could work. Damien had known about it, but it wasn't "his" place.

He'd never look for me there.

Hell, he wasn't ever going to seek me out again. The reality carved a hole in my heart. I'd loved him. Still did, and I probably always would. Wanting nothing more than to fall on my face and lick my wounds, I gathered the strands of a journey spell, calling them to me.

"Where are we going?" Zeke sounded suspicious.

"The cabin where we went after we left the boardinghouse. Do you have a better idea?" I've always included him in important decisions, and I wasn't about to stop now.

He didn't answer, so I edged nearer to him and launched my casting.

Moments later, we emerged into midafternoon sunshine in front of the primitive hut where we'd stayed before. This would be hard. Damien's scent still lingered in the air. It would be thicker inside. Not ready to face never holding him again, I sat on the front steps, folded my arms across my knees, and laid my head over them.

Zeke ran off, presumably to hunt. Or because he couldn't stand being near me. No one else could. Why should he be any different?

A presence skulked at the edges of my ward. Hecate. Damn it. She'd never give up no matter how many ways I said no.

"May as well get used to it," I muttered and got to my feet. I could do a better job holding her at bay inside because I'd wrap enchantment around the building. It would add space around me, which should make it more difficult for her to penetrate my warding.

I scanned the wooded glen around the cottage. Birds dotted tree branches. Rabbits popped their heads up from time to time. I should do a spot of hunting, but food was the last thing on my mind. Anything I ate would probably come right back up the shape my gut was in.

Eventually, I'd have to do my best to choke something down for the child. I placed protective hands over my gently swelling belly. I was about three months along. Witch pregnancies are usually ten months with mortal fathers. Hard to say how long this one would last.

Reaching inward, I searched for my son's mind. It was closed to me. After weeks of open communication, his abrupt dismissal poured salt into my raw emotions.

He'd heard Damien's power words, knew he'd leave my side as soon as the Fae could track me down. Was he in favor of jettisoning me as soon as my job as womb-mistress was done?

Awk. Did any of it even matter?

I've been a lot of things through the long years of my life, but dispirited isn't one of them. I've always picked myself up, dusted myself off, and played the ball where it lay. Even Mother's death didn't flatten me like Damien's dismissal and my familiar's harsh words.

"Stop. Just stop." I spoke aloud to steady myself and trudged up the cabin's few steps. The door was sealed with magic: Damien's magic. I stopped to inhale the pine forest scent of his workings.

Tears welled. I brushed them aside, broke the seal, and walked within.

Nothing had changed. A small stack of my possessions, my notebook, and some of Damien's magical accoutrements were still here, protected by magic I'd layered over them. A scrap of paper I'd left for him that said, *Looking for you* had been tucked over the mantle.

Hecate was close. Too close.

My first order of business was blocking her out of my business. I took more care than I do with most of my castings, winding layer upon layer around the humble hut. When I was done, I couldn't sense her.

Misery gnawed a hole in my soul. I sank into the only chair. An image of sharing it with Damien while he held me close mocked me. Since I couldn't obliterate it, I let it float by.

I must have dozed because the angle of light filtering through the only window had sharpened, changed when I next looked at it. Zeke wasn't back. Who knew if he'd ever return.

Loyalty be damned. He could have easily changed his mind.

On my feet, I layered kindling into the fireplace and lit it with a thought. Once it was burning well, I added one of two larger pieces from the hearth. I'd have to go outside and gather more wood, or it would be a chilly night.

Outside held risks.

If I was quick, perhaps Hecate wouldn't notice I'd emerged from my cocoon.

Fat fucking chance. She's nothing if not opportunistic as hell. About the only constant in her longwinded diatribes, peppered with visions of retribution, was that she needed my magic to extricate herself from a borderworld. She couldn't force my cooperation, but she could make my life a living shitshow when I kept on refusing.

Determined not to let her rule my life, I wrapped my mind in shielding and marched out of the cabin. For a few minutes, I thought I'd outfoxed her, but on my third trip gathering downed wood, the telltale scratching started again.

I hustled up the steps thinking I really should call Zeke. He was a weak spot, one she could leverage against me. Maybe. Unsure how long her current reach was, I went with "better safe than sorry," raised my mind voice, and called my familiar.

He didn't answer, but I hadn't expected him to.

Heart thudding against my ribcage, I tried again. This time, I added to my sending. *"Please. It's not safe."*

Even with him furious at me, he was still my responsibility. I didn't tell him that. It would have wounded his pride—and made him even less likely to come to me.

I dumped the armload of wood inside the door and stood on the porch scanning every nook and cranny in thick foliage as light leached out of the day. With each passing minute, panic threatened to swamp me.

I could not lose Zeke, no matter how he felt about me. I'd told him to leave, but I hadn't meant it. Not really. Hecate wasn't above using him as a pawn to get to me.

He and I should have talked about that.

Raising a fist, I shook it at the sky. "If you fuck with me," I gritted, "I will never help you do shit. Leave my familiar out of this."

"I made him too." Her voice was faint, but she'd broken through.

Goddamn it.

A flurry of white fur burst into the clearing. I ran to him. "Are you all right? She didn't hurt you, did she?"

He tossed a blood-streaked snout. *"A bit late to care about unintended consequences, isn't it?"* After shaking himself from nose to tail tip, he stalked past me and up the stairs.

"Leave us the hell alone," I shouted and bounded into the cabin, slamming the door and resurrecting the spell encompassing the shelter.

Zeke glared at me from a corner. He lay with his head on his paws and cleaned gore off his fur. Appeared the hunting had been a success.

At least one of us had a full belly. Except I still didn't feel the least bit like eating.

"Don't be selfish. The child needs food."

I busied myself stacking wood on the hearth and feeding the fire. "I'll eat tomorrow."

"How long will we be here?"

"I don't know. Not long. I'll work on a more permanent solution."

"Here is all right. Lots of game." Done cleaning himself, he curled into a ball and shut his eyes.

He'd weighed in.

There were worse places. I picked through the small bundle of possessions we'd left the first time I was here. Nothing had changed.

After plucking a few crystals from Damien's stash, I tucked them close to my body, wrapped myself in a thick coat, and returned to the chair, leaving the bed for Zeke if he wanted it.

Notebook and pen in hand, I settled in to write an

honest account of Hecate's visitations. When she first showed up, what she'd said, what I replied. If the notebook ever fell into Damien's hands, he'd have the truth.

All of it.

To ensure believability, I laced a truth spell into the pages. It would glow, proving the veracity of my words.

Bending to my task, I began.

The first night we moved back into your rooms after your illness, Hecate came to me. She expressed joy about your recovery and about our unborn son. She told me witches and the Greeks had finessed the barrier that was nearly the death of you.

I had no reason to disbelieve her...

CHAPTER 2

DAMIEN

Maeve insisted I accompany her to the council chamber. What had she meant by knowing more than I imagined? Sita reappeared in record time after Morgan left. The hawk clung to Maeve like a lifeline. I readied myself for whatever the Fae council had in mind. They wouldn't exile me—at least I didn't believe they would.

My only sin was loving Morgan—and inviting her into our midst. Hell, at one point, Logan, the head of our council, and Maeve were pushing the mating ceremony down our throats. I'd been all for it. Morgan, not so much.

A plus given the current turn of events.

My head still spun from my inadvertent discovery of Hecate in Morgan's dreams. I'd expected the witch goddess would make another appearance, given her less-than-stellar track record of showing up at the least convenient time and sowing havoc.

What knocked the wind out of my sails was Morgan holding secrets around Hecate's presence. Why would she do such a thing? Hecate had nearly been the death of me. She'd also been behind both familiars being kidnapped.

A brisk finger snap from a few meters ahead told me to step it up.

It wasn't that I didn't want to face the council, but I'd have appreciated a window to pull myself together. My emotions were raw, and I needed time to lick my wounds.

I thought I knew Morgan.

Ha! Wrong on that one. I hadn't known her at all.

At least our child would come home to Faery where he could be raised by my kinsmen. I'd made certain of it by snaring him in a geas. It would alert me the moment of his birth and pinpoint his location.

Morgan wouldn't give him up without a fight, but she'd have no choice. The geas bound her as well. She'd tried to apologize, but it was hollow, forced. She'd been caught in a deception of the highest magnitude, and—

"Get in here," Logan roared.

I hustled forward. My pace had slowed to something approximating a sluggish glacier. Carved double doors slammed shut behind me. Magic shot past, sealing me within.

Hell, who thought I was about to make a run for it?

Stopping a meter from the lintel, I scanned the large chamber. For once, its tasteful appointments—marble, crystal, woven wall hangings—didn't soothe my spirit. The dozen council members were arranged around a rectangular table. No other Fae were in attendance.

Someone, probably Logan, had decided to limit my public humiliation.

The far end of the room took on a numinous glow. Hermes and Hera stepped through a gently glowing portal. Shock punched me in the guts. They had a dog in this fight, but I'd seen more of them recently than during my millennia of existence.

Hermes was tall, regal, and bare-chested. Buff-colored leather breeks hung low on his hips. Flaxen hair cascaded to waist level; ice-blue eyes glared disapprovingly. A squared off chin and high forehead lent him a patrician air. About the same height as Hermes, Hera wore a simple lavender gown that ended at her knees. Old-fashioned lace-up tan leather boots covered her feet and calves. A copper torc circled her neck. Dark hair fell to shoulder level; silver eyes examined the chamber. Her nostrils twitched as if she'd smelled something disagreeable.

The gods never did like to hobnob with mere mages.

I rolled my shoulders back, stood tall, and nodded at them. "Been a while," I said.

"I don't believe we've met." Hera looked down an aquiline nose at me.

"You'd left," Hermes told her and directed his next words at me. "I thought we had an understanding, Fae."

"Oh, and what precisely was it?" Gods or no, I wasn't about to back down.

"That you'd stay out of our business."

"I thought I was."

"Pfft." Hera waved a dismissive hand. "Since when is inviting Hecate into your midst—"

"I didn't," I broke in. It was rude, but I was beyond caring. My heart hurt, and I'd be damned if I'd let anyone throw shade on me.

"Then how'd she gain entrance to Faery?" Hermes arched fair brows.

"It was Morgan's doing. She is gone."

Hera turned her hands palms up. "Convenient. Gone where?"

"I have no idea. I was in the process of kicking her out when she vanished. She won't be back."

"How do you know?" Hera inquired.

"Because she's deeply ashamed and can't face me." I blew out a breath. "Also, I laid claim to our son—"

"There is a son?" Hermes bellowed. "How could you let that happen?"

I'd punched him before and was tempted to do so again. My hands balled into fists. "Not seeing how it's any of your affair."

"Oh you're not," he tossed back in a singsong voice.

I turned away, intent on leaving. The Fae council was one thing, but I wasn't sticking around to be mocked.

"Stay put," Logan ordered.

"Why? You scarcely need me for—"

A truth net materialized out of nowhere and clanked around me. Could today get any worse? First Morgan's betrayal, and now my own kinsmen not trusting me.

"Did you know about Hecate's visitations to Morgan?" Logan asked.

"No." The weave surrounding me pinged with a sour undernote. The damned things were literal as fuck. "Let me amend my response," I said. "I did not know until this morning. The second I found out, I took action."

"He speaks true," Sita trilled from her spot in Maeve's arms.

Apparently satisfied, the truth net chimed happily. Once it finished singing, it clattered to the floor. Whoa. Whole lot of magical expenditure for a single question.

I glanced from the Greeks to the council.

"You must neutralize the geas around the boy," Hermes announced.

"Aye, do it now with us as witnesses," Hera urged.

I've never been especially compliant, and I wasn't about to start now. "I'll do no such thing. In the first place, that casting isn't reversible."

"You must," Maeve said.

"Why?" I'd already said it wasn't possible. Why was she belaboring the point?

Hera snorted and raised her hands. Hermes knocked them aside. "Smiting him accomplishes naught. Besides, we need him."

I didn't care for the sound of that. Dancing attendance on anyone, let alone a Greek god, rankled. What in the hell had happened to the council's plan to raise a couple of Celts to stand in on our side?

"Have you ever wondered why there are no male witches?" Maeve asked.

"No, but my son will be half Fae."

"And half witch," Hermes noted grimly.

"Not seeing the problem." Annoyance sharpened my tone.

"Male witches carry perverse power," Maeve explained. "I didn't know until I searched for answers."

"Define perverse."

"Their affinity is to sorcery, dark power."

I shrugged. "Seems like they'd fit right in with the current Coven structure. Nearly every witch I've come across has been turned to evil." Before Maeve could say more, I continued. "It's moot. The child is my son. I will see him raised properly."

"And if his enchantment merges with darkness?" Logan's question was stern.

"I'll cross that bridge when I get there."

"You cannot raise him in Faery," Logan went on. "Too risky."

They were going to exile me, after all. Good to know where I stood. "Fine. I've lived among mortals for long periods. I can do it again."

"How?" Maeve skewered me with her blue gaze. "The Paranormal Detective Agency issued a BOLO for you."

Mmph. I'd forgotten about that little wrinkle. "I'll come up with something. Perhaps a long-lasting glamour and a new set of ID."

I've always bought such items off the dark web, but Logan had presented Morgan with a driver's license and credit cards. If my kinsmen were inclined, they could save me a couple thousand bucks. Now didn't seem the time to be making requests, though.

"Relinquish the geas." Hermes was at it again.

"A. It's not possible. B. I've already refused. C. Not likely to change my mind."

Hera strode to Logan and thwacked him across the shoulders. "He's your creature. Do something."

"Doesn't work that way in Faery," Logan mumbled.

"Fine. We'll take him with us, then," Hera announced.

"I don't think so." Maeve stepped between me and the goddess. Sita left her arms and flew to my shoulders cawing stridently.

Logan stood. He has plenty of backbone when he chooses to exercise it. "Damien's son is a Fae affair. With the grace and assistance of Faery, we'll handle it."

"How?" Hermes demanded.

"We're not leaving until we're satisfied," Hera added.

"Aye, you are," Logan glanced from one to the other. "We did not invite you. If I inform Faery you are not welcome, she will see you to her gates."

Crap. Much as I wanted to see the Greeks taken down a peg, I did not want them to rain war on my people. Raising my hands, palms out, I said, "No reason for this discussion today. The child has many months yet before he's born. As an infant and small child, he will not be a threat. It will provide ample opportunity to assess the quality of his magic —and his soul."

After a measured breath, I went on, "None of us condone gratuitous killing based on incomplete data, and—"

"He's already ensorcelled you," Hera announced.

Had he?

I shrugged. "I will admit the possibility. Still, it's remote. "Ensorcelled me for what purpose?"

"Why to inveigle his way inside Faery."

"Except I won't be here," I reminded her.

"At some point you will be," she insisted.

I blew out a breath. "What exactly will he do inside Faery? I have a link with the land, and she's not warning me."

"Hecate will be with him, and—"

"Have you seen this in a vision?" Maeve cut in.

"More or less," Hera mumbled.

"It's a yes or no question," Maeve said. "Your ability is strong, but I do not believe it extends to prophecy."

"Hecate is thrilled about her grandson," Hermes said. "When we intercept her thoughts, they're full of him and how she plans to use him to further her ends."

"You cannot predict his response," Maeve insisted. "Of all the possible futures shown to me, them working in concert is not one of them."

"Maybe you didn't look deep enough," Hera huffed.

"This conversation is over." Logan didn't raise his voice, but he didn't need to. "Either you leave on your own, or I will instruct Faery to escort you beyond our borders."

"You wouldn't." Hermes looked as shocked as he had the time I punched him. Probably no one ever told him no.

"Watch me. The Fae appreciate your concern…"

"But it's premature," Maeve finished for him.

The air around me prickled unpleasantly. They'd threatened to haul me with them. Had they expected me to trundle along like a trussed goose? Maeve's injunction hadn't hit home. Neither had Logan's warnings.

I didn't require protectors. Nothing wrong with my skill. I wove warding around myself and Sita.

"Good call," the hawk croaked.

"We won't harm you." Hermes sounded wounded.

"I already told you. I cannot undo the geas. If you choose to, the odds of locating my son will all but vanish. At least this way, I will know when he's born and roughly where he is."

"Bah. Hecate will lead us right to him," Hera insisted.

"Maybe," I replied. "You're banking on her still being your prisoner and Morgan cooperating with her."

"Why would either of those things change?"

"She escaped once," I reminded Hera. "Could happen again, and Morgan is an unknown. She may well have already decided the price of collaboration was far too high."

"She betrayed you, and you're defending her?" Logan shook his head.

"She made a rather big mistake, but I have faith in her to recognize it." My words surprised me. What was more astonishing was I believed them.

"We have Fae business to conduct," Logan informed the two Greeks. "If you do not leave now, I will ensure you cannot waltz in here unannounced again."

"You're making a mistake." Hermes joined Hera and draped an arm around her.

"If it gets you out of our hair, I'll risk it." Logan's tone was acidic.

"You have not heard the end of this issue," Hermes muttered.

"I'm certain that's true," Logan replied.

With the tip of his index finger, Hermes scribed a portal. He and Hera stepped through. The shimmering gateway winked out behind them.

Breath swooshed from Maeve. "Damn it. I didn't think they'd ever go away."

"What happened to your plan to gather a few Celts to our cause?" I asked.

"It got sidelined after your injury," one of the council snapped.

"We've never needed them before," another council member pointed out followed by something that sounded like I was nothing but trouble.

"If you don't require me, I'll be on my way," I said.

"To where?" Maeve shot a pointed look in my direction.

"Not sure. Back to Earth somewhere. I'll change my appearance and name."

"The PDA can see through glamours," she reminded me.

"Only if they're looking," I shot back. "I've been MIA for months. Surely, the heat has died down to some extent."

"And the geas?" Logan furled both brows.

"It stands," I said firmly. "If it were your child, would you do any less?"

"None of us mate outside the blood," he reminded me.

"Better if you remain," Maeve said.

It's always interesting when the seer weighs in. She knows more than she reveals, but it's impossible to sort whether her suggestions come from future-seeing or some other place.

"Better for whom?"

"Why you, of course."

The way I was feeling, I could easily retreat to the *Dreaming* and sit out a century or two licking my wounds. If I did, I'd miss my son's birth and his formative years. If what the Greeks inferred was even partially true, the child might have to be destroyed.

Would I be capable of it?

Might not come to that. The *Dreaming* holds dungeons where Sidhe and Fae miscreants occupy cells. It was a far more palatable option. So long as our power trumped his, and he couldn't get away.

Talk about getting ahead of the game.

"I am leaving," I told everyone.

A few mumbled "good riddances" cut me to the quick. The council was blaming me for Morgan's defection. They felt the need to condemn someone, and I was a convenient scapegoat.

"I would like to access Faery's library from time to time. Perhaps clues exist regarding Morgan's child."

"I've been searching," Maeve said.

"Doesn't mean it's not there," I countered.

When I turned to leave this time, the double doors swung inward. I strode through.

"Do you really think she's seen the error of her ways?" Sita chirped.

Naturally, she was talking about Morgan. "I hope so, but I will not seek her out."

"Zeke would like it if we did."

I didn't reply until we reached my rooms and I was safely within, away from prying ears. "I need time," I told the bird. "For now, I'll establish a new identity, find a job and a place to live. We'll see what happens after that."

"May I come with you?"

It was an oddly formal request. "Of course. It would be safer for you to remain in Faery, though."

She left my shoulder and flew to a bureau where she perched on the edge. "You need me."

I opened my mouth to protest but shut it quickly. I had no idea what I needed, but keeping Sita close felt right.

"Thank you."

I stripped off my clothes, intent on cleaning up before I tossed a few things into a bag. No one bothered me or showed up to try to change my mind. Perhaps the "good riddance" crew had prevailed.

When I was toweling off, I noticed a small stack of things that hadn't been on the desk before. Closer inspection revealed a driver's license, passport, and a couple of credit cards. My new name was Clive Underhill. Clever since many call Faery by that name.

Gratitude cracked my wounded heart wide open. My people might be spun out about the specter of a demon child, but they believed in me enough to provide support.

"Who left these?" I asked Sita.

She rearranged her feathers. "Not a person. They just plopped down there."

Hmmm. The Fae would still help, but no one wanted to get too close.

In short order, I was dressed with a small valise packed. Returning to Seattle wasn't wise. Portland was too close.

"How do you feel about northern Arizona?" I asked the hawk.

"So long as the hunting is good, I'm all for it," she squawked.

Gathering power to me, I set a spell to take us to Flagstaff, a small enough town perhaps the PDA wouldn't be especially active. It was also growing quickly, which meant construction jobs would be easy to find. Logan may have given me credit cards, but I could earn my own way.

I'd only use them to get my new life off the ground.

Once we were in the journey channel, I went to work on my appearance. When I was done, I was about five foot ten with cropped auburn hair and a slender build. I left my green eyes the same. As an afterthought, I addressed the ear problem, shaving the points off them.

Ready as I was likely to be, I stepped out of my spell ready to craft a new life for myself and Sita. "I'm grateful you're here," I told her.

"Feel the same about you."

We stood in the desert a couple of miles north of town. I swung the valise's strap over a shoulder and started for the outskirts of Flagstaff. Sita flew ahead, diving to grab a mouse from time to time.

The best part of the past hour was I'd barely thought about Morgan at all. No matter if she eventually came around—or not—I'd get through this. I had to. Someone had to protect my son from those who'd see him dead or imprisoned before he so much as drew his first breath.

CHAPTER 3

MORGAN

Time passed. I finished writing in the notebook. Everything was there. All of it, from Hecate's first contact to her last when Damien apprehended us.

At least a week went by before it occurred to me to keep track of time. Depression hung over me like a black cloud no matter how I tried to kick its ass the hell out of there. Just getting up and moving took almost more discipline than I had, but I felt better outside—even if it was raining. I had no appetite. Chronic exhaustion dogged me, yet, when I lay down to sleep, it too eluded me.

Zeke only spoke when he had to. The babe remained silent.

Hecate had also adopted a lower profile. Was she going around me to get to my son? With her blood ties, it was possible. The thought was so unsettling I warded my womb. She hadn't exactly given up on me, but her onslaught slowed.

It also changed from her cheerful, "you and me against the world, kid," to something far darker and more menacing. I still couldn't believe I'd been taken in by her pleasantries and promises. My gullibility had cost me dearly. At night, when I lay on the lumpy mattress not sleeping, Damien's face haunted me. The expression he'd worn once the full extent of my perfidy came to light wouldn't go away.

I'd have given anything to beg forgiveness and smooth the lines in his forehead. No second chances. He'd slammed the door on me. Rightfully so. I'd have done the same were our positions reversed.

Zeke dropped rabbits in the middle of the room, his hint that starving myself was a bad plan. Of course, he was right. I've always been far too thin, and now I was eating for two. I laid a hand over my gently swelling belly. Before, when I'd done that, the child had cooed. Not any longer.

Were it not for the life force thrumming within, I'd have wondered if he'd died. Beyond television, I knew very little about trauma in families. Babies raised in the Coven had a hundred mothers. Protected from dissent and smothered with love, we taught them magic from the time they could walk.

The females, that is. Males never made it much past conception.

My babe had to be reacting to the harsh words between Damien and me. Perhaps to whatever Hecate had planted in his tiny mind. I sent soothing thoughts inward; they didn't make a dent in his silence. It was as if his heart had broken right along with my own.

Zeke seemed content, if distant. Our days fell into a pattern. We'd wake with first light, and he'd leave to hunt not returning until dusk. During the day, I gathered wood for the evening fire and hauled water from a nearby creek. The woods were full of edible grasses and herbs. I plucked them for additions to rabbit stew.

Occasionally, Zeke dragged part of a young deer carcass into the yard for me to skin out and prepare.

Hecate had to know where I was, yet no one came for me. Who would she tell? Certainly not her captors. From her perspective, I might be alienated now, but I was still her best —or only—chance of escape.

Perhaps I'd been onto something about her going around me to my son. Protections circling my womb should have put a stop to it. Since I wasn't certain she'd approached him, it was impossible to tell if my precautions made the slightest difference.

Before, I'd been able to communicate with him. I considered asking if his grandmother was around, but didn't. He was distressed enough without me grilling him.

The season was changing from the cold months to warmer ones. I could conceivably remain here until winter set in. By then, the babe would be born.

Yeah, and then Damien would show up. I'd been cocky as hell telling him he'd have to find me to pry the child out of my hands, but it had been empty rhetoric. No matter where I was, even on a distant borderworld, the geas would lead him right to me.

I didn't know much about that casting, but Hecate had shrieked its reality right after Damien drilled into my body.

Finding the geas was simple, but try as I might, I couldn't remove it. Not without emptying the contents of my belly— and murdering our child.

He'd known I'd never do that.

The geas cut both ways. A pathetic part of me didn't care how it happened. I longed to see Damien again no matter what the circumstances were.

Sad, huh?

I thought I'd been alone after the Coven booted me, but then I'd had Zeke. Soon into my exile, Damien showed up.

I hadn't appreciated the full extent of what it meant to be alone.

Until now.

More time passed. Over a month since we'd arrived here. The days were decidedly warmer. Zeke was too. My sustained avoidance of Hecate must have reassured him of my intentions. Our relationship was nothing like it had been, but he'd taken to sleeping next to me. His simple animal warmth allowed me to sleep more deeply than I had since this whole mess began. Before he shared my bed, I hadn't slept at all.

"Thanks for forgiving me," I said one evening as we sat on the front porch soaking in the last rays of the setting sun.

"You're earning my trust back," he woofed.

I ruffled his fur. One out of two since the child remained stubbornly silent no matter what I said or sang or thought. He was growing quickly, the lump of my abdomen obvious and requiring adjustment of my clothing.

A bold thought hit me between the eyes. "We could return to the boardinghouse," I murmured.

"How? You killed all those witches."

"Yes, but the PDA believes Damien did it. No one suspects me."

"Don't you like it here." He angled his head to one side and gazed at me through his mismatched eyes, twin to my own.

"I do, but I'm lonely."

"The one you really want is Damien, and he won't be at the boardinghouse. Not this time."

I cringed. Zeke is eerily perceptive.

"The cook was kind to me. So was the proprietor, once he got past believing I was a supernatural creature."

"It's harder for me to hunt there."

"We won't leave here if you don't want to. Not until much later in the year when it gets really cold."

"I'll think about it." He laid his big head on outstretched paws.

Maybe another week dribbled by. One night, I was jolted awake. Zeke, whose senses are considerably more acute than mine snored softly from what had become his side of the bed.

Sitting upright, eyes wide and staring, I searched the darkened cabin. Had Hecate finally ratted out my position? Who had she sent to do goddess knows what?

Why hadn't Zeke heard anything?

Using stealth, I dropped my legs over the side of the bed. No one inside except us. Outside could be a whole other ballgame. After shrugging into a jacket, I started for the door but stopped.

I was being stupid. I did not need to be outside to troll

for what shouldn't be there. The wolf snorted in his sleep and rolled onto his back. Should I wake him?

No reason to. Not yet.

Deploying threads of subtle seeking magic, I probed the darkness beyond these four walls. And found nothing.

Fine. Whoever was out there must be aware I was awake and had instituted measures to cloak themselves. I stared at the door. I'd sealed it with magic like I did every night. Nothing fancy like a lock or deadbolt existed. Whoever built this place hadn't worried about it being disturbed.

Or maybe they had but the locking mechanism had rotted away years ago.

Only a couple of choices: go outside to have a more thorough look or wake Zeke. I opted for the latter.

Returning to the bed, I stroked his rough outer guard hairs. "Sorry, but something might be outside."

With a muted snort, he rolled onto his belly, ears pricked and nostrils twitching. *"I don't think so."* He still sounded dead to the world, and he didn't offer to patrol the perimeter of the yard.

If he'd been worried, he'd have been out there in a flash.

I reluctantly returned to bed, but I kept my jacket on in case I needed to move quickly. It also warded off a chill leaching into my bones. I might not have located the source of whatever had dragged me from a sound sleep, but it didn't mean something wasn't out there.

Every sense I had argued the opposite.

The babe executed a full roll in my belly and landed a couple of kicks. At first, I was thrilled he was doing something, anything, but then I wondered if he was reacting to the same thing gnawing at me. Zeke was asleep again, or engaged in a bombproof imitation, although why he'd pretend sleep was beyond me.

I shut my eyes and folded my hands across my stomach. The baby moved again. *"Everything all right?"* I sent within.

After weeks of silence, the last thing I expected was an answer. When it came, it humbled and shamed me.

"Nothing will ever be again." His tiny voice held desolation and the weight of every world.

"Let me help." I stroked the hump of my stomach.

Rather than words, weeping filled my mind. Twisting onto my side, I protected my womb with hands and body while murmuring reassurances in Gaelic, the language Damien had spoken to him.

Finally, after far too long, my babe quieted.

I shut my eyes, but I was done with sleep for this night. Had something truly stumbled onto us? It might be mortals out hunting or camping or horseback riding.

Eh, scratch that last. I'd have smelled horses. So would Zeke.

The closest road to the cabin is over a mile away. The odds of someone discovering this spot—if they didn't already know about it—were thin. If our presence had been unearthed, it wasn't accidental.

Who knew about this place?

Damien, obviously. He was who'd brought me here in the first place. How had he come across it? Fae hideouts were in Faery, not on Earth. Who'd built it way back when? For what purpose? A long way from any access road, its original owner must have craved privacy.

When dawn came, I wasn't any closer to answers.

I waited until the wolf was stirring before I asked, "Did you give any more thought to moving back to Seattle?"

His head snapped toward me. *"No. Why?"*

"Someone was here last night. Probably another mage. I couldn't find hard evidence, but I'm certain of it."

"I didn't sense anything."

"You never truly woke up," I pointed out.

He shook himself from ruff to tail tip. *"I was awake enough to notice smells that didn't belong here. There weren't any."*

"By then, the person must have warded themselves." I walked to the table and drank from a cracked pitcher I kept full of water.

"We can't run every time you sense something amiss."

I set the pitcher down. "True, but we're pretty isolated. It wouldn't take much for a group to create problems."

"What kind of group?"

I didn't have an answer. Was the pregnancy making me jumpy? Possibly, but I didn't see where it would create hallucinations.

He stood at the door waiting for me to dismantle the seal. I flicked it aside and walked onto the porch, Zeke by my side. Both of us sniffed the air. All I smelled were the clear, fresh scents of a new day.

"I'm going to poke around," I said.

"I'll remain with you until you lay this foolishness to rest."

His words struck a sour chord. We don't always agree—hell, up until recently we were scarcely talking—but he'd never discounted my intuition.

"Do you know something you're not telling me?" I asked as we trotted down the steps and crossed to the place woods met the cabin's small clearing.

"Why would you even ask?"

Oh-oh. Not exactly an answer. Familiars cannot lie to their bonded ones, but they can sidestep an issue. Should I press for more?

In the end, I didn't, mostly because I didn't want to destroy our fragile détente.

A full circuit of the clearing yielded zilch. If someone had been here, they'd covered their tracks, a simple enough matter for even the most rudimentary mage.

Zeke's tail plumed. *"See. Told you no one was here."* With a toss of his head, he ran past me into deep timber.

The child rolled over again. Waves of sadness surrounded his tiny body.

If I had hackles, they'd have been at full attention. As it was, I went through the motions, doing what I did every day. No matter how I busied myself, I couldn't shake the impression we'd been discovered.

What it meant remained to be seen, but sticking around for a showdown wasn't wise. Putting myself at risk was one thing. Involving Zeke and my child quite another.

When he returned just shy of dusk with a freshly killed rabbit for me, I said, "Unless you're dead-set opposed, I want to return to the boardinghouse."

He dropped the rabbit on the porch. *"Why there?"*

"Mostly because it's the only spot I know. They'll let me work for room and board. We're not welcome in Faery. No Coven would have us."

Angling his head to one side, he regarded me. *"Are you truly that unhappy here?"*

"No, but after last night, I don't feel safe."

"But nothing was here," he insisted.

I stared at him but stopped before probing his mind. Zeke was hiding something from me. I was sure of it but unwilling to force a confrontation. Not after how rocky things had been between us.

"You may be right." I chose my words with care. "But I'm vulnerable pregnant, and I've had the oddest feeling all day."

"What kind of feeling?" Was he mining to assess if I knew more than I was saying?

The lack of complete trust between us was new, uncomfortable ground.

"Like someone is out there."

"I already told you there's not." He punctuated his words with a howl.

We'd reached a standoff. "Even if you're correct—and you may well be—I still want to leave. We've spent weeks here."

"We're safer here than anywhere else."

The babe was restless. Did he react to lies? Was that what all his recent activity had been about?

For the first time since the Coven exiled us, I longed for the presence of other witches. Women who'd lived through childbirth. Women who'd support me.

May as well long for the moon delivered on a platter.

I sank to a crouch in front of Zeke. "If I leave, will you come with me?"

He looked away, never a good sign. A minute ticked past, followed by one more before he said, *"Not much choice."*

"Of course, there's a choice. We'd still be bonded, but nowhere is it written we have to be together every moment."

Still facing away, his ears and tail drooped. *"You would trade me for mortals?"*

Damn it. I'd hurt his feelings. "I'd like to have both. I will take you somewhere to hunt every day."

"Let's remain here through one more moon cycle, and then I will go with you."

It was a reasonable request. Why was I having such a hard time saying yes?

"I fear Hecate may have located us," I blurted.

"She's imprisoned. She has no teeth."

"She can bend others who are free to her will. What about Circe or Medea?" It was a stretch since neither goddess had been seen anywhere for at least 500 years.

"Never heard of them."

"They used to work with Hecate."

"If they were so tight, they'd have freed her long since."

"I don't know. About any of it. All I'm trying to do is keep us safe."

"So is Damien." My son's voice from out of left field was such a shock I tumbled onto my ass.

Zeke heard him too. *"Do not speak his name,"* he growled.

Huh? Zeke has always been Damien's biggest cheerleader. What in the unholy fuck was going on?

"But he was here," the babe cried, followed by heartbreaking sobs.

I'd wanted the truth, but now that I had it, I wished I'd left well enough alone.

"Were you ever going to tell me?" I asked Zeke. Clearly, he'd been feigning sleep the previous night.

"No." He didn't bother with telepathy.

"Why not?"

"Because you'd have reacted exactly like you are. If we stay here, maybe he'll come back."

"Did he talk with you?"

"No."

Zeke can't lie outright, not to me. I breathed a little easier. At least he wasn't after Zeke, like the witches had been, aiming to lure him from my side.

Last night must have been a reconnaissance. To have Damien so close, but hidden, creeped me out. "Was Sita with him?"

"Yes."

Shudders racked me; my throat felt raw. I ached for Damien, but surely if he'd meant well, he'd have shown himself, not skulked around like a thief. The same went for Sita. I'd done my best to love Mother's familiar, but she'd shut me out as thoroughly as Damien.

For all I knew, he was hatching up a plan to activate the geas. Maybe the Fae had determined a way to support the babe outside my body until he was developed enough to be born.

Humans had NICU units. No reason they couldn't be replicated with magic.

"That settles it," I said. "We leave in the morning."

Unwilling to engage in further dialogue, I picked myself

up out of the dirt. My child continued to sob as I stumbled up the steps and into the cabin. Clearly, a single parent wasn't enough. My heart cracked open for him. Child of a home broken beyond repair, would he ever find peace, let alone joy?

Zeke didn't follow me inside, but he heard me when I said, "If Damien shows up again, you will alert me."

No woofs, no growls. Nothing to suggest he'd comply. If I felt anything like what had jolted me awake the previous night, though, I'd be more savvy about what to look for.

CHAPTER 4

DAMIEN

Settling in Flagstaff was simple since I'd made a home for myself among mortals many times. Thanks to Logan's generosity, I selected a partially furnished one-bedroom apartment in the older section of town. Within an hour of arriving, I'd tacked down a job. No one ever requests references for construction work.

If they had, my previous foreman would have told them they'd be lucky to have me.

The next day, I arrived at the jobsite at six in the morning. The foreman was a bit nonplussed by my lack of tools, but I explained they'd been stolen in Seattle, and I was gradually saving up to replace them.

He fell for my lies because he loaned me a decent set that probably belonged to him.

After a week, we fell into a routine. Sita left at dawn with me. She spent her days hunting while I worked. The money was good, and my expenses much lower than in Seattle. If I kept myself busy, the pain in my heart and soul receded but never totally left me.

I missed Morgan. Sita did as well. We talked about her and Zeke at night over supper. Wondering where they were, what they were doing, and if they were safe. That last part worried me.

It shouldn't have. Morgan can run magical rings around me. Still, she carried my son, and concern for them both gnawed at me.

I'd expected to see someone from Faery, but no one bothered us. After my initial expenditure, charging first and last month's rent to a credit card, I'd covered every expense. And I'd pay Faery back next time I stopped by.

A month clipped past followed by half of another one. Uncomfortable sensations pricked me more and more often. Were the Greeks tracking Morgan? Had they already found her, perhaps locked her away awaiting the child's birth?

Even worse, had they ripped the child from her body and destroyed it?

Crap. I had to get a grip. I'd have known if the latter possibility was more than my worst imaginings. The geas would have informed me.

I hadn't been working long enough to request time off, so, one night after dinner, I said to Sita, "Feel like a field trip?"

"Where to?" The hawk ruffled her russet plumage.

"I want to look in on Morgan."

After a surprised squawk, Sita asked, "Why?"

"Not sure I can put my finger on it, but she might be in danger. Something's been nagging me for a while now."

"What if Hecate's there?"

"If she is, we'll deal with it. I plan on being as stealthy as possible. If this goes according to plan, she'll never know we were there."

A couple of beak clacks. "Where is there?"

"Finding her is our first task. It might take us more than one evening."

Sita took a chunk out of the mouse she was eating. Once it slid down her gullet, she said, "Ready any time."

It took us five nights to locate Zeke and Morgan. In the end, since I couldn't find them any other way, I returned to the outskirts of Faery and tracked an extremely faded trail they'd left.

Surprise cut deep when it led straight to the cabin where she and I had sought refuge after fleeing from a Seattle boardinghouse. The humble hut looked the same as when I'd last seen it.

Still deserted.

No fell forces lurked in shadows. More importantly, no sign of Hecate.

"Remain silent," I reminded Sita and deepened the invisibility around us.

Morgan had taken a chance lighting here, but it turned out to be a solid choice. A rush of consciousness barreled into my mind.

My child, blindly seeking refuge. Had Morgan been unkind to him? I couldn't imagine her as anything but a gentle and loving mother. Guilt jabbed. If I truly felt that way, how in the hell could I wrest the babe from her arms?

Zeke found me next. He didn't say a word, withdrawing

as soon as he ascertained who'd broken the peace of his refuge.

"*Missed you,*" Sita cooed, presumably to Zeke.

Aw crap. What part about concealing our presence hadn't sunk in.

Remaining was risky, so I reversed my casting. More than anything, I wanted to stay, to soak up Morgan's energy and imagine a time before our relationship had broken apart.

Would Zeke tell her I'd been there? Or the babe? He was capable of primitive communication.

My spartan living room took shape around us.

"Sorry," Sita chirped. "I've missed Zeke so much."

I stroked her feathers. "It's all right. I know."

"Hecate wasn't there," the hawk pointed out.

"I didn't sense her, either."

"Do you suppose Morgan came to her senses?"

I had no idea. Even if she did, could I forgive her for inviting Hecate into our midst on the sly?

Trust is a funny thing. Once broken, it's damned hard to put it back together and not always see the cracks.

"At least they're all right," I murmured. I'd set out to reassure myself and been successful.

Sita returned to her mouse. "Can we go back tomorrow night?"

I started to say no, it wasn't a good idea, but the words wouldn't come. I wanted to go back worse than anything. It wasn't wise. It would put me—and by definition, Faery—at odds with powerful Greek gods.

Had Logan and the council been successful raising any

of the Celts? Even if they had, it didn't mean they'd be more kindly disposed to welcoming Morgan back to Faery.

I lasted four days before I scheduled a return visit to the cabin.

It was empty. Her scent lingered inside. I stood inhaling it and missing her so acutely it made my chest ache. She hadn't left a note, but then why would she? Either Zeke or the babe must have told her we were here. It had frightened her, and she'd sought a spot I didn't yet know about.

"Why did they go?" Sita squawked as she flew around the room.

"It's the geas. She's afraid of me." The words were no sooner out than their truth stabbed me in the heart. I'd been hurt, furious, and reacting all over the place when I'd staked a claim to our child that didn't include her.

"Hecate hasn't been here," the hawk announced. "I just checked."

I had too, but it might not mean anything other than Morgan being careful about her trysts with the witch goddess. "Let's look through the woods too," I suggested.

An hour later, I was satisfied. No trace of Hecate clung to anything in the vicinity. It didn't mean Morgan couldn't have traveled to hobnob with her maker, but somehow I didn't believe she had.

"We're stopping by Faery before we go home," I told Sita.

"Why?"

"To see if Maeve knows more than she did when we left."

"I'm sad," Sita cooed. "I shouldn't have said anything to Zeke. They left because I didn't keep my beak shut."

"It wasn't you. The babe recognized me straight away. If Zeke knew nothing, the child would have told Morgan we were here."

"Still sad," the hawk insisted. "They have no nest, no family, nowhere to go."

"You're not still angry with her."

"Guess not," was followed by a muted beak clack.

Switching up destinations, I brought us out in Faery and headed for the library. On a whim, I activated the faux bookshelf that led into Maeve's private domain.

An old-fashioned oil lamp burned on the table. The seer glanced my way and beckoned to the bird. "Figured you'd be by sooner or later. How are things going in mortal-land?"

Sita flew into her open arms, cooing softly. The seer stroked her feathers.

"I'm well," I replied. "Working, saving money. Please tell Logan I'll repay the funds I used."

"Pfft." She waved a dismissive hand. "Faery isn't in danger of heading into receivership. He doesn't care."

It's always jarring to hear ancient creatures using modern lingo. "He might not, but I do."

"You didn't come by to engage in idle chitchat. Or talk about money. What brings you home?"

Never could slide anything past her. "Have you seen anything further?"

She chuckled. "Of course. New visions rise daily. Sometimes hourly. What are you interested in?"

"You must know."

"If I did, I wouldn't have asked." She snapped her fingers. "Come on. What is it?"

I told her about visiting Morgan—twice. And finding no trace of Hecate. "Does it mean she recognized her error?"

Maeve pushed the scroll in front of her to one side and reached for a nearby mead bottle. Two glasses sat on the table, so she must have known I'd stop by. If not today, then soon.

Once she'd filled both tumblers, she pushed one toward me. "So many things you could have asked."

I downed half the glass. "Like what?"

A shrug. "Have the Greeks returned? Did we ever find a Celtic ally? Have I scryed your son's future?"

"Yes, I want to know all those things too."

She nodded briskly. "No on the Greeks. Sort of on the Celtic front. Arianrhod might help us, if we're desperate."

"My son?" I prodded.

"I've seen him grown, which means no one will snuff out his young life."

"It might mean that. Not all your visions come home to roost."

"True enough, but this one will."

I resisted slamming my mostly empty glass on the table. Fucking seers and their fucking riddles. "And you know this how?"

Another shrug. "I just do. He will be very powerful, your son. Also, best I can ascertain, there's naught in the way of evil within him."

Tell me something I don't know.

She shook a finger my way. "Uh-uh, none of that."

"If you don't like the message, stay out of my head," I groused.

"What do you want?" she asked in as soft a tone as she ever used.

What did I want? "Probably the impossible. I want to trust Morgan again. I want a life with her—and our son."

"The Fae council won't like it. They don't trust her, either. Not after her shenanigans with Hecate. But they shouldn't rule your decisions."

I stared at her. What was she trying to tell me?

"To live your own life." She answered my thoughts. "We all make mistakes. I'm certain Hecate was very...persuasive. Nothing quite like shared blood or—in this case—shared essence to sway a person."

"How can I ever be certain?" I blurted.

"Of what?"

"Her loyalties."

Sita squawked from the confines of Maeve's arms. Hard to interpret what she meant. Either outrage I was even considering anything resembling a reconciliation, or outrage I still harbored doubts about Morgan. Our search for Hecate had been thorough and turned up nothing.

"Tincture of time," Maeve said flatly. "It's how trust is rebuilt, one day at a time."

"What about antagonizing the Greeks and maybe getting us into a war?"

"Those are considerations, more the war angle than the Greeks. Been mighty quiet on the witch front."

"Because they must know Morgan and I split up. If we

get back together, I bet they'll be back at it with their nasty hex bags and dirty spells."

"Could be. Was there anything further?"

A dismissal if ever I've heard one. We needed to get going, anyway. It was probably time to get up and head to work on Earth's side of the veil.

I got to my feet. "Yes, one more item. You say you've seen my son grown. Did it come with seeing Morgan and I together?"

"Sometimes." She smiled, with a whole lot of teeth and little warmth. "Welcome to my world where not much has clarity."

Sita winged to my shoulder. I'd wondered if she'd choose to remain in Faery. It was clear she adored Maeve. "You can bide a while if you'd like," I told the hawk.

She stroked the side of my face with her beak. "My place is with you. Maeve said so."

Interesting. They'd had a conversation, one beyond my reach. Feeling like an anachronism, I made my way to the veils and pushed through them. Dawn was indeed breaking.

I felt torn. Part of me wanted to return to the cabin and track Morgan. She probably did her best to mask her trail, but I'm one of the best trackers the Fae have ever spawned. I also had the geas and blood thrumming through my son's veins to guide me.

The other part urged me to hustle home and get to work. I was still new at this jobsite, too new to start missing days. The reason I've managed as well as I have blending in with mortals is I've learned not to draw attention to myself.

Being a bad employee would attract the wrong kind of notice.

Far better to be one of the workers no one ever gave a second thought to.

"Why are we standing here?" Sita cawed.

"No reason. On our way home now."

I didn't quite make it to work on time, but I wasn't more than ten minutes late. The foreman was deep in discussion with a civil engineer about a structural issue. He never even noticed my arrival.

Tonight would be soon enough to discover Morgan's current location. This time, I'd talk with her, test the waters. I wasn't quite ready to forgive and forget, but surely a middle ground existed.

One where we at least started talking with each other again to discover if anything remained of our love.

For all I knew, she was done with me. Trust cuts both ways. My geas must have trashed hers. The Greeks had insisted I neutralize it, but that spell lacks a counterspell. I didn't have to activate it, but I couldn't stomp it out, either.

No reason to leap ahead of the game. I'd work my shift, maybe close my eyes for an hour, and do what I could to find her.

Do not get your hopes up, a stern inner voice warned.

No kidding. Except my life was an empty shell without her. I'd kept on keeping on and hated every minute of it. If this would be my existence from now on, I'd figure something out.

Get used to it, somehow.

Maybe one day, a hundred years hence, it wouldn't hurt

as much. I might have imagined it, but something suspiciously like Hecate's raucous laughter nagged at the edges of my hearing.

It unnerved me enough I nearly dropped a wooden plank off the scaffolding I stood on. Was the witch goddess pulling strings from the sidelines? Anything was possible. Still, she had no ties to me, and—

Bullshit, she doesn't. The child shares blood with us all.

Fear for the unborn babe coated my tongue with a metallic taste. I had to find Morgan, if only to warn her.

"Hey, Underhill, look sharp," a voice sounded from below.

It took a moment to recognize my current name. "Sorry," I yelled, getting a better grip on the board that had nearly gotten away from me.

No more laughter, but I warded my mind just in case and returned my attention to work. No point getting lost in what-ifs. I'd know soon enough if I could even find Morgan. Once I did, we'd talk.

What if you can't? The inner voice was back.

I'd deal with it. I wasn't sure how, but no one can hide themselves that well. If I struck out, I'd enlist aid from somewhere.

"One step at a time, mate," I mumbled.

"What was that, Underhill?" the same guy called.

"Nothing." Grabbing another board, I set about nailing it into place.

CHAPTER 5
MORGAN

Zeke was still sulky, but he joined my spell the following morning. I gathered my pathetically few belongings from the cabin, including my notebook—I'd hand it to Damien to read if an opportunity ever presented itself—and did my best to obliterate any trace of us having been here. After sobbing himself to sleep, the babe had retreated to silence.

Perhaps he shared Zeke's impression about Damien not being able to find us if we left. I had more faith in the Fae than that. He's an ace tracker and motivated as hell. If he wanted to find us again, I had no doubt he'd pull it off.

I brought us out in the back of a park a few blocks from the boardinghouse. It gave me an opportunity to create a glamour for Zeke that turned him into a shaggy brown dog. Next, I fashioned a faux leash.

The rounded hump of my belly posed a problem. Did I

alter it with a glamour? If I did, would my son believe I'd never wanted him? He was fragile as it was.

"What are we waiting for?" Zeke demanded, tail swishing this way and that.

"Trying to decide if being pregnant will make them more or less likely to offer me work."

"But you are," he woofed.

"Yes, but I can make it appear otherwise."

"I see."

When I folded my hands over my belly, the child was still as death. *"I love you,"* I sent inward.

No response, but I hadn't expected one.

After rocking from foot to foot for a few minutes, I snagged the end of Zeke's leash and started for the parts of the park people used. I didn't want to lie my way inside the boardinghouse, so pregnancy was part of the package.

Smythe would take me or not. If not, I'd try elsewhere. Charles, the cook, had a soft spot for me—and Zeke. Maybe he'd go to bat on my behalf, if Smythe was on the fence.

I didn't feel much like smiling, but I did anyway, experimenting with variations that oozed sincerity as I covered the few blocks to the boardinghouse. The carnage from the night I'd left had been cleared away.

Of course, it had. No one leaves blood and gore on city streets for months. Suddenly cautious, I checked for hex bags. Breath rattled from me when I didn't find a one. Maybe the local Coven had given up on me ever retuning.

Good. Made my life simpler.

After a slight hesitation, I started up the boardinghouse steps and knocked firmly on the battered front door.

"Hold your horses," issued from within followed by muttering about residents who couldn't hang onto their keys.

Smythe swung the door inward. His eyes widened. He hadn't changed one whit, but then I'd only been gone a few months. Tall, spare, and in his fifties, he had a bald pate and rheumy brown eyes. Jeans hung low on his hips. A plaid lumberman's jacket covered a stained T-shirt. Scuffed motorcycle boots rose to just below his knees.

"Never thought I'd see you again. Where's the other one?"

Zeke woofed and wagged his tail, ever the politician.

Smythe's thin lips formed what might have been a smile. He patted Zeke's head. "Not you, buddy, Damien."

An idea, so obvious I should have thought of it in the park, rose to the fore. "He's out of the area working. Had to go home for a while because his father was sick. He'll be back in a few weeks."

"I see." His gaze traveled downward, stopping at my stomach. "Mmph. In a family way, too. So will Damien be paying for your room? I assume it's why you're here."

Oh-oh. Logical assumption given my lie. "He should be, but for now how about if I work in the kitchen again like before?"

Smythe's eyes narrowed. "Are you certain he's coming back for you, missy?"

I nodded as I remembered the proprietor's pet name for me. "Not sure when, but he will be here."

I took a peek inside his mind. He thought I might be lying but wasn't willing to go to the mat. Besides, the cook, Charles, had been complaining about needing an assistant.

Here I was, ready to work.

"Alrighty. Let's begin with one month starting today. Your old room is empty. Key is on the board."

I resisted hugging him. He wasn't the huggy type. "Thank you very much. Shall I begin with lunch prep?"

"Charles would like that." He clapped his hands together. "Best get a move on, missy. See you later today. There's a spot more mending to be done. I'll leave it next to the machine."

"I'll get to it between lunch and supper," I promised and skirted past him. The key to my room hung on a numbered board. I grabbed it, and Zeke and I trotted up the stairs.

"Pretty easy," Zeke said.

It had been. Should I be suspicious? Eh, I lacked the energy. Comes a time when you have to trust someone. The odds of the Coven laying a trap for me with Smythe's help were slim to none. The man hated anything magical, and he liked me. If anyone had stopped by with a bargain involving good things for him in exchange for bad things for me, he'd have turned them down flat.

"Where are we?" The babe's voice shocked me. Had he finally forgiven me?

I waited until we were inside and I'd set my few things on a dresser before answering. "This is the place Daddy and I met."

The tight ball in my stomach relaxed and turned over. The fact Damien knew about this place must have reassured him. After a glance at a cheap analog wall clock, I hustled down to the kitchen with Zeke.

Charles was bent over a board chopping vegetables and potatoes. At the sound of the swinging door opening, he straightened and grinned my way. A harried middle-aged man wearing a stained white apron, he stood about six feet tall, had a paunch and a mostly bald head. Clear blue eyes had more than a few miles on them.

"Smythe said you were back. I missed you. Everything all right?"

"Yes, all is well." I smiled too, feeling more centered than I had since Damien kicked me out of Faery. "Put me to work."

He stepped away from the board. "Finish these. When you're done, boil up some macaroni."

"How much?"

He frowned. "Two boxes."

We worked together in a companionable silence with Zeke curled in his usual spot by the kitchen door. After lunch, I offered to take care of all the cleanup, so Charles could shop.

We settled into the same routine as before, so much so it seemed we'd never left. Charles possessed a mild type of magic, but I couldn't quite figure out what he was. Maybe a brownie, except they never leave the Old Country.

We'd been at the boardinghouse a few days. I'd just returned from Zeke's evening walk—so far he hadn't complained about not being able to hunt—when the babe started doing flipflops.

Was danger afoot?

Alert to any alteration in the status quo, I hustled us into the boardinghouse and up the stairs to our room where I proceeded to seal us in with magic. Had the Coven posted beacons, or a roving sentry?

We'd been here long enough for someone to have discovered us.

What would I do if they had? Running—again—didn't sit well. I couldn't spend the rest of my days fleeing amorphous threats.

"Do you sense anything?" I asked Zeke.

He'd ditched his glamour and had his paws on the sill, staring into darkness. *"Not sure."*

He faced away from me, but he was hedging. After centuries together, I read his body language.

Not much point getting undressed, not until I homed in on what the fuck was up. Fae enchantment, bursting with damp pine scents, swooshed into the room as Damien stepped through a glowing portal with Sita riding on one shoulder. She proceeded to fly around the room, cawing hoarsely.

"Some things come full circle," he observed from a couple of feet away.

Zeke ran to him, tail wagging furiously. Damien opened his arms, and the wolf rose on his hind legs, wrapping his paws around Damien's shoulders. The babe made little cooing noises.

"I suppose," I agreed, silently urging him to stay where

he was. An inane desire to throw myself into his arms, feel the press of his muscled frame against my body, rocked me to my core. In that moment, I would have given anything to trade places with Zeke.

Back on the floor, the wolf licked every square inch of available flesh. Yeah, I wanted to do that too.

Sita swooped to Zeke's back, landed, and pecked his head lightly. It made my heart glad to see them together.

What in the unholy fuck was wrong with me?

I pulled it together, or tried to. Everyone was delighted to be reunited. I didn't trust this merry little tableau for one second.

I should be wary, on my guard. Damien wanted something. This wasn't a social call, not after how our last interaction had blown up.

His trademark fair hair hung loose to waist level. Green eyes zeroed in on my belly. He's a few inches taller than my six foot height and broadly built. Despite the khaki trousers and white shirt I had no problem visualizing him in all his naked glory. Muscles slab his shoulders, arms, thighs. He carries himself with a simple elegance that's always made it tough for me to breathe.

He arched a fair brow, still staring at me. His gaze made me wish I'd combed my hair and put on clothes not stained from my stint in the kitchen.

"Why are you here?" I asked. May as well get the preliminaries out of the way. It wasn't as if we were a couple anymore.

"I wanted to see how you were doing. You still have enemies."

"Kind of you. As you can see, we're doing all right. We'd still be at the cabin were it not for your visit."

"Sorry about that. Didn't mean to spook you."

Do not engage, my inner voice snarled.

I wasn't in a listening mood.

"What gives you the right to stalk me?" I demanded.

In one of my many too-little-too-late moves, I tossed a sound shield around the small room. I'd told Smythe Damien and I were still an item. The man has ears like a lynx. It wouldn't do my case any good if he overheard us arguing.

"Nothing, but I couldn't stay away."

I blinked stupidly at him. The baby cooed some more before saying, *"I want Daddy."*

I felt like telling him he'd have Daddy soon enough. Would he pine for me when the shoe was on the other foot? I'd never know, and it made me sad.

"What do you want?" I did my damnedest to cling to watchful and wary.

"Mostly I wanted to see you, make certain you and my son are all right."

"Is there some reason we wouldn't be?" I bristled.

He shrugged. "The Greeks want our son dead. Virtually every Coven has it in for you."

I flapped a hand in his direction. "Spare me. I've managed this far. On my own." I stressed those three words. Maybe he'd pick up on the not-so-hidden message I'd cut Hecate out of my life.

Zeke was rubbing his head against Damien's thigh, making little grunting noises like he does when he's beyond happy. Sita cooed like a dove. The babe did a few more flipflops as he tried to push me closer to Damien.

Everyone was willing to forgive, forget, and move on.

Except me.

I'd catch hell from Zeke—and the babe, who really needs a name—but I stood tall. "If you got what you came for, you can leave."

Zeke snarled at me, showing a mouthful of teeth. The hawk clacked her beak.

Suddenly, I was just tired. Of everything.

"Nothing has changed since you discovered I'd been hobnobbing with Hecate—" I began.

"Oh?" The arched brow inched upward. "Unless I'm mistaken, you cut her out of your life."

"So what if I did?" My tone was surly.

He angled his head to one side, eyes never leaving me. "It's a pretty big 'so what.' Means you've made a choice to—"

I held up a hand. "What is means is I have no idea who to trust. She might be on the up-and-up, but she used me. I'm done with anyone who isn't honest with me."

"How do you know she used you?"

"Because she was delighted when you and I broke up. It's probably what she wanted all along. She pretended to care, told me all the things I'd been waiting to hear since she made me, but with sketchy ulterior motives."

I paused to suck in a breath. "Her goal is escape. She needs me for that, or says she does."

"What were you going to do once she was free?"

"Be together. Make the Covens stronger. Weed out witches turned to evil."

"Do you have any reason to believe that last isn't true?"

"No," I admitted.

"So, like all of us," he went on, "she's a blend of self-serving and altruistic."

I shook my head to clear my thoughts. "What? You're defending her?"

"Not entirely. Merely pointing out we have no idea what makes her tick."

I sank to the edge of the bed. Confusion reigned. "But you kicked me out of Faery, dropped a geas on our child, all because I'd spoken with her."

He shook his head. Light danced through the silk of his hair. "Nay. 'Twas the subterfuge that stunned me. If you'd told me the first time she appeared, we'd have dealt with it."

"How?" I snarled. "After what happened to you, you'd have either forbidden further contact or used my connection with her to track her down and harm her."

"Maybe. Hard to say what I would have done in retrospect. You never gave me a chance."

"Kind of like you pulled every future chance out from under me when you exiled me?" I dropped my head into my hands, too weary to spar with him. "Go. Just leave us alone," I mumbled.

Instead, he walked to me, bent, and placed a hand on my belly. Our son pressed against the wall of my womb, seeking comfort from Damien's touch. Where his fingers splayed across my stomach, sparks seared me. I craved his touch as much as I ever had.

Any of the pretty words I'd used to delude myself I'd get over my attachment to him rose up and slapped me hard. I could live without Damien, sure I could. It was what I'd been doing, but I'd never be whole.

Never be truly happy.

When the day came for him to run off with our babe, I'd have nothing left to live for. Still, I'd plod on from day to day, month to month, year to year in a gray haze forever kicking myself for letting Hecate draw me in.

He withdrew his hand and straightened. "I'd like to be your friend if you'll let me."

Oh-oh. Slippery slope. Say no and be done with it.

Rather than no, "What exactly does that mean?" emerged from my mouth. Stupid, weak woman. Pathetic too.

"I'm not sure." He crouched in front of me, his voice soft. "What I do know is I miss you. I struggled with myself about dropping in. Let it go for weeks before I finally couldn't stand it any longer and tracked you to the cabin. Even then, I felt bad for invading your privacy, so I left without making contact."

"Zeke and the child knew you were there."

"Blood calls to its own, and Zeke has always liked me."

He was so close, almost touching me. Yes would have been the easy answer, but I couldn't risk myself like that. Not again.

I swallowed around the lump blocking my throat. "What used to be between us is so broken, it's not fixable. If we did get back together, you'd always wonder if I did it to avoid the geas."

"I might, but I'd get over it."

"Eh, talk is cheap." Breath rattled from me. I stood and crossed the room to put some distance between us. "I might make another mistake," I said. "Big ones seem to be my specialty. I couldn't stand for you to shit all over me again, no matter what I did wrong."

"If it had been anyone but Hecate—" he began before stopping himself.

"No matter who or what," I said, "you didn't even give me the benefit of the doubt. You smeared me with the same brush the sisterhood did and kicked me to the curb. Did I deserve it? Yeah, probably. Not what the Coven did, but what you did. Still, you could have asked questions, heard me out. Instead, you were judge, jury, and executioner, all in one package. I can't risk that again."

"I understand."

When I looked at him, his shoulders had slumped in defeat. Damn me, but I wanted to comfort him, smooth away the lines spiraling out from the corners of his eyes.

Not my place, not any longer. The child wailed; I had no way to comfort him. Zeke faced away from me with Sita still clinging to his back.

"I don't know if I can be friends," I murmured. "It's in my best interest, particularly after you call in the geas."

"Can't we raise him together?"

"If you wanted that, why saddle me with a geas?"

A muscle danced beneath one eye. "I'm far from perfect, Morgan. I was hurt, angry, reacting all over the place. I'm sorry. If I could retract the geas, I would, but nowhere is it written I have to activate it."

Son of a bitch, he really means that.

I wasn't ready to jump back in. Maybe I never would be.

"I don't know. It's too much. Please leave. Give me space to think things through."

"Sita and I are in Flagstaff."

My mouth twitched. "Do you think I need assistance locating you?"

"Eh, guess not." He walked toward me and held out a hand.

After an uncomfortably long pause, I clasped it. Warmth traveled from my palm up my arm to my heart. Longing for him pierced me.

"Thank you. Hopefully, this will be a new beginning for us," he said.

I don't know if I could have let go of him. Mercifully, he released my hand and turned. Before he walked through the portal that hadn't entirely winked out, I called, "Wait."

He stopped and I grabbed my notebook from off the dresser and thrust it at him. "Everything is in here," I said. "It's spelled so you'll know what I wrote is the truth."

Damien took it and tucked it away in a jacket pocket. "I'll read it as soon as I get back." He vanished along with his portal, as if they'd never been here.

I looked away. Had I done the right thing? My words in the journal bared my soul. Too late now. He was gone.

The child's wails had quieted. Zeke skewered me with his mismatched eyes. *"Good you trusted him with your writing. It will work out if you let it."*

"How can you know."

"I just do."

On that note, I stripped off my clothes, grabbed a robe and threadbare towel off a rack, and plodded down the hall to the women's bathroom and a hot shower.

I'd dreamed of Damien finding me and more or less apologizing. Now that he had, I had no idea what to do about it.

DAMIEN

Walking away from Morgan was one of the hardest things I'd ever done. She'd requested space, though, and I'd honor her needs. At least she'd waited until we talked before asking me to leave.

It was something.

And she'd given me a journal.

She could have barred me from her chamber the second I set foot inside. She'd looked weary, but resolute. Weeks had passed, long enough for the hump of her belly to become noticeable.

Touching my child had damn near reduced me to tears. I longed for him, and he missed me. He wanted us to be together. All of us. Morgan and I should select a name for him. Perhaps it could be our next task.

"Why did she return to the boardinghouse?" Sita cawed. We were back in my humble abode in Flagstaff in plenty of time for me to catch a couple of hours sleep—after I'd taken a peek at Morgan's journal.

"It's familiar, and they'll let her work in exchange for a room and food. Not many places will do that."

"She could hunt. Then she wouldn't require mortals for anything."

The hawk's tone left no doubt how she felt about humans.

"It's what she was doing before we disturbed her at the cabin." Guilt pricked. Although we'd established the beginnings of a truce, Morgan could easily return to the hut in the South Cascades.

Or another location of her choosing.

Not bothering to undress since I'd be up in short order and on my way to work, I stretched out on the sofa. It wasn't as lumpy as the bed. My kinsmen in Faery never could understand why I preferred life on Earth to Faery with its bounty of creature comforts.

I'd never tried to explain. Faery lacked challenges. Every day was the same. All my needs were catered to even if I did nothing. After hundreds of years where nothing ever changed It was tough to find a reason to keep living.

It didn't bother anyone else, but I grew restive, uneasy. It was why I'd volunteered to live on Earth and spy for my people. At least I was doing something productive.

Sita retreated to her usual perch on top of a dresser. She wasn't asleep, but she wasn't inclined to talk. Our visit had raised questions. The hawk missed Zeke. She'd probably gotten past her ire with Morgan. Her original bondmate, Zoelle, had kept secrets and pretended to be Morgan's blood mother. Since she was dead, killed by witches in cahoots with darkness, Morgan represented the last link to the hawk's bondmate.

Morgan hadn't mentioned being cursed. Was she still convinced of it? Before my lengthy illness, the specter of doom had loomed large.

Would I go back to the boardinghouse?

Not right away. The ball was in her court. What would I do if she didn't seek me out? Was I strong enough to stay away?

Probably not.

I removed the journal from my jacket pocket and settled in to read. It didn't take long, not more than an hour. By the time I was done absorbing words that glowed silver with her truth casting, shame spilled through me.

I should have asked questions. Should have done a lot of things. Morgan wasn't innocent, but she'd been trapped between misplaced loyalty to Hecate, who truly had played her, and her love for me. In a backhanded way, she'd been trying to protect me as I recovered from the Fae death coma.

When I riffled through pages hunting for one particular place, they were blank. Apparently, she'd spelled the notebook with more than a truth spell. Rightly so, no one needed to see what I'd just read. I set the journal aside.

Rather than sleep, which wouldn't happen this night, I replayed our conversation. We'd both admitted to mistakes. If we maintained that level of honesty—

Sita quorked unhappily.

"What is it?"

"We didn't check for witches or hex bags. We should go back."

"Surely, Morgan knows to assess harm in her immediate vicinity. Zeke too."

"He told me he was worried even though he lacked evidence."

I rolled to a sit. "What exactly did he say?"

The hawk chirped a few times before adding, "Something shadows us, but I've never caught them outright."

Mmph. More of a wolfie intuition than hard facts. Still, he was canny. The babe had been so overcome to have me close, he'd been one step up from incoherent. No help from that front.

"We need to go back," Sita pressed.

"Maybe. First, I'm going to go to work. Tonight, we'll do a reconnaissance, but we'll stay far enough away we don't kick off anyone's radar."

"What if something bad happens, and we're not there?"

I finally understood what she was angling for. "If you want to keep the watch, I'll join you later this afternoon."

She was gone before I quit talking.

Was I making a mistake? Jobs came and went. As the old saying goes, "I was looking for a job when I found this one." Still, I'm not into gratuitous bridge-burning. Determined not to make a nuisance of myself by landing on Morgan's doorstep for a second time within the span of a few hours, I changed into work clothes and took a bus to the jobsite.

For once, I was nearly an hour early. No reason not to get

started. When the foreman showed up, he joined me on a scaffolding. "No overtime unless I requested it, Underhill."

"Not angling for extra pay. Couldn't sleep, so I decided I'd do some good here."

"Women problems?" He jabbed me in the ribs.

I snickered. "You don't know the half of it, mate."

"Ha. Bet I do. Damned twats. Can't live with 'em, can't live without 'em."

On that cheerful note, he rappelled to the ground and started dishing out the day's orders.

The day crawled by. My mind was only half there when we had our usual co-op lunch. No word from Sita, but she would have had to return to talk with me. No one could manage telepathy from such a distance. It was why Maeve had gifted Morgan and me communications crystals quite a while back.

I still had mine. My bet was Morgan had left hers in Faery at the bottom of a bag with funds and ID provided by Logan. Not that she'd have brought the crystal even if it were uppermost in her mind the day we'd had our big blowout.

Probably the last thing she'd have wanted with her since I'd threatened to grab our child and cut her out of his life.

Christ, what a moron I was.

The afternoon passed uneventfully. We'd be done with this project next week, but the firm employing me had jobs to keep us busy for well over a year. Construction is kind of like the Old West Gold Rush. High stakes, high returns, not enough men to meet the need.

I started back to my apartment on foot. Before arriving, I

ducked into a handy alley and teleported to Seattle. A logical entry was a park not far from the boardinghouse. As soon as my portal dissipated, I called Sita.

Even though I waited through a count of ten, the hawk didn't answer.

I tried again, this time targeting Zeke with my mind voice. Still no reply.

Something cold and damp took root at the base of my spine. After warding myself well, I covered the short distance to the boardinghouse. A cursory examination of the grounds revealed nothing. Not a hex bag or whiff of witch. Odd since Morgan would have kicked off the latter, and she lived here.

Or she had yesterday.

Crap. Should I return to Faery for reinforcements? Even one more Fae would make a difference.

I needed more information first. Lots more. If Morgan had another change of heart and had run from me—again— no need to sound any alarms.

No clues jumped out at me after I'd completed two transits of the building. I raised my mind voice again and called the hawk and wolf. When they still didn't answer, I executed a mini jump spell that landed me in Morgan's room.

Empty.

Her spicy witch scent reassured me she'd been here as recently as this morning. What had happened? It was closing on the dinner hour. Was she in the kitchen? A scan would reveal my presence, but I was so worried I didn't give a fuck and zeroed in on it.

The cook's head snapped around. Too late, I remembered he carried magic as well. He straightened and faced the direction of my probe. "What have you done with her?" he snarled.

Not a conversation I wanted to have from a distance. One more mini jump landed me in the kitchen. "Not a damned thing. I can't find her or Zeke or my hawk."

He narrowed his blue eyes. "Fae, eh?"

"You already knew as much."

He harumphed. "So I did."

I cut to the chase. "Was she here for breakfast preparation?"

He nodded. "Lunch for a while, but something soaked up her attention. I asked if anything was wrong. She said, 'maybe,' and took off out of here with Zeke on her heels." After a brief hesitation, he added, "The hawk you asked after was with them."

"You say it was around noon?"

"Yeah." He walked closer and thumped me in the chest. "Are you sure you don't know where she is?"

"Positive."

"She carries your seed. You should have—"

I chopped a hand downward. "Spare me. I'm going to launch a tracking spell from here."

"Are you any good at them?"

"The best the Fae has. Let's hope it's good enough."

"No matter what, tell me—"

I was gone before he finished speaking. Tracking is a two-step process. On the one hand, I'm in a journey channel. On the other, I'm manipulating a beam following my quarry. Since I don't feed a destination into the journey spell, I have no idea where I'll come out.

Until I do.

Had Morgan left of her own volition? From what Charles said, it was possible. If so, she'd have cloaked herself and Zeke. Probably Sita as well.

Fae magic isn't the strongest. My dual effort took so much time anxiety chewed a hole in my guts.

It took perhaps a quarter hour before my spell wound down. I snatched a quickie ward into place. Popping out in an unknown location has a tendency to startle any mortals who might be wandering about.

And I was a wanted man. I'd given the PDA the slip, but it didn't mean they'd stopped looking for me.

Reason number forty-three why I should have returned to Faery for reinforcements. I tested my link with my homeland and breathed easier when it thrummed to life.

A familiar neighborhood blossomed around me. I was on Queen Anne Hill, not far from the Coven guild house. Thank Danu I was warded since the streets were full of people. The after-work crowd milled about in search of dinner or the evening's entertainment.

If my spell had run true—and I'd never had one go astray—Morgan should be close. This time, rather than Zeke or Sita, I called her.

"I. Do. Not. Require. Help."

Tension bled from me in a whoosh. Thank all the gods, she was all right. *"Is Sita with you?"*

"Yes."

I could have packed up my spell and returned first to Charles to reassure him and then to Flagstaff.

Could have.

Instead, I asked, *"Can we talk a moment?"*

"Why?"

"Because no matter what you're up to, this expenditure of telepathy is bound to draw unwanted attention. We're better off talking."

"If you hadn't shown up, it wouldn't be a problem."

A perky Australian shepherd—one of Zeke's alter egos—ran to me. Clearly, my ward wasn't an impediment for him. I followed him two blocks down and between two older buildings.

Morgan crouched a hundred yards into the declination, but she straightened as I walked toward her. Damn it. My ward was less than worthless here, so I chucked it. Sita flew to me and attached herself to my shoulder, talons digging deeper than usual.

"You can leave now," Morgan said.

"Can I? Charles said you charged out of there as if an entire army dogged you. What happened?"

"Not seeing where it's any of your affair," she said stiffly. "Damn it, Damien. Didn't we decide I'd come to you, not the other way round?"

"We did, but it was before Sita vanished. And before I read your notebook. Thank you for sharing it with me."

"Um, okay." Color stained her cheeks, tinting them rose.

We might talk about her journal, but it wouldn't be today. She was uncomfortable, and I still didn't know why she'd ended up here. "What was I supposed to do with Sita?

She showed up. I couldn't very well leave her in the boardinghouse."

"You could have sent her back to me."

The hawk cawed indignantly. "No one orders me about."

Fine. I'd veered offtrack anyway. "You still haven't told me what got your dander up enough to leave during meal preparations."

"Yeah. Probably shouldn't have. I need that job more than they need me."

She was so close, I couldn't stand not touching her, so I dropped my hands onto her shoulders. "Let me help. I'm here."

She twisted from beneath my touch. "Don't."

We stood almost toe to toe. The babe sang, calling to me. She must have heard it too. To hell with it. I wrapped my arms around her and steeled myself for a slap or a blast of magic.

Neither happened.

After a moment, she leaned against me and returned my embrace. "You're hard to say no to."

"Told you that the first night we met."

"You did, didn't you?"

"Uh-huh."

"I felt something closing on the boardinghouse. It was dank, heavy, not right. Zeke had been warning me, but he lacked specifics, so I didn't pay him much heed."

She tightened her arms around my back. "I couldn't ignore what I sensed, and I was afraid it wouldn't bode well for everyone in the house, so I left to draw it away."

"Why come here? You're awfully near the Coven guild house."

"Because it's where I tracked the source. This is as close as I got. No reason to walk right into the lion's den."

"Did you have a plan?" I pressed.

"Watch and wait. They must know I left the boardinghouse. If not this minute, then soon."

"Which makes this dangerous for you. Maybe they set beacons."

"I'd have sensed them."

She felt perfect in my arms. Holding her felt right in a way nothing else had since she walked out of Faery.

"Why didn't you call me."

"How? I didn't have time for a side trip to Flagstaff."

"You could have sent Sita back."

Morgan shook her head. "Too risky."

"The thing that's after you, what does it feel like?" I tangled my fingers in the silk of her hair.

"This isn't a good idea," she mumbled, let go of me, and stepped back a pace. Her tresses slid through my hands.

"Maybe not." I grinned crookedly. "But you sure feel good."

"You too. Too good," she blurted before clapping a hand over her mouth.

"Whatever's after you," I pressed. "Any idea what it is?"

A slow nod. "Yeah. Feels like Banshees and a couple of Kelpies."

Interesting. "No witches?"

"No, but they could be concealed behind spells."

"Any idea why the Coven called out the cavalry?"

"Maybe they want to make sure I don't give them the slip this time."

My mind tracked back to the last time they'd tossed a noose around Morgan's freedom. Only a desperate hail Mary that had nearly cost my immortal life had saved her.

"Have you heard anything from Hecate?"

She cast a pointed glance my way. "Funny you should ask. It was her who warned me they were getting too close for comfort."

Which side was the goddess on?

Certainly not the Fae side, but it was conceivable she wanted Morgan for more than help breaking her out of prison.

"Did she say anything else?"

"She would have, but I shut her out. Again. She doesn't get it, but I truly am done."

Zeke barked, low, urgent.

I spun in time to see a horde running toward us. Banshees led by three Kelpies.

Crap odds. Our only chance was to flee.

"Lend your magic," I urged and kicked myself for not leaving a portal open.

"Mine's quicker." Cinnamon, vanilla, and bayberry surrounded me. The alley exploded leaving us floating in darkness, but not for long. In a lightning-fast transition, her room formed around us.

"We need to go to Faery," I protested.

"What? And bring my troubles into your lands? That's stupid. The Fae hate me as it is without me dragging them into an impromptu war." She shook her head. "I have to deal with this myself."

I drew myself up tall. "I am not leaving."

She burst out laughing. "Of course, you aren't."

A frantic knock was followed by Charles standing in the doorway. Even his slender magic made short work of locks.

"Thank all the gods you're unharmed." He stared me down. "Where'd you find her?"

"On Queen Anne Hill with a pack of Banshees."

"But they never leave the Old Country."

Fuckity fuck. I draped a sound shield around the room and pushed the door shut with a shot of magic.

"What will you do?" he asked Morgan.

"Not sure. We'd just begun to talk about it."

"I want in on that discussion. Done in the kitchen for now."

"Not sure it's a good idea—" Morgan began.

"Not your decision," he said gruffly. "I am not without resources."

It was indescribably rude, but I manned up and asked, "What are you?"

He grinned and morphed into something I recognized in the instant before he resurrected his glamour. He was far stronger magically than I'd given him credit for.

My mouth clacked open and shut a time or two. "What in the hell is a Dark Fae doing here?"

"Long story. But you missed the important part. Our magic is additive, and Morgan needs all the help she can get."

I started to point out the two halves of Faery hadn't

worked together in centuries, but if he was willing, so was I. Maybe I'd never have to tell Logan and Maeve...

Nice try. They'll find out. Hell, Maeve's probably already seen this in her ball.

Faery doesn't have many rules, but one is we're to report all Dark Fae sightings immediately. I was already out of compliance since I should have teleported to the council chamber immediately.

Do not pass go. Do not collect 200 dollars.

I'd deal with the fallout later.

Charles cared about Morgan. It counted for a lot. No way was I leaving. Not with her and my son under attack.

CHAPTER 7
MORGAN

So much for going it alone. Back in wolf form, Zeke had already sashayed to Charles and was rubbing his head against his thigh.

May as well just go for it since I couldn't shake my entourage. "I'm sick of running," I announced.

The men, who'd been absorbed in sizing one another up—or whatever it is men do—spun to face me.

"We've been down this road. What do you have in mind?" Damien asked.

"I'm going to storm the gates of the local guild house. Should have done it after those bitches killed Mother. Better late than never."

"Those will be crappy odds," Damien muttered.

"I'll have the element of surprise, and I'd really rather do this alone."

"Not without me," Zeke woofed.

"Or me," Sita chimed in.

"You can't face an entire Coven by yourself," Charles protested. "Let me raise a few brothers. I'm not the only Dark Fae living outside Faery."

His statement earned a furled brow from Damien.

"Absolutely not." I did my best to be firm. "Non-negotiable." If the guild house was overrun with Dark Fae—or any Fae—the witches not yet turned to evil would never listen to me.

About anything.

Damien hadn't weighed in, but from the look on his face he was solidly behind the consensus: either don't go or bring an army.

Last thing I wanted was to alienate every witch worse than I already had. After weaving a careful shield around my mind, I spread my fingers in front of me and floated a diversion. "Maybe it wasn't such a good idea after all."

Would they fall for it? If they did, I'd sneak away while Charles was cooking and Damien was (hopefully) back in Flagstaff. Taking the familiars along would be acceptable. After all, they were part of witchdom too.

I wouldn't need much time. Not more than half an hour to kick some serious ass and determine if anyone in the guild house was on my side.

Hecate scratched at the gates of my ward.

Fuck. She's as persistent as Damien. Maybe worse. She had warned me about today's problem, but for all I knew she was part of the planned attack. She's sly, that one, and could easily be playing both ends against the middle.

"Stop worrying about me." I flapped my hands in a shooing motion. "Go back to Flagstaff, Damien. I'll be in the kitchen at my usual time for dinner prep. Sorry about lunch."

Charles narrowed his eyes. "Not entirely true."

"It's close enough," I argued. "Please, leave me alone." I augmented my words with compulsion. Didn't make a dent. Neither man budged.

Zeke ran to the window and put his front paws on the sill. I kicked myself for not pulling the curtain closed. As a stopgap, I made Zeke invisible but maybe not in time.

"Told you we should have gone to Faery." The beginnings of a spell wafted around Damien.

I stole a peek out the window. Double damn. Instead of Banshees and Kelpies, cloaked witches bore down on the boardinghouse. They were still a block or so away. Despite their shielding, I saw them clear as day. Superior magic has its plusses.

I did not want a repeat of the last slaughter in this location. It would drive the PDA nuts. "You shouldn't be here," I hissed at Damien. "The PDA might nab you again."

Charles' dark brows crawled up his forehead. Apparently, he hadn't known about Damien's woes. But then, why would he?

My salvo to Damien was the last thing I said before I engaged a jump spell that landed me in front of my erstwhile sisters. Zeke had been ready and inveigled his way into my casting. Sneaky of him.

I had seconds before Damien, Charles, and Sita would charge into the fray.

"Stop right there," I shouted. Drawing myself up to my full height, I faced eight women I'd once called sisters.

Before they could trap me in enchantment, I swept the lot of us into a travel channel. In the space between two breaths, it spit us out at the rear of a nearby park, the place containing a gateway into a parallel world.

I jettisoned my ward and pushed us through.

Zeke growled, hackles and fangs on full display.

Shanna's eyes widened. "How in the goddess's name did you transport all of us?"

"Same way I killed five of you."

"We thought the Fae did that."

"Nope. Yours truly."

It snagged their attention. "You will quit hounding me. If you don't, I'll show up at the guild house and mow through whoever stands in my way. Is that clear?"

"Eh, you got lucky that night," Shanna muttered.

"I did, huh?" A slender thread of my skill looped around her throat. I snugged it tighter. When she clawed at her neck, gagging, I asked, "Had enough? I've never liked you. Wouldn't take much for me to end this."

Gasping for air, she wheezed, "Take it away."

As a compromise, I loosened it marginally. I rather enjoyed Shanna on the receiving end of torment.

"The Greeks were right about you," another witch mumbled. "You've turned pure evil."

I'd have laughed if it didn't mean removing my attention from my would-be attackers. "Not me. I was minding my own business when you exiled me and murdered Mother. How could you have? Zoelle never did anything wrong."

"She lied about your origins," Lorena announced.

The slender flame of an idea ignited. Know thy enemy is good advice. "How so?" I pressed.

"She claimed you were hers."

"And so, I was. She was a most excellent mother."

"The prophecy implicates you."

"Oh? Which one?"

"You know which one."

"If I did, I wouldn't have asked." Time was wasting. Soon, Damien and Charles would pop in. Sita too. Damien shouldn't be seen anywhere in this vicinity, although he might be marginally safer on this side of the gateway we'd crossed.

Or not. If we traversed it, the PDA could too.

"That you're a latter day queen who wants power over us all," Lorena growled. "You helped imprison Hecate, our true goddess."

Wow. Interesting. The Greeks had done a real smear job to cover their tracks.

"I could give a flying fuck about power. I want to root out the darkness that's encroaching into every Coven. Many of you—Shanna for example—have welcomed sorcerous ways."

I cut off a squawk of protest by tightening the noose still around her neck.

"My task, and one blessed by Hecate, is to clean up the Covens. All of them, not just this one."

"You're lying," another witch snarled.

"And you're pregnant," another blurted. "By that Fae. The child is a boy. He must be destroyed."

"Never going to happen," I gritted.

"Kill them all," Hecate broke through and shrieked into my mind.

"Who was that?" Lorena sounded rattled.

May as well give them grist for the mill. "Hecate. She rides shotgun most of the time."

They were stalling, trying to divert me. A spell wound its way around me and Zeke. I could not let the ends close. Even my power wouldn't be enough to intervene if it did.

"I do not want animosity—" I began.

"Could have fooled us," a witch snapped.

"You came after me," I reminded them. "What I desire is free rein to clean up the Coven. Aren't you interested in who bonded with evil?"

"Oh, and I suppose you're the one to tell us," Shanna croaked.

Heartily sick of her, I yanked on the noose until she fell to the ground twitching and unconscious. Spinning to one side, I sidestepped the entrapment casting.

"Where are your familiars?" Zeke demanded.

Good question.

No one answered.

Damien and Charles pelted through a gateway that blasted out of the ether. Power rained from upraised hands. Whoa. Charles hadn't been kidding when he said the two halves of Fae magic were additive.

Witches fell to their knees as wounds blossomed all over their bodies. Blood sank into the ground. The earth groaned beneath the onslaught, but I might have imagined it.

Once upon a time, witches were guardians of the natural world. Did Earth mourn us? Hell, did she even miss us?

Sita flew from witch to witch, pecking with abandon and knocking out eyes. In between attacks, she cawed, "You killed my bonded one. Slaughtered her."

Zeke added moral support by biting a few nearby appendages.

A couple of witches lurched to their feet and launched a feeble counterattack. The air hummed with expended power.

Crap. This was exactly what I didn't want to happen. Not that they were anywhere close to offering up cooperation, but any window I might have had to establish détente had slammed shut.

Hecate's chorus of *"Kill them all,"* reverberated through my skull. I couldn't keep her at bay and have enough power to manage here.

Good to know.

Probably wasn't lost on her, either.

What in the hell happened to salvaging the remaining good witches? Had it fallen by the wayside? Or had the witch goddess slipped into madness?

A power word wedged its way from my throat, followed by several more. I felt dirty, but they had the desired effect. Everyone stopped dead and stared at me.

"I'm. Done. Running. I will return to the Coven with you. When I'm done, it will be clear of taint. Everyone responsible for killing Mother will be dead."

Damn but I liked the sound of that.

"Kill them all." Hecate was back. More likely, she'd never left.

"Never going to happen. Live with it."

"Like hell you are," Lorena spat in response to my edict. "You can't stop me."

"We'll meet you there," Damien announced. "Charles and I will begin the sorting process."

"No. Men," a witch shrieked.

"Too bad about that." I shrugged. "Remember, you came after me. Where are the Banshees and Kelpies?"

No one volunteered to speak, so I selected Rebecca, one of the weaker sisters, and invaded her memories. Moaning, she grabbed her head, but she wasn't able to block me. Images poured through my mind. Blonde hair sheeted to midback; Hazel eyes fluttered shut. Like the others, she was garbed in a black robe sashed in green. It covered a stocky build with defined shoulders and a thick waist.

"Watch it," I told the men. "The Banshees and Kelpies bide in the basement, hiding in a tunnel system. It's actually a shortcut to travel to and from the Highlands. Explains how they got here."

Charles, who'd released his glamour and gained several inches and a full head of dark hair in the process, laughed. "Banshees have to obey us. They're faeries."

Oh yeah, I'd forgotten that pithy piece. "Well, the Kelpies don't."

"We'll feed them a few witches." Damien grinned nastily. "Should appease them. A win-win."

It did not jive with my hopefully peaceful takedown. Except how peaceful could anything be that broke into a guild house and obliterated a goodly percentage of its residents?

"Do not go ahead of me," I cautioned the men.

"Why not?" Charles was getting into this. I knew less than nothing about the Dark Fae, but Damien had indicated their power was significant and they tended to be nasty.

"Because I'd like a few of the sisters to be on my side."

He laughed uproariously. "Never going to happen."

Damien laid a hand on his arm and bent to speak into his ear.

The babe swished from one side of my belly to the other. I took stock of the witches sprawled on the green and the two on their feet. Eight in all. Shanna was pure evil. What about the others?

I repeated what I'd done with Rebecca, trolling through minds. I wasn't delicate, but I was in a hurry. For all I knew, reinforcements were on their way. I wanted this to play out in the guild house, not an open verge where the PDA could pour in at any moment.

It didn't take long. Shanna and Lorena had long since sold their souls to darkness. The other sisters were merely misguided and plagued by incomplete information.

I flirted with ending the two evil witches and being done with it. Then we could teleport everyone back to the guild house and begin the process of rebuilding—once I'd culled through the sisterhood. It had been my original goal, but I'd been sidetracked by my search for Hecate.

"You're not thinking." This time it was Damien in my mind.

"Leave me alone."

"They will never accept you. Not if you start out by killing them," he insisted.

We'd had this conversation before. I wasn't in much of a listening mood this time.

"I'm open to suggestions but make it snappy. You're a sitting duck out here. Even the witches are convinced you killed those five outside the boardinghouse."

"Take the wicked ones and scrub their magical centers."

I hadn't even considered it mostly because it had such a low probability of success. I was more likely to break a witch, drive her into madness. Still, it was a show of good faith. I could demonstrate I was trying to salvage everyone —whether it was successful or not.

It might buy me a few points.

"Terrible idea," Hecate sputtered.

"For the love of Danu, shut the fuck up."

I must have shocked her because she stopped battering at the edges of my mind.

"Risky," Zeke woofed. *"Gives them an opportunity to overpower you while you're occupied."*

The wolf was right. It argued for including Damien and Charles, something I was loathe to do. The witch who'd spat out the words, *No men*, was serious as fuck.

Perhaps it was time for many changes. I didn't totally understand the prohibition against male witches. My child wasn't evil. I'd know if he channeled darkness. High time I drilled into the issue.

I gestured to Damien and Charles. They joined me.

"Keep an eye on the rest of them, I'm going to experiment on Shanna to see if I can separate out the taint from the rest of her magic."

I didn't wait for agreement. She was already unconscious. It would expedite my task. Hopefully.

"Ward yourself," Damien said tersely.

He was just bursting with good ideas. Evil freed from one witch could easily enter another. My task was twofold. Cut out the bad shit and neutralize it before it found a new home.

No precedent for this, so I stood over Shanna and augured into her magical center. Usually the seat of our power consists of shades of pretty colors winding together like strands of DNA. Magical centers are places of constant movement.

Hers had huge segments that were coal-black, and the undulating strands were mired in ominous brown muck. Holy godhead. This would take hours.

Time I didn't have. Every moment Damien remained out in the open was dangerous for him.

Since I was inside Shanna's magic, I started clipping offending bits. But then I had to stop to nullify them.

"I've got that part," Charles said gruffly.

Clip. Toss. Clip. Toss. Sweat beaded my forehead and dripped down my sides despite a fairly chilly day. For every scrap of evil I freed, two more cropped up to take its place. What the fuck? They had to be layered.

Changing things up, I scooped rather than taking the surface layer. Some healthy strands came away too, but I was moving much faster.

She wouldn't have much magic once I was done, but it was her own damned fault for courting darkness.

Finally, I wiped my forehead with my forearm and stepped back.

"I've never seen anything like that," Damien muttered.

"The witch was pure evil." Charles shook his head. His boots were smeared with muck where he'd stomped out the parts I'd extricated.

The other seven witches had fallen silent as they watched me work. They didn't need a roadmap to understand what I'd done—or that the sisterhood was in deep trouble.

Lorena looked away. "Just kill me," she mumbled. "I am not going through that."

Rebecca stared at her and made a sigil against evil. "You too? How? I looked up to you."

Lorena didn't answer.

Charles hustled to where she crouched. "Are you certain, witch?" At her nod, a glowing saber flickered to life in his hand. He carved out a spot beneath her breastbone, encased the seat of her power in spells, and set fire to it. Greasy black smoke smelling like rotten flesh choked me.

Lorena didn't make a sound as she crumpled to the earth. Sita plucked out an eyeball, chomping merrily.

We'd leave her here. No reason to drag her back to the Coven. She didn't deserve any type of ceremonial leave taking.

Was my magic up to the task of bringing us all to the guild house?

Guess I'd find out. I coaxed a journey spell into being. Before it hit velocity, Fae magic slotted with mine.

The green dropped away replaced by the common room in the Coven guild house.

Horrified shrieks greeted me, along with epithets. I cut through the cacophony.

"Hear me out. I mean well, and this Coven will be better off once I'm done."

"She speaks true," Rebecca said in a trembling voice. Another witch seconded her impression.

"She can't mean well. She brought men into our fold. Fucking men. Get them out of here now." Lilith strode forward, crystal ball in hand.

"Not a chance," I snarled. "If you're truly a seer, you've seen this in your ball. You know how it plays out. Time to offer up your badly tarnished soul for redemption."

She turned to flee; Damien nabbed her in a golden net.

No rest for me, not for hours. Time to get back to work. I was doing what I should have done all along. Salvaging the sisterhood—and avenging Mother—was way more important than the deranged witch goddess still shouting instructions from the sidelines.

CHAPTER 8

DAMIEN

Who would have thought I'd ever partner with a Dark Fae? Certainly not me. So far, it was going decently. I've mentioned how much stronger Dark Fae are than me. I never could have obliterated the evil Morgan dredged from Shanna. Not by myself. Nor could I have ended Lorena. I'd helped Charles, but he'd have been fine without me.

At some point, I'd have to come clean with the Fae council, but I'd worry about that later.

Interesting Lorena chose to end her immortal existence rather than explore a chance for salvation. Either she was so steeped in evil she preferred it, or watching Shanna stripped of sorcery had rattled her badly.

Perhaps a little of both.

My irritation with Morgan at forging an independent path without discussing it first gave way to waves of admiration. She was strong, principled. And she was holding Hecate at bay. It was wrong of me, but I'd done spot checks. The witch goddess didn't sound any more sane than she had my last go round with her.

Had the Greeks tortured her to the point her faculties fled?

My attention shifted to a bevy of witches pouring into a large room. Couches and easy chairs dotted its expanse along with tables and bookshelves. To be more than dead weight, I scanned auras.

Charles joined me. "Never thought I'd see the day I'd partner up with one of your ilk."

"Funny, I was thinking the same but in reverse. Let's make Morgan's task simpler. That one"—I jabbed a finger at Lilith, the Coven's seer—"is tainted."

"Ha! More like immersed." He drew his dark brows together into a thick line. "Damn me. She's a shapeshifter, not a witch at all."

I stared at the seer holding her crystal ball at eye level between her and Morgan. Try as I might, I couldn't peel enough layers to find anything that wasn't witch.

Zeke barreled into her from the right knocking her to the carpeted floor. The crystal ball went flying. It shrieked when it hit the floor, an eerie caterwauling no magical accoutrement should have been able to produce.

Crap. Was it sentient? All Maeve's props only worked through her magic.

The wolf's paws were on Lilith's shoulders; he snarled, displaying every tooth. It should have been enough to keep her on the floor.

"Fuck," Charles shouted and executed an impressive

leap that landed him next to them. Colors flowed from his hands and wrapped around Lilith, except it wasn't her any longer. She'd morphed into an alligator-esque creature with snapping jaws.

Zeke held his ground.

Morgan extended her hands. Viscous strands married with the colored webbing already trussing Lilith.

Witches were closing from all four sides. Time to determine who batted for our team. I erected a hasty barrier around Morgan, Zeke, and Charles to keep the horde at bay while I culled those who'd embraced evil. Not that I could do much more than segregate them, but it would be a start.

"Help me," I called to Sita. She'd lived with these women and should know the bad apples.

"I will," Rebecca ran lightly to my side. "Now I know what to look for, it's those five." Her cheeks were streaked with tears she'd shed after discovering Lorena, obviously a mentor or role model, had deceived her.

"Two more," Sita cawed. "Ronnie and Anya. They imprisoned Zoelle. Probably helped murder her."

"Nooooo," Rebecca cried. "No one told us she was dead, only that she'd moved elsewhere."

"She's dead, all right," I confirmed. "I was in the room when it happened."

Working with Rebecca and a few other witches who'd clearly had a stomach full of duplicity, I herded the tainted witches into a cage, crafted and sealed with magic.

Would it be enough to hold them? I sure as hell hoped so.

The alligator had shifted into first a lion and then a

bobcat. Morgan was having a hell of a time hitting a moving target.

"Knock her out," I yelled.

"Been trying. Can't," she panted.

"Told you"—Charles' voice carried—"she's a shapeshifter, but one of the elder ones, so she's not limited to a single form. How in the hell did she enter this Coven?"

Morgan's mismatched eyes widened. She hadn't heard Charles' assessment when the two of us had been talking.

"Fuck it, then," she growled. "I figured she was possessed. Zeke, to me."

Reluctantly, the wolf abandoned his post. He'd been taking chunks out of fallen witches, but he'd been wounded too. Blood dribbled from cut places in his shaggy pelt.

Morgan focused a beam of black light on the Coven's seer. It penetrated the center of her forehead, leaving a hole two inches across. The bobcat shifted to an eagle; the hole closed.

"What the fuck?" Morgan hit the eagle with more black light. It flinched but didn't fall over.

Sita flew at the eagle from the side, latched her talons onto its shoulders, and drove her beak through the side of its neck. Blood flowed.

Half a dozen witches rushed forward, intent on rescuing their seer.

I stepped between them and Lilith. "Do you really want to save her? She's not a witch. She deceived you all."

"Why should we believe you," a witch with long red hair demanded.

"Because I'm telling the truth. Look for yourselves."

"It's ridiculous. She's been part of this coven for centuries. Something possessed her."

"Look well," Sita cawed from her perch on the eagle. "Witches aren't shapeshifters. How can you explain her transformations?"

"There must be a logical answer," the redhead insisted, still intent on breaking through to Lilith. "Might be illusion or possession."

"It's not," Sita cawed.

The crystal ball still moaned piteously. I was loathe to touch it, but I surrounded it with a probing spell. It shrieked louder. Running on instinct, I tightened up my casting until it surrounded the ball.

The stone cracked; a tiny leprechaun leapt out shaking both fists at Lilith and shrieking, "Free. Free. Finally, free, you horrid bitch."

He executed a somersault and landed in front of me, bowing low. "I am forever in your debt, Fae. If my people can ever provide anything of use to you, you have only to ask."

"Appreciate the thought, but freeing you was an accident. I had no idea you were in there."

"Doesn't matter. She captured me from my home, separated me from my kinsmen, after pretending to be our friend."

"Why?"

He puffed out his chest. "For my seer ability. She had none and needed me so she could pull off her charade."

"Why not refuse?" Charles called from his post over the eagle.

"She hurt me if I said no." The creature hung his head. "After a while, I gave up."

The leprechaun was growing as he spoke. Soon he was closer to normal size. Had Lilith damned him with a shrinking spell before she'd encased him in her ball? He capered to this side and that. In the midst of an impressive leap, he vanished.

"Hard to believe," the redheaded witch muttered.

"Nothing like seeing the evidence." I turned to face the women. "Can you keep those witches"—I swung an arm to encompass the bunch we'd trapped in a cage—"from escaping?"

"When did you do that?" A woman with cropped white hair stared aghast at her sisters beating on the sides of my trap.

"As soon as I determined who needed to go."

"He's lying," one of the detained witches cried.

"And a Fae. And a man. You can't trust him," another shouted.

"Grab Morgan. And that wolf of hers," a third suggested. Compulsion ran through her words, thick and saccharine.

"Aye, we've been on the hunt for them for months." The first witch nodded.

"Shut up. All of you," Morgan thundered. Wresting the light sword from Charles, she drove it through the eagle's feathered breast. The bird lashed its beak back and forth, snapping at anything close. The only place she managed to inflict damage was a nearby low-slung table.

"I hate this," Morgan muttered and grasped the sword's

hilt. Bending, she whispered a power word. It ran down the hilt and into the bird.

"Keep it coming," Charles urged. "A couple more like that, and she'll finally be dead."

"Not that way. It costs me," Morgan growled. Hands spread, she angled more black light right at the eagle's neck. Sita had opened it enough to create weak points. Her enchantment separated the wounds until the bird exploded. When the parts settled, they were arms and legs. A torso and a head.

I kept an eye on the segments to make certain they didn't edge toward one another. I'd heard of phenomena like that with truly ancient and evil sorcerers.

Morgan staggered upright. Sweat streaked her forehead. Circles etched beneath her eyes. How was our son surviving this?

Wearily, Morgan faced the women who'd been part of her family. They stared back. "I am not done," she said. "Who else carries the stain of evil?"

No one had been watching over my cage. Everyone's attention had been rivetted by the battle to dispatch Lilian. A startled gasp suggested leaving the witches to their own devices had been a major oversight.

"They're dead," someone cried.

"How is that even possible?" another chimed in.

I strode to my working. Sure enough, bodies littered the floor. My nostrils twitched. Hemlock. I'd had no idea witches were sensitive to it. Where the hell had they gotten hold of it?

"Is hemlock fatal to your kind?" I searched the room, hoping for an answer.

"No," the redhead mumbled. "It shouldn't be. Unless they weren't really witches, either. Shit." She sank into a chair and dropped her head into her hands, rubbing her temples.

I could relate. My head was pounding too.

A stream of blue-hued power flowed from Charles' outstretched palms as he examined the fallen witches. "Ha. Not dead after all. This is something akin to the Fae Death Coma, except they did it to themselves."

Sneaky. I'd have withdrawn my magic. Someone would have carried the witches off somewhere. While the Coven prepared to dispatch the bodies, the women would have teleported the fuck out of there. Except if it was anything like the Fae coma, it would have to wear off.

"Morgan?" I glanced her way.

"It's a type of stasis. They could have shucked it whenever."

The redhead was on her feet. "We can handle this from here."

The witch with cropped white hair said, "Aye, this is our problem." Facing Morgan, she bowed. "Appreciate you bringing it to our attention. We will ensure they can't do any further harm."

"A bit late for Zoelle." Morgan's tone could have etched glass.

"I am truly sorry about your mother. We had no idea she was dead."

I had the presence of mind to toss a truth spell over her before she was done speaking. It chimed sweetly.

"So it wasn't all of you?" Morgan asked.

The witch shook her head. "We are not in the habit of slaughtering our own, or have you forgotten?"

Morgan rolled her shoulders back. "Since you kicked me out, I've had reason to question everything."

"Understandable. Would you like to return?"

Morgan hesitated, eyes rounding into moons. Clearly, she hadn't expected an invitation. Placing a hand on her belly, she said. "No. I will give birth to my son and raise him. He will have no chance at all inside any Coven."

"What if we made an exception?" The witch's tone was sweet, but something swarmy lay behind it. I didn't trust her.

"Not even then."

"Are you certain you'll dispatch your corrupt sisters?" Charles asked. Snagging an end of my truth spell, he tossed it over the entire room.

"Define dispatch," the redhead said.

"Ensure they're defanged and can do no more harm."

"If you're asking if we'll turn them into Shanna," the white-haired witch replied, "I checked. She's naught but a vegetable."

"She may come around," Morgan argued. "Don't you want the Coven to be safe? How can it be when it's become a magnet for dark sorcery?"

"I told you, we'll figure it out," the witch said stiffly. "Pick up the pieces. 'Tis a sad day for us all."

"Sad because you finally had to face up to the truth?" Morgan shook herself from head to toe. "I did you a favor."

"Not feeling like it at the moment," the other witch muttered. "We need time to grieve, to process—"

"Don't take too long. I plan on returning to check on your progress."

"Who made you the witch police," someone called from the rear of the room.

"Hecate. If she had her way, I'd have killed you all for allowing evil to penetrate your ranks. But I'm not her."

"Prove it," someone yelled.

Morgan pinched the bridge of her nose between her thumb and forefinger. I catapulted to her side. "Do not let her break through. You'll never contain her again."

"Damien's right," Charles said.

Zeke rubbed against Morgan's side.

"Drop a truth net over me," Morgan invited.

None of the witches moved, so I crafted one. Once it was in place, Morgan said, "Hecate has made my life a living hell. She's co-opted my dreams and my waking mind too. I expend scads of magic to keep her at bay. Her incessant chant of 'kill them all' is a constant I've had to live with."

My spell chimed enthusiastically, ample evidence of truth. I dismantled it.

"Believe me now?" Morgan inquired.

Silence hung heavy in the well-appointed room.

"Fine. I'm leaving. If you allow those witches to escape, you will face my wrath, and it won't be pretty."

"What about the other Covens? We can't be the only one," the white-haired witch said.

"It's a long story," Morgan replied. "This where I should have begun. Instead, I wasted months trying to locate Hecate. My plan is to weed darkness from every Coven."

"Big task for a single witch," someone observed.

"It is. While you're processing and grieving, see if you can find it within yourselves to designate a witch or two to help."

No one snatched up the bait. Why? Didn't they care about how far the sisterhood had fallen?

The beginnings of Morgan's spell caught me up. I added to it. So did Charles. In the blink of an eye the three of us plus Zeke and Sita were back in Morgan's room.

Charles rubbed his hands together. "Haven't had that much fun in ages. Thanks for an enjoyable afternoon. Got to get to the kitchen or dinner will be late."

"Nice try," Morgan said. "Augment your efforts with magic."

He winked broadly and adopted his usual glamour. "Our little secret. See you in the kitchen soon."

Once he was gone, I said, "Could have gone worse."

"Yeah. Could have gone better too, but I'm not complaining. I finally did something besides stew in my own soup about Hecate."

"Why'd you decide to approach your Coven?"

A shrug. "I always wanted to, but there was never an opportunity. I finally figured out there never would be unless I made one."

Zeke was licking my hands. Sita perched on the dresser. "Today was good," she chirped. "We finally avenged Zoelle."

Morgan stroked the hawk's plumage. "Yes, we did."

I started toward them, but stopped.

"What?" Morgan asked. "Isn't it about time for you to return to Flagstaff?"

"Is that what you want?"

She closed her teeth over her lower lip. "For now, I think so."

It hurt. I'd have far preferred to stay. "Would you mind if I talked with our son before I go?"

She tilted her head to one side. Clearly, she hadn't expected that request. "Okay."

I placed my hands over her belly and opened my mind to the babe, reassuring him we'd always keep him safe. In the middle of our conversation, I raised my gaze to Morgan. "He has a name. Did you know?"

She shook her head. "What is it?"

"Niall. I'd thought we needed to name him, but he's named himself. The kidnapped leprechaun disturbed him."

"I can see where it would have." Morgan exhaled sharply. "All those years, and none of us had a clue Lilith was anything but what she appeared."

After a few more minutes, I let go. I should have left it be, but I asked, "When will I see you again?"

Her lips parted in a soft smile. "Soon. Come back whenever you'd like."

I wrapped her in my arms and held her for a few precious moments before setting a spell in place to take me back to Arizona. "Are you coming?" I asked Sita.

"Would you mind if I stayed here?"

"No, I wouldn't mind at all."

As my journey casting swept me away, I felt certain my

family would be together again soon. Sita had forgiven Morgan, and Morgan had forgiven me. Hecate was still an unknown, but we'd deal with it together.

Charles had been an unexpected gem. The Fae council wouldn't see it that way. I should report in, but it could wait until after work tomorrow. I inhaled a quick meal and sacked out on the couch.

Must have been more tapped out than I imagined because by the time I jolted awake, I didn't have time to take a bus to work. A mini jump spell spit me out near the jobsite. Only a few minutes late, I grabbed my gear and got to it.

"What's up, Underhill? Get laid last night?" Someone elbowed me.

"Why would you think that?"

"You're whistling and entirely too happy for a Thursday."

I hadn't realized my joy was spilling over. Trying for the male version of a Mona Lisa smile, I said, "I'll never tell," and pounded a few more nails home.

CHAPTER 9

MORGAN

It would have been easy, too easy, to ask Damien to stay. We'd just been through hell at the Coven guild house and were riding high on what had been mostly a success. Why hadn't my erstwhile sisters been more enthusiastic about helping me address the other Covens? There were a lot of them, maybe sixty scattered around the world.

It would easily take me years to address the problem, and that assumed each Coven stayed "fixed" after I dropped in. They might not. Once evil has taken root, it's tough to eradicate it for good.

I stripped out of my filthy clothes, grabbed a robe and a towel, and trotted to the bathroom for a quick shower. As I stood under hot water, I laced my fingers over my stomach.

"How are you, Niall?"

"Good. My father was here."

His reply ran a sword through my heart. What would he

do if Damien and I didn't repair our fractured relationship? Would I ever be enough for our son? It wasn't looking that way.

A question danced through my mind. I fiddled with wording before coming up with, *"Does your grandmother talk with you?"*

"Sometimes."

Damn it. I'd been afraid of that. Done cleaning up, I toweled off and hustled back to my room. I'd have killed to know what Hecate was filling my son's mind with, but I didn't want to press him. All the blood and carnage he'd borne witness to today had been enough.

Dressed in my only other set of clothes, I prodded Zeke. "Want to come to the kitchen with me?"

He stretched out each leg and yawned before joining me as I left the room. Sita was asleep. As an afterthought, I returned long enough to crack the window so she could hunt.

Charles grinned at me after we slipped through the swinging door. "If you're tired, you can sit this one out. I have dinner well in hand."

"Nope. I'm good."

Zeke retired to his usual spot but not before polishing off a bowl of scraps Charles had set out for him.

Charles pointed to the makings for a salad. I started chopping. "How'd you end up here?" I asked.

"Had a falling out with the Unseelie prince. He made demands I wasn't willing to meet, so I left."

A whole other infrastructure I knew nothing about. "How long ago?"

A shrug. "Hard to know exactly. This isn't the first spot I've been." He nailed me with his blue gaze. "All I'm willing to say."

I poked the edges of his mind, but it was closed to me.

Unfortunate. I had scads of questions. Like, what was his real name? Were the Dark Fae looking for him? Did he have to work? Or was he like Damien and merely choosing to pass the time?

"The sisterhood didn't appear particularly grateful. Any idea why?" he asked as he stirred an enormous pot of stew.

I could have borrowed a card from his deck and not answered, but their reticence had bothered me too. "I'm not sure. Particularly given Lilith's long deception, I would have expected a warmer welcome."

"Perhaps they'll come around."

"Doubt it. Best case, they'll stop spying on me."

I tossed greens with a vinaigrette dressing. "Have you known about me from the beginning?"

"Yes."

"Why didn't you say anything?"

He set the spoon down, walked to me, and spoke near my ear. "You didn't figure out what I am. It's better that way. You cannot tell anyone I am here. No one."

"But you showed yourself to the entire Coven."

"They didn't exactly see me. I'm a master at concealing my identity. You had no idea I carried any magic at all."

Not totally true, but I hadn't looked very hard, either. I'd been too sunk in my own problems to seek out power in unlikely places. "It's not me you need worry about, but Damien is likely to mention you to the Fae council."

"Why would he do that?"

I took a step back. "Is there some reason he shouldn't? The two halves of—"

The kitchen door swung against its stops. Smythe stood with his hands on his hips. "Is dinner ready?"

"Yes. Sorry. Of course." Charles walked back to the industrial range, hefted the stewpot, and carried it past Smythe to the serving table. I followed with the salad. A tray of sliced white bread sat on a sideboard. I returned for it and a few slabs of disgusting margarine.

Some of the other residents waved hello, but most kept to themselves. This boardinghouse was definitely a "don't ask, don't tell" zone. Everyone sat on secrets.

Before Smythe interrupted us, I'd been about to mention the animosity between the two branches of Faery. His appearance had stilled my tongue. Just as well. Conversations about who we really were should be held behind shielding.

I waited until everyone had served themselves before filling a bowl with stew and a plate with salad and retiring to a stool in the kitchen. Per usual, there was barely enough to go around. I felt certain Smythe's instructions ensured the perennial lack of leftovers.

As I ate, I asked myself why I hadn't picked up on the extent of Charles' magic. I'd spent enough time with him, but it never occurred to me he was much beyond what he appeared. The depth of his deception was a testament to his skill.

Smythe wandered into the kitchen. "Why was dinner late?"

I glanced at him without bothering to set down my fork. "The stew needed more time."

"Seemed tender to me."

I smiled and pushed waves of calm his way. "Because we cooked it an extra half hour."

"How's that mending coming?"

Oops. "I'll get to it as soon as I'm done cleaning up the kitchen."

"See that you do." On that cheery note, he left.

Charles pushed through the doors on his heels. *"Did he ask after dinner?"* At my nod, he went on. *"What'd you tell him?"*

"That the stew needed more cooking time."

The Dark Fae grinned. *"Good woman."*

Done eating, I attacked the dishes. Charles left. I frequently didn't see him after he'd finished meal preparation. Now that I knew more, I wondered where he went. Not back to Faery. It sounded as if he'd been exiled—kind of like me—even though he said he'd chosen to leave.

I made a mental note to tell Damien to hold Charles' secret. It offered a ready excuse for me to go to him, but I wouldn't have time until much later tonight. Probably better to wait until between breakfast and lunch tomorrow. Surely, he wouldn't find time to sandwich in a trip to Faery before that.

Zeke followed me out of the kitchen. Rather than go to my room—and the sewing—right away, I took us out for a walk. We hadn't gotten two blocks when witch energy bore down on us. I dropped a shield into place and readied defensive magic.

A piss-poor idea in the middle of Seattle, but it beat being ganged up on.

"*Only one,*" Zeke woofed.

I relaxed marginally but kept my guard up.

Rebecca melted from between two parked vehicles and caught up to me. I kept my barrier in place. "What is it?"

"It's only me. Test my intentions."

"Not here." Zeke might not have been done with his evening constitutional, but I herded us down a deserted side street and whisked us to my room. She didn't fight me, and I didn't sense any other witches in the vicinity.

"This is where you landed?" Rebecca blinked as she observed my modest surroundings.

I took a chance and released my shield. "Yup. This is it. I didn't have much choice. No money. No ID. No—"

"I get it. I'm sorry for what happened to you. It wasn't my doing, but I didn't speak up on your behalf, either."

Zeke, who'd been standing between us, hackles at half mast, retreated to the window where he placed his paws on the sill staring into the darkness.

"Why are you here?"

"Even if no one else volunteers, I will help as I can with the other Covens."

Gratitude welled. "Thank you. It's not without danger."

"I'm well aware."

"What about everyone else?"

She raked her fingers through heavy blonde hair. "They've been arguing ever since you left."

"About?"

"What to do. Lilith's trickery stunned the sisters. And, of course, we now lack a seer."

"You never had one," I pointed out. "Lilith picked and chose which of the leprechaun's visions to share. For all you know, she made shit up."

"There is that." She laid a hand on my arm. "Are you sure you don't want to come back?"

"To a place where I won't be able to keep my child?"

"But it's a boy. Male witches—"

"He's half Fae. And he's not evil," I broke in, not wanting to have this conversation.

"I could argue on your behalf."

I patted her hand before stepping away. "Don't bother. I'd have to watch my back. It's not appealing."

"What will you do with him?"

It was an odd question, so I drilled into her mind to see what lay behind it. Curiosity jumped to the fore.

"I will love him and raise him to the best of my ability."

"Will the Fae be involved?"

Another unusual question. "Why wouldn't he be?"

Dots of color stained her cheeks. "They aren't thrilled about mixed-race children."

"How do you know?"

The color deepened. "I looked it up."

"Why are you so interested in me?"

Her entire face turned a deep rose. "It's not that so much, but we all lived in the same place. You're the only one who dug deep enough to reveal the rot permeating our core."

"Don't give me too much credit. I'm also the only one

who got the boot. If it hadn't happened, I'd still be fat, dumb, and happy like the rest of you."

Sita whisked through the window, the remains of a mouse in her curved beak. When she saw Rebecca, she dropped it. An outraged squawk emerged.

"How dare you come here."

"It's all right," I told the hawk. "She means well."

Rebecca bowed before the hawk. "I am most humbly sorry about your loss. I may not have spoken up in Morgan's defense, but I did make my misgivings known regarding plans for Zoelle. At the time, I believed she was merely relocating at the behest of the Coven. If I'd had any idea what their true plans were, I'd have moved heaven and earth to intervene."

"Whatever. Your intentions didn't do much good," Sita cawed.

I tossed a sound shield around the room.

"No, they didn't." Rebecca straightened. "I should leave. What has happened within our home hurts my heart. Witches are not supposed to be at one another's throats."

"It won't improve until we carve out the evil that's taken root," I warned.

"Like I said earlier, I stand ready to assist."

Once she was gone, I sorted through the stack of ripped garments and sheets Smythe had left. I'd figured out the sewing machine my last go round here.

Midway through my second piece, Zeke said, *"She really was alone."*

He'd never left his post gazing out the window.

"There's hope," I told him and Sita. "If one witch can come around, others may as well."

"When will you check on the seven?" Sita rustled her feathers.

"Tomorrow sometime."

I took stock of the sewing pile. Too much to finish tonight, but if I made a dent in it, Smythe would probably be satisfied. Tomorrow would be busy between dropping in to warn Damien to hang onto Charles' secret, stopping by the Coven, and taking care of my tasks here.

"She was nice," Niall cooed. *"I want to be a witch."*

"Why not one of the Fae?"

"I want to be Fae too." He sounded sleepy, content in his watery home.

When I was done with a ripped sheet, I laid a hand over my belly. *"You can be whatever you want, darling. The world will be wide open for you."*

"Only if you and Daddy are together," he informed me.

I returned to the stack of sewing, machine humming merrily. Did I carry a young seer in my belly? He'd sounded certain when he'd pronounced that bit about his future only being secure if Damien and I were a team.

Or were his words wishful thinking?

All children long to be raised by both parents. Why would my son deviate from that path? Magical or no, he was attached to us both.

A familiar clawing at the edges of my mind had to be Hecate. She'd been quiescent since the scene at the guild house.

"They have moved me, Daughter. I do not know for how long,

but with your help I can escape. I am beneath the ruins of Fort William's Castle."

Fuckity-fuck. She was at it again. I debated ignoring her, but she repeated her plea. I pushed the mending aside and swathed the animals and me in layers of warding. *"I do not trust you. Your interference nearly cost me Damien."*

"I am sorry for that. I had no idea how attached you were. I do not blame your lack of faith in me. Were the tables turned, I wouldn't trust me, either. Hermes and Hera were force-feeding me bella donna and fermented rye seeds. I have not been in my right mind, but I can think clearly again."

"You called Damien a pesky Fae and said my hand was well-played to rid myself of him."

"So I did. It was a mistake."

"Do not fall for any of it," Zeke growled.

"Damien wouldn't approve," Sita cawed.

I clapped my hands over my ears and deepened my ward. It took a long while before I blocked out her voice. When my mind quieted, I was panting, and sweat rolled down my sides.

Determined to make better progress than I had, I returned to the mending.

"We're going to visit Damien tomorrow morning," I told the animals.

"And tell him everything," Zeke woofed.

"Yes, I will tell him everything. No more secrets."

The wolf plopped on my feet, his way of telling me he'd hold me to it.

CHAPTER 10
DAMIEN

I'd been working for a couple of hours when the distinct scent of witch brought my head snapping around. Had word spread through the Covens? Were they after me now too?

"Can we talk with you for a few minutes?" marched across my mind.

It sure felt like Morgan. I pushed a seeking spell in an arc and located her, Zeke, and Sita. Something must have happened for her to have tracked me to the jobsite.

I found the foreman and did my best to look punky. "Not feeling tiptop. Might have a touch of food poisoning from last night. Mind if I take a half-hour break? I'll make it up at the end of the day."

He eyed me up and down. "Okay, and Underhill..."

"Yeah?"

"Stick to ground work until you're certain you're not dizzy."

I mimed a salute. "Aye aye, sir. For what it's worth, I'm a shitty sailor."

He snorted. "Get out of here."

I didn't wait to be asked twice. Not wanting to appear too chipper, I trudged down the hill from the jobsite, angling in the general direction I'd sensed Morgan. She met me at an outdoor café on a busy corner.

Too many people to really talk, so I gestured for her to follow me to a deserted lot at the end of the block. Zeke, wearing his shaggy brown dog glamour, trotted next to me, nosing my hand. Sita moved from Morgan's shoulder to my own. We were far more memorable than I'd have liked.

How many couples travel with a dog and a hawk?

"Good to see you," I ventured.

"I can't stay long. Please don't tell the Fae about working with Charles."

I took a step back. "Can't do that."

"Why not?"

"It's one of our laws. He knows as much. It would put me in a terrible position if I hung on to the information and Logan or Maeve found out."

She shut her eyes briefly. "Why?"

"The short version is we don't trust them. The feeling is mutual. He's supposed to report in same as me. It ensures separation between the two halves of Faery."

"Erm, he didn't exactly admit it, but they may have kicked him out."

Shock ricocheted through me. "Shit on a shingle. That's unusual. He must have done something hideous."

"Can't you please just leave him out of this. He helped

us. Speaking of which, Rebecca showed up and offered to assist with clearing the Covens of taint."

"That's a spot of positive news. Maybe others will come around."

"I'm hoping but not holding my breath. About the other?"

I didn't want to lie to Morgan or overpromise. "I won't bring Charles up, but if Maeve's already seen him in her crystals, I won't deny the association." I turned my hands palms up. "How can I?"

"Mmph. I see the problem. Okay, I'll let him know. We need to leave now. Maybe we can connect later today or tomorrow."

"Not so fast," Zeke woofed.

"Tell him." Sita clacked her beak.

My stomach formed a hard painful knot. Suddenly, the tale I'd spun about feeling ill entered the realm of truth. "Tell me what?"

Breath steamed through Morgan's clenched teeth. "Hecate showed up again. This time, she sounded sane. Says they moved her and it's my one opportunity to help her escape."

I unclenched my jaw before I broke a tooth. "Thanks for telling me."

She rolled her eyes. "Pressure from the peanut gallery aside, I would have, but today I'm short on time."

"Where is she?"

"Beneath the ruins of Fort William's castle."

I visualized the wreck of what had once been a clan

stronghold. "It would have to be pretty far beneath since there's nothing left of the place."

Morgan flapped a hand. "It's not on my agenda today."

"Are you even considering it?

I had to hand it to Morgan. She faced me squarely, holding my gaze. "I'm not sure. If I do go, it won't be without you."

"And us," Sita squawked.

"Goes without saying," Morgan told the hawk.

I switched topics. "Why are you so busy today?"

"This trip to talk with you. Finishing an ungodly stack of mending. Meal prep and serving. And I plan to do a spot check at the guild house to make certain those seven witches didn't break free."

"I'll stop by later this evening if it's all right."

Zeke woofed happily. Sita rubbed her beak on the side of my head. At least, the animals endorsed me.

Morgan nodded. "Yeah. That's fine. I might not be especially energetic, but we can touch base."

I wanted to hold her, bury my hands in the silk of her hair, but she blew me a kiss and was gone.

My allotted half hour was more than up. I rejoined the crew and worked out the day plus the time I'd missed. When I let myself into my rattrap apartment, Maeve was waiting.

I hung my coat over a hook. "To what do I owe the pleasure?"

She narrowed her blue eyes. "Something you'd like to tell me?"

Oh-oh. She already knew. So much for keeping Charles a secret.

"The, erm, cook at the boardinghouse is more than I originally thought."

"Is that right? When were you planning to show up in Faery and let us know?"

"For Danu's sake, I only found out yesterday." It was a lie, but a small one. I'd known Charles was some iteration of mage, but not the exact type.

"You should have dropped everything and hightailed it to Faery."

"Excuse me." I swept past her, snatched a bottle of mead, and poured us both glasses. "If you saw the Dark Fae, then you also saw us kicking ass at the Coven guild house. It took hours, but it's cleansed."

"You could have come afterward."

"My magic isn't as strong as either Morgan's or his. Took everything I had left to come here and fall on my face."

"Shit excuse."

Maybe it was, but I'd hang my hat on it.

"What do you know about that particular Dark Fae?" she pressed.

"Nothing."

Magic drilled into me, withdrawing after she satisfied herself I wasn't holding secrets. She grabbed her glass and emptied half of it. "If the Dark Fae is who I think, the Unseelie prince banished him to Earth."

"Any idea why? He seems a decent enough chap, and his magic is robust."

"Pfft. It should be. He was part of their court before he pissed off the dragons by stealing one of their eggs."

"What? Why?"

"No idea. Perhaps he fancied himself a dragon-rider. The Dark Fae have a longstanding relationship with dragonkind."

My eyebrows shot up. I hadn't known that. "Was the egg recovered?"

"Luckily, yes. It wasn't harmed. Still, the theft created a breach until the Unseelie prince acted swiftly to toss his kinsmen out of Faery."

"Explains why Charles—"

"Oh is that what he's calling himself these days?" she inquired acidly.

I'd figured it wasn't his real name. The Dark Fae have always favored fancier titles. "Explains why he buried himself at an obscure boardinghouse." I finished my thought.

"Did you ever consider it's why you also picked that spot? Magic calls to its own."

I hadn't, but then I'd only known the extent of Charles' ability these past twenty-four hours.

"We have to tell them," Maeve went on.

"Huh? Tell who, what?"

She polished off the mead and poured another couple of fingers. "We must let the Unseelie court know. They've been hunting him for years."

"Not very hard," I mumbled.

"This is not our problem. But sharing his location is our responsibility."

"Morgan may have alerted him."

"How?"

I plopped onto the couch that doubled as my bed.

"Morgan stopped by this morning to ask me not to tell anyone about Charles. I told her I couldn't do that."

She narrowed her eyes. "You left something out."

Fucking seers. "Yeah. I did say I wouldn't bring him up, but warned her it was likely you'd been following us with your glass. Under direct questioning, I was clear I'd follow our laws."

"Some of them. You conveniently ignored the one that states you must report any and all Dark Fae sightings as soon as possible."

I turned my hands palms up. "So, sue me. It's out in the open now."

"If Morgan hasn't warned him, you will not, either."

I should have agreed and wished her a good evening. Should have.

Instead, I asked, "Did anyone ask why he'd stolen the dragon egg?"

"That's Unseelie business," she gritted as if even saying the name made her feel dirty.

"Was there anything else?"

"Isn't this enough? Logan has to make a trip to their court. He'll downplay your lack of an immediate response and pretend you followed the rules."

"Be sure to thank him for me."

"Return to Faery and thank him yourself."

Logan's temper was legendary. "If it's all the same, I'll give it a few days, wait until the heat dies down."

She shook a finger at me. "You will not warn him."

"No, I won't. My bet is he's already gone."

A shrug. "We'll see. Even if he is, the others can probably track him."

"Have you seen anything further about Hecate or the Covens?"

"Nothing new. It surprised me when Morgan grabbed the bit between her teeth."

"She's been talking about it since they murdered her mother," I reminded Maeve.

"More power to her. Evil must be weeded out wherever it rears its head."

"Have the Greeks returned?"

"No, but they won't stay gone. They want your child dead."

"Didn't the council establish a connection with Arianrhod?" Getting the Celts involved to give us an edge against the Greeks had been my idea.

"We've covered that ground. Yes, sort of. No guarantees she'll dirty her hands with us, though. Depends on her mood."

Maeve plopped her glass on the table. "Don't wait too long to thank Logan. Might improve his temper."

"Tomorrow night," I promised.

"Why not tonight?"

"I told Morgan I'd check in with her."

"Make sure she butts out of anything related to the Dark Fae."

I muffled a snort. "I'll try, but you know Morgan."

"She will soon be mother to a half-Fae child. Loyalty to Faery and respect for its rules must be instilled—"

"Stop. Just stop. You're angry, and rightfully so, but

Morgan and I are feeling our way. Nothing is certain, not even whether we'll resurrect our relationship."

"It changes nothing."

Before I could respond, she was gone. This was why mages didn't mate outside their ranks. One of the reasons, anyway. Crossing all the Ts and dotting all the Is was tough enough when you were born with them. The odds of wrenching compliance from Morgan about anything Fae-related were slim to none.

I took a quick shower and changed into fresh clothes before launching a journey spell to Seattle. Zeke and Sita greeted me. Morgan must still be in the kitchen cleaning up.

"Half the witches escaped," Sita cawed.

"Yes, the Coven underestimated their power," Zeke growled.

"Where's Morgan?"

"Right here." She strode through the door. Anger hardened her features, and her dark brows swept upward like crow's wings.

I started toward her, but she held up a hand. "I have to return to the guild house."

"I'll accompany you."

"Not the wisest decision. Men make everyone nervous."

"But I'm a mage."

"Same difference."

I tried another tack. "How'd they lose the captives?"

"Not sure. No one is fessing up. I plan to change that."

"How? By torturing them?"

"If it's needed."

Gah. What the hell had happened since this morning?

I closed a hand around her upper arm. "Listen to

yourself. When we left yesterday, you had the beginnings of new ground with the sisterhood. One even volunteered to help you. If you're too heavy-handed, you'll blow it."

"I. Don't. Care." She punched the air. "Let go of me." She wrenched away.

Riding on instincts that have rarely failed me, I pushed into her magical center. A wave of enchantment boomeranged, slapping me so hard I staggered.

I'd wanted to be wrong, but the force behind that blow came from Hecate.

Zeke growled and stood across from Morgan, hackles quivering.

"How could you?" the wolf snarled.

"Give it a rest. I made you too," Hecate shot back courtesy of Morgan's vocal cords.

"Fight this," I pleaded.

"What if I don't want to?"

"It's not you talking, but her." Sita clacked her beak and took to the air keening mournfully.

"I need her," Morgan informed me. "I'll give her back when I'm done."

Crap. Must be to escape from beneath the ruined castle in Fort William. "If I give my word to lend my magic, will you leave?"

The Morgan who wasn't laughed maniacally. I wasn't at all certain Morgan's assessment about Hecate's mental state was solid. She sounded madder than a swamp witch.

I debated my options. On my best day, I wasn't strong enough to stand up to either witch alone, let alone their combined skill. No one in Faery would hear me, or they might, but Logan was pissed and Maeve not far behind.

"You're welcome to leave anytime." Morgan/Hecate crossed her arms beneath her breasts.

"Not a chance."

Zeke dropped to my side, still growling.

"Was she like this before she left for dinner?" I asked him.

He shook his head.

Fuck. Charles must be gone. Morgan had let down her guard, and voila. Since she'd been formed from Hecate's essence, it would be tough to fight an outright takeover.

"Fine." She shrugged. "Then I'm out of here."

Power swirled around her turning the air shades of blue and violet. I muscled my way to her side. She spun, clearly intent on losing me. But, if she was leaving, I'd piggyback onto her spell.

"Go away."

"Nope."

Deep in my mind I heard my name. Barely more than a whisper, it had to be Morgan doing her damnedest to break through.

The door slammed against its stops and then slammed once more. Charles strode into the room and draped a sound shield around all of us. He shucked his glamour and snarled at me. "I am helping her, not you. You betrayed me."

"You know damn good and well I had no choice."

"There is always a choice."

"We can argue the fine points later. Tell me how I can help."

He pushed past me. "Who said I needed your puny assistance? How in the hell do your kind even get to be called mages?"

Sita landed on my shoulder. "Do not talk to Damien like that."

"Give it a rest, hawk."

The Morgan who wasn't twisted away from Charles. Enchantment bubbled around her as she tried to launch a travel spell. He sliced right through it, grabbed both her shoulders, and shouted power words in the ancient language of our people from back when we were still one.

It was damned impressive. Had that long-ago falling out been worth it? I had no idea why we'd parted ways. But then, I'd never asked, either.

A shadow detached itself from Morgan's midsection. Zeke lunged at it, jaws snapping.

"Don't kill her," I cautioned.

"*Why not?*"

"She's part of Morgan."

"Your turn." Charles was panting from effort.

I got the picture, surrounded the shadow with layers of enchantment. and tossed it into a journey spell heading for what was left of the castle in Fort William. May as well ensure she was whole again, reunited with her physical self.

Charles let go of Morgan. She crumpled to the floor, moaning softly. "Christ. I was soooo stupid. Never again."

"You bastard." Charles stood in front of me thumping my chest with a fist. "If you hadn't ratted me out, I'd have been in the kitchen, and this never would have happened."

"Let's get one thing clear. I did not rat you out. When I

got home from work earlier today, our seer was waiting in my apartment. She'd already seen you and knew we'd been working together. There was no percentage in trying to lie my way out of it.

"Hell, mate. You know the law as well as I do."

He took a step back. Morgan pushed to her feet. "Thank you. Both of you. Please don't fight. Crap. I still can't believe she did that. I'll have to be warded every minute."

"So, you didn't invite her in?" Zeke woofed softly.

"Most assuredly, no. My mistake was feeling sorry for her and allowing her to talk with me."

I turned to Charles. "I'm sorry about how this turned out. Maeve, our seer, tells me you stole a dragon's egg and were banished because of it."

He rolled his shoulders back. "That egg contained my son. The dragon couldn't incubate it. Liaisons such as ours are forbidden. So I took the egg to give it a chance at life."

"Why didn't you explain that to your prince?" I asked.

"Pah. Can you explain anything to whoever runs the Fae show?"

"Sometimes."

"What happened to the baby dragon?" Morgan asked.

"My prince returned it to dragonkind. I have no idea, but my bet is its mother ensured it never hatched."

"I'm so sorry," Morgan murmured.

"I am too," I told him. "But if you didn't ever check, you can't know for certain."

"Eh. It's old history. I have to get moving. The Unseelie guardians could show up any moment. They'll dump me in the dungeon in the *Dreaming*."

"Go." Morgan made shooing motions. "Damien and I will cover your tracks here."

"Thanks. Perhaps our paths will cross again. My true name is Balthazar." A swoosh of Fae-imbued power washed through the room. When it cleared, he was gone.

Morgan headed for the door. I cleared her room of all traces of Balthazar. With a name like that, my bet was he was one of their royalty. Over the next quarter hour, we purged the boardinghouse of anything that might lead the guardians to our friend.

Back in her chamber, I said, "Were you planning to return to the guild house?"

She shook her head. "Not tonight. It's what got Hecate so spun out. Those missing witches. Her anger jumped the divide and enabled her to take over. Sooner or later, it's bound to occur to her that I'm her ticket to freedom in more ways than one."

"I'm not leaving you alone. We can remain here, but it would be best to return to Faery."

"Why? They'll just grill you about Balthazar. Those guardians he mentioned will know he flew the coop, and they'll blame me and you."

"Okay, so we'll remain here. I'll join Zeke on the floor."

"No." She wove her arms around me. "If you've truly forgiven me, we can share the bed."

Still shy of the fragile bond growing between us, we curled up together fully clothed. I lay behind her and kept a hand over her rounded belly. Niall cooed happily. Tomorrow would bring its own set of problems, but, for now, I kept watch while she slept.

MORGAN

It took a long while to fall asleep, even with Damien holding me. Damn but he felt good stretched full length against my back. I didn't fully appreciate how much I'd missed him until that moment. Niall's delight was palpable. The poor kid had been through hell, and he wasn't even born yet. After everything he'd borne witness to, he couldn't be looking forward to life outside the protection of my womb.

I'd been just plain naïve while in the kitchen preparing dinner. Cooking is not one of my talents. I'd never turned out a meal for fifty people before. I had a couple of cookbooks open and was figuring out how to change recipes designed to feed four or six.

While I was scratching out equations doing math, Hecate started chatting up a storm about inconsequentials. I barely paid attention, answering yes or no at intervals. We made it through preparations for the evening meal. She even had a decent suggestion or two.

Who knew she was a cook?

Once dinner was over, and I was clearing the dishes, she widened the breach she'd created in my magical center and jumped. The whole thing was over in seconds, leaving me gasping and doing my damnedest to dislodge her.

No luck. The harder I tried, the louder she laughed at me.

"I made you," she chortled. "Any tricks you play won't work."

Maybe not overt tricks, but if I pretended acceptance, I might catch her off guard. It was a sure bet I couldn't say a word to Zeke or Sita. Given my track record, they'd never believe I hadn't invited her in. Deep within me, Niall had fallen silent.

What did he know about his grandmother? Had she made promises I wasn't privy to?

I might have hidden my predicament from the animals, but Damien picked up on it right away. Thank all the gods he believed me. I don't deserve that level of trust, yet he offered it unstintingly.

The rest is history. Charles—er, Balthazar—showed up and kicked Hecate's scheming ass all the way back to Scotland. Actually, Damien did the kicking once she was separate from me.

I thought about Charles and his half-dragon child. I'd had no idea dragons could mate with mages. Was the result a dragon? Seemed logical, since mages were born not hatched.

Except for me. Not that I was hatched, but neither was I born.

Perhaps, once the dust settled, we could at least determine what had happened to his child. Shouldn't be all that hard. Maybe Maeve could hunt it down through her psychic channels. Looking backward is far easier than forging predictions. At least, it's what Lilith always said.

Even if she cheated and used a leprechaun to spawn her prophecies, the same principles had to apply.

I must have slept at some point because when I opened my eyes, dawn was breaking. Time to hit the kitchen and turn out something credible for breakfast. I should tell Smythe Charles was gone. Maybe he'd tap someone else to help me.

The gentle rise and fall of Damien's breathing soothed me. I tried to get up without waking him. No such luck.

"Where are you going?" The arm he had around me tightened.

"To work. Breakfast won't make itself."

He rolled me to face him. "Morgan. You're not thinking. You don't have to work. I'll take care of you and our child."

"What will the other Fae have to say?"

"I don't give a flying fuck."

"Trouble follows me. I'm loathe to bring it into Faery. I'm still cursed, or have you forgotten? And there's the niggling matter the Greeks would prefer if Niall wasn't born."

"They can find you anywhere. You're safer in Faery. They're concerned he'll be a conduit for darkness."

"Well, he's not. If he carried evil, I'd know it better than anyone." I splayed a protective hand over my belly. Once the babe was born and others could test his magic, we'd put that ridiculous notion to bed once and for all.

It took discipline—a lot—but I untangled myself from Damien's embrace and perched on the edge of the narrow bed.

"Smythe was kind to me. He didn't have to take me back. I'm going to finish the mending and cook until he can find someone to fill in."

"Give him a timeframe. Otherwise, he won't try very hard."

I scratched my head. "Like what?"

"Two weeks."

"But it's scarcely any time at all."

"Two weeks' notice is standard practice for mortals."

So much I still didn't know. "All right. I'll chase him down this morning."

"How can I help you?"

I'd been on my way to the door intent on washing up in the bathroom down the hall.

"What about your job?" I turned to face him.

"It's not important. I'm easily replaceable, but I will stop by to let him know I won't be returning." Damien unfolded his long body and got to his feet. "How about if I take the animals out?"

Zeke was on his feet in an instant, tail pluming. Sita untucked her head and flew to Damien's shoulder.

"Thanks. It would be a big help."

"What about the Coven? I can check on them, maybe help track down the witches who escaped."

"They'll never let you inside."

"They did before."

I rocked from foot to foot, undecided. Was I ready to start knocking down precepts that had been part of every Coven since the dawn of time?

Damien grinned. It made him look young, innocent. "I caught that. Tell you what. I won't be pushy about it, but I'll bring the familiars and knock politely. Maybe they'll welcome a spot of assistance from a different type of mage."

"Perhaps so," I murmured. "See you later."

Fae magic hit me dead in the guts the second I pushed the door to my room open. A pair of Dark Fae hustled past me and into the room. They were shielded, but I saw right through it.

Oh-oh. So much for hitting the kitchen early.

I turned and marched back inside, shutting the door behind me and tossing a sound shield around everyone. Zeke was growling softly. Sita clacked her beak.

Damien wore his amiable expression. "Aye, mates. What can I do for you?" he asked in Gaelic.

"You know goddamned well what you can do. What have you done with Balthazar?"

A shrug. "He left. He's his own Fae."

I took in the two mages. They had to be the guardians Charles had alluded to. Like all Fae, they carried an otherworldly beauty. One was fair, the other dark. Slightly built, like most of Damien's kinsmen, their ears rose to points, and they were dressed in modern garb: trousers and woolen shirts. Rather than footwear, they were barefoot.

The dark-haired one's curls were close-cropped. The blond's hair fell to his shoulders.

"Fine," one growled. "We'll track him."

"Closer than we've been in eons," the other muttered.

I didn't exactly have a dog in this fight, but it had never stopped me before. "Why not leave him be?" I inquired.

Two sets of silver eyes bored into me. "How did this become your affair, witch?" the blond sneered.

"He was kind to me."

The mages exchanged glances. "Not the Balthazar we remember. What did you do? Ensorcel him?"

It wasn't worth answering, so I retreated to, "Leave him be."

"Not your decision to make." The dark-haired one faced Damien. "Did you report this sighting to your council?"

Damien rolled his shoulders back until he towered over the mages. "To our seer. She saw as much and sought me out before I could work in a trip to Faery."

"But our laws are clear," the blond sputtered. "You must drop everything and—"

Damien flapped a hand his way. "I would have gotten around to it. Some of us have jobs here."

Shock waves rolled from the Dark Fae. "You work? For mortals?" The blond sounded scandalized.

"I have for many years."

"Why?" The other mage narrowed his eyes.

"Doesn't matter."

Time was blazing past. At this rate, breakfast would be more than late. "Please leave. As you can see, your kinsman isn't here."

"We will inform our prince," the dark-haired one said.

"About what?" Damien sounded weary.

"Your dereliction of duty."

Damien turned his hands palms up. "Faery knew within hours of my discovery. Knock yourselves out."

A spell bubbled around them, igniting in a puff of silver smoke. When it cleared, they were gone.

"He has enough of a head start, he might outfox them," Damien muttered as he readied himself to take the familiars outside.

I hoped so. I'd come to appreciate the Dark Fae, and his story about protecting his yet-to-be-hatched child had touched my heart.

"I'll find you in the kitchen," Zeke told me.

"Mind if I spend the day with Damien?" Sita cawed.

"Not at all," I told the hawk.

Out of time to clean up, I flew out of the room intent on the kitchen. Damien and I hadn't made specific plans for later, but we'd find each other. We were starting to feel like a couple again. Lying next to him through the night had gone a long way toward healing the rift between us.

A rift I'd caused. And one I'd cure no matter how many years it took.

Smythe stormed into the kitchen after a breakfast that was half an hour late. Mouth open, presumably to ream us out, he stared around the room. "Where is Charles?"

I shrugged. "Not sure. He hasn't been here since lunch yesterday."

"Is that why dinner was late too?"

I nodded and turned away from the sink where I'd been doing dishes. Soapy water was dripping on the floor, so I snagged a threadbare towel and dried my hands and forearms.

"Why didn't you say something then?"

"I thought maybe he'd come back." I was improvising, but he had no way of reading my mind.

Smythe's expression shaded from annoyance to speculation. He examined me until I wanted to throw a bolt of magic his way and run out of the room. Zeke unwound himself from his spot near the door and sashayed to Smythe, tail wagging.

He's good at breaking up tension, but Smythe wasn't sidetracked. "When is the baby due?"

Whoa. Out of all the questions he could have tossed my way, I wasn't expecting that one. "Um, not exactly sure. Maybe five months."

He drew his dark brows together. "Have you seen a doctor?"

Another out-of-left-field query. Probably better to lie so he didn't drag me to a clinic himself. "Sure. Just not for the last couple of months."

"I see. Are you planning on staying here after he's born?"

Another cut-to-the-chase question. "Not sure. Probably not."

"Why? Did you get a better offer?" He angled his head to one side. He'd never actually slacked off on examining me.

What I wanted to do was tell him it was none of his business. Instead, I murmured, "Things are kind of up in the air."

"You'll stay on and cover the kitchen, right?"

Finally, a question I'd expected. "Probably not. This is hard for me by myself. Never been much of a cook. When I was following directions from Charles, it was fine. By myself, not so much."

"So how long will you stay?"

Zeke wagged his tail again before plopping on his hindquarters, tongue lolling.

I blew out a breath. "I can give you two weeks' notice."

He took a step back. "Why, you ungrateful twat. I took you in when you had nothing. Provided a bed and food, and this is how you repay me?"

Great. This was going downhill with the speed of a runaway train.

I wafted threads of a calming spell his way, but the harsh set to his features didn't abate.

I could have told him if he was going to be a dick about it, I'd be gone as soon as I cleared my few possessions out of my room. But I didn't possess all that many allies. Alienating the few I did have wasn't wise.

I deepened the calming spell. "Sorry to disappoint you, but I am not a cook. And I'm not especially interested in learning to be one. Even if I was, I'd need someone to teach me. Those books"—I swept an arm toward the cookbook shelf—"presume a person knows the basics. I don't."

His shoulders slumped. "Yeah. Probably right. Guess I'll

troll through who lives here. Maybe someone else would be a better fit. You will give me two weeks, maybe three?"

"At least two," I agreed and hoped to hell I wasn't lying. If elements heated up with the Coven or Hecate, I might vanish into the ether, my good intentions swept away by more pressing exigencies.

I returned to my sink of cooling water. After a few minutes, the swish of the swinging door told me he'd left.

Zeke returned to his spot near the back door. *"Could have gone worse,"* he observed.

"Could have gone better," I countered. "It took a piss pot of calming to settle him down."

I'd just drained the sink and was draping my towel over a hook when the characteristic feel of Hecate scratching at the edges of my magical center sent me into a panic.

Screw me once, shame on you. Screw me twice, shame on me ran through my head as I made the central core of my power as impregnable as I could.

"I'm sorry. I won't take over again," she said.

"Give me one reason I should trust you," I shot back.

"The escaped witches. I'm the only one who can find them."

"I'll take my chances."

Zeke head-butted me. *"Stop talking to her."*

"Working on it," I replied.

We hurried out of the kitchen. Presumably, I'd have heard from Damien if his field trip to the guild house went south. I should return to the mending and finish it, but it would keep. Surely, there'd be a spare moment to address it before I left the boardinghouse.

Niall kicked a time or two as he repositioned himself.

When would he be born? Some of the sisters would surely know, but I didn't trust any of them to actually touch me.

"Where are we going?" Zeke asked as we trotted upstairs.

"To the guild house as soon as I grab a coat."

One of the other residents shot me a strange look as we passed on the stairs. Of course he would, since, from his perspective, I'd been talking to myself.

"Sorry," I mumbled. "Old habit," but he was long gone.

Once I'd made the mistake of teleporting from my rooms —well, more than once. On one occasion, Smythe hadn't seen me leave, but he couldn't find me, so he'd stationed himself outside my room. When I returned, courtesy of the fire ladder and hallway, he'd accused me of sorcery.

To avoid a replay, I zipped up my coat and retraced my steps down the stairs. Zeke padded next to me, doggie glamour on display.

We kept up our pretext of a girl and her dog until we hit the back section of the park, the part that skirted worlds. From there, I teleported. Hecate had been strangely silent since accosting me in the kitchen.

Her absence made me nearly as edgy as her presence, mostly because I had no idea what she was plotting, or when she'd show up again. Holding wards drained even my level of ability, but the alternative was so unpleasant I kept my protections in place.

Rather than the front door, I brought us out behind the large Victorian. The yard was deserted and provided a decent vantage point to scan the interior. If every Coven was as much trouble as mine was proving to be, it would take several lifetimes to address all of them.

That was assuming they remained fixed—not a given at all.

Why me? Magic was second nature, but the specter of spending every iota of energy on an ungrateful sisterhood rankled. I'd been quick to sign up to salvage my kinswomen from evil, but the reality was far starker than I'd imagined.

Zeke's ears pricked forward. He stood stock still.

Oh-oh. Not a good sign. I pulled my head out of my ass and threaded a beam of seeking magic through the thick wall a few feet away.

Muffling an outraged shriek, I barreled toward the rear door. Zeke's teeth around my calf slowed my momentum.

"Let go of me," I hissed.

"*We have to think this through,*" he woofed.

"Nothing to think about. Sita's in a cage."

"*Unless we want to join her, we need a plan.*"

"*Let me help,*" Hecate pleaded.

"*Go fuck yourself.*"

Zeke snarled, hackles raised.

"*Meet me in the alley where I rescued you.*" Damien's mind voice sounded strained.

Tension wrapped me in prickly folds. Was it really Damien? Sounded like him, but my last stint in that alley had nearly been the death of us both.

"*No. Meet me at Faery's gates.*"

"*Done.*"

I built a hasty spell. The location of the veils was protected. As a witch, I'd never have guessed where to look. Hecate knew where they were, and she could pass the information on to whomever she was working with.

Eh, maybe this would be a decent test. We'd see who was actually waiting when we got there.

How the hell had the Coven nabbed Sita? Had they even let Damien past the front door?

"We'll find everything out soon," Zeke woofed.

"Depends who meets us." Feeling less sure than I had about much of anything, I kindled my spell and prepared to call Logan if things went south.

Or not. The Fae had their own problems.

I'd caused them enough trouble. Whatever awaited us, I'd deal with it myself. Faery's gates had been the only location I could come up with that might sort Damien from whoever might be masquerading as him.

Goddess's tits. Would I ever trust anything again? Or anyone?

CHAPTER 12

DAMIEN

Whenever something is too easy, it rouses my suspicion. Why in Danu's name didn't I hesitate when the guild house door opened for me? A witch I remembered invited Sita and me inside. She was even smiling, a dead giveaway if I'd been on my toes.

Had the group ensorcelled me?

Witchy enchantment can be sneaky like that. They often win, not by brute force but by deception. It should have been at the forefront of my mind. Why in the hell wasn't it?

I can Monday morning quarterback all I want. It didn't change the fact they baited a trap, one I fell into headlong. Sita is smarter than I am, or maybe she's programmed to distrust the sisterhood who'd signed her bondmate's death warrant.

Morgan was convinced most of the sisterhood wasn't yet tainted, but I still should have been more on top of my game. I asked if they'd corralled the missing witches. My hostess replied, "Not yet, but we're closing on them."

It had sounded promising, too promising.

"How can I help?" I asked without probing for details. Something else I should have done.

Sita, who'd been perched on my shoulder, took to the air. A moment passed before I deduced her destination. Another bird—presumably a familiar—had entered the far side of the large room. The owl hooted a greeting; Sita cawed back.

If I'd been paying attention, I'd have noticed witches exchanging a few worried looks, but that came later. For now, I was fascinated by the two familiars greeting each other like long-lost friends.

"Bella. To me." A round witch of medium height with unkempt black hair ran into the room holding a set of jesses.

The owl hissed and clacked her short, curved beak. She and Sita flew to a ceiling beam, well out of reach of any of the witches. Power shimmered around them as they spoke.

The witch who'd greeted me, Christine, pushed long red hair behind her shoulders. "Come," she invited. "Join me for tea and refreshments. They're laid out in the morning room."

Laid out, eh? Had they known I was coming? Lilith, their seer, was gone. Or was she? Had the pieces of her reconstituted themselves? A cursory glance around wasn't overly reassuring. Most of the witches huddled in small groups. No one looked at me.

The birds appeared happy to be reunited. I didn't see the harm in a spot of tea. Some of the best deals are brokered over meals, and I wanted the sisters to view me as an asset, not a threat.

Yeah, fools are made not born. Had I not been so gullible, I wouldn't have lost Sita, but I'm getting ahead of things. I told the hawk where I'd be, but she was so deep in magical dialogue with the owl, she didn't acknowledge my existence.

In a backhanded way, I was happy for her. Granted, she had Zeke, but hobnobbing with a sister bird must be satisfying on many levels. Misreading the owl's intent was my first mistake. Or perhaps Bella had been on the up-and-up. She'd clearly given her witchy mistress the slip and not shown the slightest inclination to be trussed with jesses.

My second mistake was following Christine into a large room with cut crystal windows. Sunlight poured through them, creating colorful prisms that danced on the ceiling and walls.

She poured a rich tea, fragrant with cinnamon and berries, and waved me toward a selection of delectable pastries. Most of our food in Faery isn't nearly this elegant. Once I was settled with a delicate cheese Danish and another pastry topped with strawberries and whipped cream, she sat across from me and nibbled on her own selections.

We spoke of this and that, but whenever I attempted to steer the conversation to the fallen witches, she deftly redirected me. It was sinking in she was stonewalling me when my head felt odd: floaty and not all there.

Too late, I recognized the telltale signs of poison and

lurched to my feet. Desperate, I focused power inward to protect my magical center, but I was clumsy.

A day late and more than a dollar short.

Christine watched me with all the interest of a feral cat waiting for a mouse caught in a trap to stop writhing.

"Why?" I choked out.

Her pleasant expression shattered, replaced by disgust. "We loathe men. You have no place in our midst."

I barely heard the last words. My senses were failing, hazed over by a sticky gray web. I cycled through magic, trying to cling to consciousness.

It fled anyway.

When I came to, my head pounded as if I'd drunk an entire vat of mead. My mouth tasted wretched. Groaning, I held my head between my hands to keep my skull from imploding and rolled to a sit. Waves of blackness threatened to send me right back to sleep.

Not going to happen. The fucking Coven had my bird.

Maybe the renegade witches had all broken free and taken over.

Waves of nausea swamped me. I took shallow breaths, willing them to pass. My magic was mostly intact—Christine had missed an opportunity to strip my power—and I pushed it through me seeking residual bits of toxin and destroying them.

At some point, I staggered to my feet and walked this way and that as I finished clearing the witch's venom from my body. It had to have been the tea. She hadn't drunk any.

Clarity was returning. Where was Morgan? Crap. I had to warn her. She wouldn't fare any better than I had since she was my almost-mate—and carried my child. The sisterhood would have no way of knowing about our estrangement.

I'd figured out where I was. Christine hadn't pulled out all the stops and dumped me on a borderworld. Nope. I was only a few blocks from the guild house. And then I remembered witch magic wasn't capable of lengthy teleport spells.

It was a longshot, but I raised my mind voice seeking Morgan. *"Meet me in the alley where I rescued you."*

After a pause so long I convinced myself she wasn't close enough to receive telepathy, she replied, *""No. Meet me at Faery's gates."*

"Done."

I readied myself to travel. Leaving Sita behind grated, but I'd never storm the gates again on my own. They'd laugh in my face. Bella had seemed to care about Sita. At least they had each other—until I worked out how to rescue the hawk.

Faery's veils came into view.

Morgan and Zeke were already there. The wolf raced to me, put his paws on my shoulders, and licked my face. His lupine features twisted in disgust. *"What happened to you?"*

Morgan joined us. "Thank the goddess, it's you. I thought it might be a trick." Her nose crinkled. "Really? They pulled that old hoax on you? Damn it, Damien. Didn't you realize after the first swallow it wasn't right?"

"Knew I recognized the smell," Zeke woofed. *"It's daffodils and oleander."*

No one likes to be chided for their stupidity. "Wasn't thinking they'd harm me," I said stiffly.

Morgan raked fingers through her dark hair. "You never should have gone alone. I knew better, but I assumed since you'd already been there, they'd at least play fair. What happened to Sita?"

"An owl flew into the main living room—"

"Bella?" Morgan cut in.

I nodded. "They seemed friendly."

"They were the best of friends," Morgan confirmed. "I don't get how Sita ended up in a cage."

"A cage? Damn it. I missed that part. When I left for tea with Christine, the birds were thick as thieves." The full import of her words hit home. "You went by the guild house?"

"Why wouldn't I? I'd have charged inside, but Zeke talked sense into me." Her mouth twisted into a wry expression. "Christine, eh? Charming, isn't she? Never, never trust any witch who invites you to a meal. They always have ulterior motives."

"You could have told me before."

Maeve rustled through Faery's veils. "Are the two of you ever going to stop nattering and come inside?"

Morgan set her mouth in a tight line. "Are you sure you want me within? Bad luck seems to be my new BFF."

"I wouldn't have invited you if I didn't mean it," the seer snapped. Her gaze settled on me, and she gripped my upper arm. "Off to the healers with you. Pronto. How in Danu's name did you manage to slop down enough poison to flatten you? Didn't you—?"

"Enough." Heartily sick of women pointing out my

flaws, I stalked through Faery's veils. If they followed me, fine.

"Meet us in the second small dining area once you're done," Maeve called after me and took off along a corridor with Morgan and Zeke.

I'd been dismissed. My macho egotistical side almost said fuck it and trotted after them. A wiser part set a path toward the infirmary. I was far from at the top of my game. If a potion or spell could dissipate the remaining toxin, the rest of today would play out better.

The infirmary was empty, but not for long. Blue-robed healers converged on me clucking and cooing. At least they didn't dun me for not seeing through what was apparently a tried-and-true witch trick. Men had been shanghaied into Covens in the days before sperm banks.

I felt sorry for each and every one of them.

After a time, the healers shooed me away. Before I left, they dropped an amulet around my neck that looked like black onyx. An early warning system, it would turn color in the presence of many different substances toxic to Fae.

Great. No one trusted me to take care of myself.

Logan, Maeve, Morgan, Zeke, and a couple other Fae were sharing a meal when I joined them. I wasn't especially hungry, but I filled a plate anyway and sat at an oblong wooden table.

Zeke cast adoring eyes my way. I wasn't fooled and tossed him a choice bit of meat.

I'd barely taken three bites when Logan said, "We'll have visitors presently, and—"

"Who?" I wasn't in the mood for surprises.

"Us." The two Dark Fae from the boardinghouse stepped through a portal.

Logan shot to his feet. "I told you to wait another thirty minutes."

"We decided not to." The dark-haired one shrugged.

"Not as if we report to you," the blond added.

"Perhaps not," Logan said stiffly, "but while in my court you will respect my wishes."

"So, shoot us." The blond grinned engagingly.

"What do you want?" I asked and got to my feet, grateful for the boost of healing I'd received in the infirmary.

"What?" The dark-haired one arched a brow. "No pleasantries, offers of spirits, or victuals?"

I exchanged glances with Logan. This was beginning to feel like a game, one where I wasn't apprised of all the rules.

"We haven't been on a breaking-bread-together basis for a long while—" Logan began.

"Short-sighted of us, perhaps," the blond broke in. "I'm Alexander."

"My name is Rolf," the other Dark Fae volunteered.

What in the hell had happened since they'd stormed out of the boardinghouse? Had Charles turned himself in? Seemed unlikely.

"It would help if you'd shed light on why you're here," I mumbled.

"It's not related to the earlier matter," Rolf said.

"What earlier matter?" Logan asked.

"The one that sent you to the Unseelie prince with explanations," Maeve clarified.

"Oh. That. Been trying to forget about it." Logan frowned.

I made a mental note to ask him about his trip to the other side of Faery, but later.

"Don't get me wrong. We're still annoyed Balthazar was gone from that shithole hotel because you warned him," Alexander said sourly.

"Wrong," Morgan spoke up. "I was who warned him. What you did to him was unfair. Don't you realize—"

"Hush," I shouted into her mind. My bet was the other Dark Fae had no idea about his affair with a dragon, and Charles probably wanted that piece to remain a secret. Try as I might, I couldn't force myself to switch from the name I knew to his Fae one.

"Realize what?" Alexander turned the full force of his silver gaze on Morgan.

"Nothing. I misspoke."

"Like hell you did," Rolf muttered. "I heard that one"— he jerked a thumb my way—"order you to stand down."

"No one orders me to do anything," Morgan sputtered.

"We're getting off course." Logan stepped in. "Earlier you said your visit had naught to do with your missing kinsman. If not that, then why are you here?"

Alexander hooked a chair with a foot and dropped into it. Rolf mirrored his motions. "Do you suppose we could get a spot of mead?" he inquired.

Logan snapped his fingers. A tankard and a tray with several glasses floated in and landed on the table. The Dark Fae helped themselves.

I looked longingly at the carafe, but maintaining a clear

head took precedence. I didn't trust our dark half, and I'd already gotten myself in trouble once today by being too trusting.

Once burned, twice shy.

Alexander clanked his mug on the table. "We are here," he announced, "because it has come to our attention we have a common enemy."

"Which one?" Maeve inquired dryly. "We've been collecting them of late."

"Witches came to us," Rolf said, "with, erm, incentives to turn against our own."

"They assumed we'd side with them," Alexander added, "since everyone knows of the schism betwixt the dark and light halves of Faery. Interestingly, on their heels, a handful of Greek gods showed up with still more incentives to ensure the child percolating in yon witch's belly never draws breath."

"Our seer foretold the child," Rolf went on. "Part of his role will be healing the rift between us."

I stared at Maeve. "Have you seen the same?"

After a pause, she reluctantly nodded.

"Why didn't you say something?" Morgan demanded.

"Because that particular bit only showed up in the last day," Maeve replied.

"Not the topic at hand," Logan cut in.

"For me, it is," Morgan informed him.

"Stop. Just stop." I held up both hands, swallowed incredulity, and asked the Dark Fae, "You're here to make peace with us?"

"Nay, merely to sow the initial seeds," Rolf clarified.

"Peace will require far more than a single visit," Alexander added.

"Does this mean you're not angry about Balthazar?" I glanced from one to the other.

"Not exactly," Rolf replied. "He's still missing, but he has been for centuries. He still cannot live freely, and he's gone to ground somewhere else."

"Not as if we exactly lost something," Alexander said.

"He lost a lot," Morgan spoke up. "He was kind to me."

"Pfft. Balthazar doesn't have a kind bone in his body," Rolf growled.

"Maybe he changed," Morgan murmured. "People can, you know."

"I recognize your need to defend him," Logan said, "but could you please stand down for now?"

Something about his tone must have registered because Morgan nodded.

Logan poured mead for himself and lifted his mug. "To the beginnings of peace."

Rolf and Alexander echoed his sentiment. I grabbed my own mug in time to join the toast. A swallow of mead wouldn't hurt. Faery hasn't been unified in my memory. We would be far stronger united than the way we'd operated time out of mind.

"What exactly did the sisterhood promise?" Morgan asked once a second round of toasts had gone down.

Alexander angled his head to one side. "They brought clear tubes filled with a golden light. According to them, the tubes could be held in abeyance until one of us required a magical assist."

"Except we're not weak like our Seelie cousins," Rolf cut in.

I winced, but it's tough to argue with the truth.

Zeke woofed sharply. Morgan sank a hand into his pelt, murmuring, "I know."

"Know what?" Alexander eyed her.

"If the tubes contain what I believe they did, you escaped a nasty witch deception. The enchantment in the tubes would have weakened you, rendered you vulnerable. Worse, when one is cracked open, it sends a message to whichever sister created it to show up and feast on the spoils."

She exhaled briskly. "We can absorb power from others. Rather than enriching your ability, the tubes would have drained it."

Rolf shook his head. "Doesn't make sense. After the first one damaged us, we'd have wised up and destroyed the others."

"If you figured it out," Morgan said. "What you'd likely have found is a confused kinsman with a witch pretending to offer assistance."

"There are far more direct ways to thwart an enemy," Logan said.

"Sure, but witches deal in subterfuge. They're rarely direct. Look how they killed Mother."

"They murdered one of their own?" Alexander was on his feet, a horrified look marring his even features.

"Aye. Wasn't pretty," Logan said.

"Beware of witches bearing gifts," Rolf muttered.

"We'll have to file this away," Alexander agreed.

I almost hated to ask, except I wanted to know. "What did the Greeks promise?"

Rolf smiled, kind of a shit-eating grin. "Why, all of Faery just for us."

"Mmph. Wonder what they planned to do with us?" Maeve mused.

"The same thought occurred to us," Alexander said.

"While the thought of dominion was appealing," Rolf added, "we're far from stupid."

"Even we're not so coldhearted as to wish ill fortune on our own," Alexander said.

"Could have fooled me," Logan mumbled.

The Unseelie prince must have given him hell when he visited his court.

"Where do we go from here?" Maeve asked.

"I need to figure out what happened to the tainted witches from my guild house. And rescue my hawk, Sita," Morgan said.

"Don't witches have property rights over familiars?" Rolf asked.

Zeke snarled.

"Didn't mean it quite that way," Rolf explained. Not mollified, Zeke snarled again.

"Yes and no," Morgan replied. "Your point?"

"Seems to me you can simply knock on the door and demand your bird."

"I don't believe it will work, but it's worth a shot. If they even open the door for me." Morgan started out of the room with Zeke trotting next to her.

"Hold up. You're not going alone," I blurted.

She turned. "You are not going back there. Not after what they did to you earlier."

"I'll accompany you." Maeve finished the mead in her glass and stood.

"It's not necessary—" Morgan began.

"In this instance, I believe it is." Maeve spoke over her.

"Help us hammer out the beginnings of détente with our Unseelie cousins," Logan invited me, except it was more like an order.

I ran lightly to Morgan and wrapped my arms around her. "If you're not back in a couple of hours, I'm coming after you."

"Hell, we'll all come," Alexander said. "The Unseelie army has grown soft."

I chose not to mention we scarcely had troops any longer. Tough to be serious about training when centuries had passed since our last conflict.

"You can coo at each other later," Maeve said. Her words had barely registered when the women and wolf were gone.

"About that détente," Logan said.

"More mead, and we'll hammer something out," Alexander replied.

I cleared my throat. "Should we include your prince?"

"No," three voices thundered in unison: Logan, Rolf, and Alexander.

Alright, then. Apparently, his subjects didn't like the prince any better than Logan did. We've never gone the royalty route. Hopefully, the Unseelie prince wouldn't simply assume he'd end up lording it over us all.

It wouldn't go well.

I searched my memory, but, try as I might, I couldn't recall his name.

"Damien."

I glanced at Logan. "Yes?"

"Gather the council and whoever else you find. May as well include as many of our people as we can."

"Grand idea," Rolf said. "We'll do the same. Do you have a larger room?"

"Right this way." Logan walked out of the dining room.

I turned the other way, intent on rounding up as many of my kin as I could find to witness a truly monumental twist in Fae history.

CHAPTER 13

MORGAN

"That was an interesting development," Maeve murmured.

"Which one?"

"That the Unseelie had a come-to-Jesus moment."

Her use of modern phraseology made me smile. "Do you trust them?"

"Not entirely. Still, I can't see what's in it for them to lie about this."

"I'm at a disadvantage," I told the seer, "since I don't know them."

"Not sure I do, either, after all this time."

We reached Faery's veils. I set a spell in motion to drop us near the guild house, but not too close. It was night on Earth, rather late from the looks of the moon and a few scattered stars.

"What are you going to do?" Maeve asked.

I shrugged. "March up to the front door and knock, I guess."

"Why not teleport inside?"

"Because I have no idea what we'll find. For all I know, someone opened a channel to Hell, and demons are consorting with the sisters."

"Who was the witch who volunteered to help you?"

"Rebecca."

"Let's reach out to her, assess the lay of the land."

It was such a solid idea, I was ashamed I hadn't come up with it. "We could try to talk with Sita too," I ventured.

"Let's do that first. I trust her more than any witch."

The truth in her words stung. Once—and not all that far back—the Coven had been the center of my universe. If someone had told me a year ago they were capable of the events that had transpired, I'd have labeled them daft.

We were crouched in the shadow of a deserted building. Queen Anne Hill has quite a few of them.

"I'll try to raise Sita," Zeke woofed softly. *"I can leverage the bond between familiars. Perhaps the sisters won't notice."*

"Go for it," I told him. "Find out where they're holding her."

Zeke moved a few paces away.

I placed my mouth near Maeve's ear. "If Zeke locates her, we should try to extricate her before we storm the fortress."

"Solid. I like it. It will take a bargaining chip off the table. Do we even want to dig deeper once we have the hawk in hand?"

I nodded. "When Sita is safe would be the time for me to

raise Rebecca. Hopefully, she'll have information we can leverage to approach the situation."

"If they haven't imprisoned her," Maeve muttered darkly.

The words *that's absurd* stuck in my throat. They'd murdered Mother, which meant any loyalty that used to exist was dead. Hopefully, Rebecca had the good sense to keep her mouth shut and her impressions to herself.

Zeke shoved between Maeve and me. *"She's still in that cage, but in the basement near the freezers. No one else is there."*

"What's the cage made of?" Maeve asked.

"Metal."

I'm not sensitive to iron or any of the other elements, but I'd have to expend a lot of power cutting through the bars. Enough to draw unwanted attention. So much for a remote approach.

"Are you certain she's alone?" I asked.

He bobbed his shaggy head. *"I talked with her. Told her we were here."*

Crap. "Did anyone hear you?"

He head-butted me. *"I used the familiars' tongue. Even if someone heard it, they wouldn't know what we said."*

"Maybe not, but they'd know someone reached out to Sita," Maeve noted.

"I'm going inside. There's a recessed stairwell that will spit me out in the basement. Means I won't have to expend magic to enter the building."

"I'm coming." Zeke took off. He knew the entrance I'd described.

Maeve started after him.

I caught up with her. "Your magic will be our undoing."

"Not if I don't deploy it," she retorted and shrouded herself. If I hadn't just been looking at her, I'd never have known she walked beside me.

I sucked in a breath to steady myself and started down the stairs. Zeke waited at the bottom. I borrowed a page from Maeve and concealed us as best I could. Each witch has her own distinct energy signature. Hiding from other witches is tough.

In and out, I told myself and twisted the knob. Luck was with me. It wasn't locked, but then none of the guild house doors ever were. Not with anything as prosaic as a deadbolt. If we wanted to bar entry, we utilized magic.

Not we. Not anymore.

On that grim note, I entered the building, scuttled the length of a hall with a concrete floor, and pushed open the door to a small pantry outside huge walk-in freezers.

Sita was on the floor of a large iron cage sitting on a table. She ruffled her feathers but remained silent as I assessed the cage—and a heavy padlock with its hasp around the door.

What in the hell had happened to the owl? Bella had always been Sita's friend. I had a hard time believing she'd set her up. I let my hand hover over the lock. Sure enough, someone had spelled it to warn them if it was tampered with.

Zeke pushed against me. I laid a finger over my lips to keep him from whining or snarling or making any noise at all.

Maeve was up to something beneath her shroud, but my attention was focused on the hawk.

No food. No water. Shame on those who'd left Mother's familiar to wither.

Fury scoured a path through me. It lent strength to my enchantment as I quietly cut through two bars on the opposite side of the cage from the padlock, catching them before they clattered to the concrete.

Sita didn't wait for an invitation. She scrunched, making herself small as she pushed through a hole barely large enough to accommodate her. I grabbed her, pulling to move things along. It must have hurt, but she didn't make a sound.

The second she was safe in my arms, Fae power swirled, burning bright as Maeve got us the hell out of there. So that was what she'd been up to.

"Nothing like leaving your calling card," I sputtered when shadows consolidated around us.

"What were you planning to do?"

"Leave the same way we came."

"Wouldn't have worked. You were intent on your task. Shortly after you cut through the first bar, it alerted someone. They were closing on us. We barely made it out of there."

"Not possible. I'd have felt something."

"She's right," Zeke cut in. *"I detected them too."*

Why hadn't I? "Any idea who?"

"Ideas, yes. Clarity, no," Maeve replied.

I'd sort it out later. Sita struggled in my arms. I loosened my grip. "Are you all right?"

"Yes."

"How'd they capture you?"

"It can wait," Maeve said, followed by, "We're far too near the guild house."

Power bloomed around us.

"What about confronting them?" I demanded, still incensed they'd dumped more suffering on Sita's feathered head.

Instead of answering, Maeve swept us into another teleport spell. This one spit us out inside Faery near the council chamber. The hallway was full of Fae, both light and dark.

A blue-robed healer met us and held her hands out for Sita. "Let me take her to the infirmary, please. She needs nourishment, and we must ensure nothing has contaminated her magic."

"Are you willing?" I asked the hawk. She'd been through enough. If she preferred to remain with me, I wouldn't force her from my side.

"Yes. The last few hours have been difficult," she cawed.

Damien loped to us and scooped Sita into his arms. "I am so sorry," he told her. "If I'd had any idea, I'd never have left you."

"Bella is dead," Sita croaked. "She died trying to save me."

Fuck me. Not only were the sisters killing their own. They'd moved on to familiars. I had a hard time believing Rynda, the witch bonded to Bella, had stood by while her owl was murdered. When Sita was better, I'd mine for details.

The healer stood next to Damien until he reluctantly transferred the hawk to her arms. "I'll return her as soon as I can," she said and walked away.

Zeke trotted after them. *"I will stay with Sita,"* he informed me. *"We can mourn Bella together."*

Damien wrapped an arm around my shoulders. "What happened?"

"One more close call," Maeve gritted. "We have to return, but with more than two of us."

"We'd have done okay," I told the seer.

"Not my assessment."

"What about the meeting Logan called?" I asked Damien, curious to ascertain how détente was developing in Faery.

"Fairly well. Better than my expectations," he replied.

"It's a grand opportunity to conscript a few Dark Fae to fight alongside us." Maeve raked a hand through her hair. "Something malicious bided at the guild house. Witches were there too, but hellspawn outnumbered them."

Confusion made my head fuzzy. "What happened? Even if all seven witches escaped, the others outnumbered them."

"Anyone's guess." Maeve made a face. "Does it even matter? Darkness gathers. The guild house has turned into a launching pad. We must intervene while it's still possible."

A staunch whistle summoned us into the council chamber.

Knowing Logan, he had an agenda and wouldn't take kindly to us interrupting. Indeed, he spent the first few minutes stressing the historic significance of the two halves of Faery gathering in the same room.

By my count, maybe twenty Dark Fae were bunched in a group on one side of the council chamber. It reminded me of news articles I'd picked up online about school integration where African American youth were bussed to a previously all-white school where they proceeded to stick together.

The Dark Fae were here but treading on eggshells. Made sense since this wasn't their turf. If the Unseelie prince was among them, I couldn't sort him from the group. And then I remembered one area of agreement had been not telling him.

How robust could any détente be if it didn't include their head of state? It would be like not including Logan and Maeve.

I flexed my hands to work out the kinks. Damien stood next to me. We hadn't bothered with seats. The political climate in Faery wasn't my concern. I shouldn't even be here. Where I was needed was kicking some serious butt in the guild houses.

Except Maeve had been right. Even with two of us, we'd have been outgunned. For me to try it alone was a suicide mission. I could kill several, but eventually they'd take me down.

The group had just exchanged names and the roles they played. Many sets of eyes drilled into me. I shrugged. "Token witch and Fae mother-to-be." I patted my round midsection.

Niall had been quiet for many hours, but he rolled into the hand cupped around my belly.

"The young prince is why we are here," Alexander explained.

Alarm bells tolled. The Unseelie prince wouldn't take kindly to another with a royal title. "Not a prince," I protested. "Damien's and my son."

"We disagree," Rolf said. "He will draw our two people together. The process has already begun."

Maeve strolled to the front of the room and drew a good-sized crystal ball from her robes. Holding it between her hands, she said, "The babe will not be born for a few months. Perhaps as many as five or even six. Meanwhile, we face a common enemy. It will provide ample testing ground to learn to work together."

"What mutual enemy?" Another Dark Fae, this one with a riot of russet curls falling to the middle of her back, stared at Maeve.

"Bear with me and watch," Maeve said as the crystal hung suspended in front of her.

Scenes played across its surface. My viewing angle wasn't great, but I saw the guild house. Its lower floor was filled with Banshees. One Kelpie, wearing his human form, was entertaining two witches.

I sought familiar faces. All of the captive witches were free. Others huddled in small groups. Try as I might, I couldn't locate Rynda. Had she chosen exile once her owl was dead?

"Looks like a witch problem," the female Dark Fae noted. Swiveling to look at me, she said, "Why aren't you handling this?"

Same question I'd asked myself. "We were there, but we were only two. It wouldn't have been enough."

"The presence of evil is a problem for everyone wielding white magic," Maeve corrected her.

"What did you have in mind?" Alexander asked. "Unlike our more fragile cousins, we've missed a good war."

"Don't you dare speak for us," someone called from the other side of the gallery.

I sucked in a breath, hoping the first war didn't break out in this room.

"I'd like to know too," Logan muttered and cast a pointed look at his seer.

Maeve waved a hand; the crystal went dark. "Our magic used to be additive. When I was very young, there was little difference betwixt Dark Fae power and ours. When we went our separate ways, somehow the Dark Fae walked off with the lion's share of our mutual talent."

"Now, you wait a minute." Rolf's tone was chilly.

"Not casting blame," Maeve hastened to add. "Merely stating what occurred. The guild house contains a gateway. I verified my suspicions when Morgan was freeing Sita. We must shutter it and ensure none of the wicked creatures continue to spread their poison."

"I'd heard the problem was widespread," another Dark Fae spoke up. "Not simply one Coven, but all of them."

I nodded. "You're correct. Perhaps not every Coven, but this must be addressed one guild house at a time."

Alexander was on his feet. "Word will carry, and the remaining houses will either go to ground or mount a defensive perimeter that will make our job much more difficult."

"They can't all contain gateways to Hell," someone called out.

"She knows where the guild houses are." Someone pointed a finger at me.

"You're suggesting we attack all of them simultaneously?" I asked as I rolled the idea around in my head. "It would take a lot of us."

"How many?" Alexander persisted.

I did a quick tally. "North America has eighteen Covens. South America has fourteen. Europe and the UK are home to another dozen. I'm not sure about China, Russia, and Southeast Asia."

"Let's start with the ones in North America," he proposed. "Maybe six of us for each, so we'd need 108 mages, that's 54 from each of Faery's houses."

"A coordinated approach," Logan said. "It could work. And it might encourage other Covens to mend their ways since word will spread." He cleared his throat. "We do have an army, but its skills are a wee bit on the rusty side."

"Same for us," Rolf said, "but what a grand opportunity to practice."

"Nothing like a good war to solidify our partnership," someone cried. Others took up the chant of, *War now. War now.*

Not that I was in a sour-grapes mood, but I could see this going two ways. Maybe it would shore up the Fae and their newfound bonhomie—or it could rip it apart before it even got off the ground.

I leaned close to Damien. "Who will lead each of these groups?"

"Good point," he murmured.

Logan whistled. When it didn't quiet the crowd, he banged on the table. Finally, as a last resort, a blast of magic swooshed overhead leaving a trail of red sparks in its wake.

Everyone in the room stopped what they were doing and stared at him. Logan jumped on the table and faced the room. "If we can't even pay attention to one another," he observed dryly, "we have no business planning an offensive. First off, are you certain you don't want to include your prince? I'm assuming it's still Xavier."

"What do we need him for?" Alexander arched a fair brow.

"Were the situation reversed, I would take umbrage were I excluded," Logan replied. "If we're serious about resurrecting our relationship, everyone must be on board."

"While we're at it"—Damien leapt into the fray—"how will leadership for the eighteen groups be determined?"

"Why, of course, we would assume that role," Rolf replied. Surprise ran beneath his words as if he'd never even considered another option.

"Quite the assumption," Damien shot back.

Logan held up both hands. Power crackled between his palms. "Enough. I suggest drawing straws or voting for a leader."

"If each group is three of us, and three of you," a Dark Fae pointed out, "it will be a draw every time."

"Perhaps not," Logan said. "This is why Xavier should be here. Some items could be hashed out betwixt him and me."

"Without your council?" a voice cried from the back of the room.

The chamber devolved into many voices talking at once.

"This will never work," I told Damien. Not much worry about being heard over the din.

"It might. Give things a chance to die down. There are hundreds of Fae. We only need a few."

Difficult as the next steps would be, I wanted to collect Zeke and Sita and return to the guild house before something worse happened. Like the surrounding neighborhood falling into a putrid sinkhole.

"What in Danu's name are the lot of you doing here?" a voice thundered.

My head whipped around. A tall, broad-shouldered man stood framed by a silvery portal. Built a lot like Damien, he had dark hair that had been braided in many small rows and woven with colorful jewels. A white fur cape sat on his shoulders. Light-brown leather trousers were cinched around his waist. A heavy golden chain with a robin's-egg-sized opal hung around his neck. His chest and feet were bare.

Logan jumped lightly off the table and strode to the newcomer, hands extended. "Xavier. It's been far too long."

The Unseelie prince ignored him. "I asked a question," he boomed. "Why are you here? Eh, never mind." He clapped his hands. "Return to our side of Faery. Immediately. I shall deal with this later."

Power shimmered around him, adding a reddish haze to the air.

"Sit and have a drink with me," Logan invited.

"Why would I want to do that?"

"Because it's high time our people formed a united front. Evil is afoot. We shall address it together."

"No. We will not." Another hand clap. "Back to your homes. Now."

No one moved.

"Appears you have an insurrection on your hands," Logan noted.

"Nothing I can't fix." Xavier's silver gaze landed on Alexander and Rolf. "Where is Balthazar? I sent you to retrieve him."

"We're working on it." Alexander didn't bother to stand in front of his liege.

"I suggest you work harder."

"We were planning a war. It's far more entertaining." Alexander smirked.

"Against whom?"

"Fallen witches, for starters," Rolf replied.

"Why not start with her and her half-Fae spawn?" Xavier pointed at me.

Damien started forward, but I jumped between him and the Unseelie prince. "I am not a fallen witch," I informed him. "I've been victimized by them. There is a difference."

"Not from where I sit."

"Then look harder." I swung an arm to the side. "Your people don't seem wildly enthusiastic about following your commands. They were excited about planning an offensive to bring the Covens to heel."

"We could do this together," Logan suggested.

A loud groan rose, presumably from the Dark Fae. Damn but it must be horrible being saddled with an immortal leader you hated. Wasn't as if he was ever going to go anywhere.

Xavier walked toward me. Damien positioned himself by my side, a protective arm around my shoulders.

"This is all your fault," Xavier pronounced.

I gazed around him to the Dark Fae in the chamber. "Do you agree?" I asked in a loud, ringing voice.

A chorus of nos rose, sweet music to my ears.

I shrugged. "Seems your subjects don't agree with your assessment."

Blotches of color stained his cheeks. I'd just publicly humiliated him. Not the wisest move, but I was beyond caring. He'd accused me of selling out to evil. If Zeke had been here, he'd have lunged for his throat, prince or not.

Logan and Maeve flanked Xavier. "About that drink," Logan murmured.

"Aye," Maeve added. "You can tell me how Kaylynn is these days. I've missed her since Faery split."

They'd offered him an opportunity to save face. He could have tossed it aside. Instead, he walked out of the room with them.

Once they were gone, Alexander surged upright. "Back to planning our offensive, mates."

Voices rose and fell.

Perhaps this would turn into something viable after all. I nudged Damien. "Going to check on Zeke and Sita."

"Return when you can. We'll be at this for a while."

"Will Maeve and Logan return?"

He shrugged. "Probably. Once they're done mollifying

Xavier. He always was a problem. One of the reasons going off on our own was appealing."

"Were you around then?"

He grinned. "Nope, but history has a way of making itself known."

I slipped out of the room. Apparently, witches weren't the only iteration of mage with skeletons in their closets. Zeke reached me half a corridor from the infirmary.

"She's better," he woofed. *"But it was nip and tuck."*

"How so?"

"The sisters planted a locator. It had to be removed."

I doubled up a fist and shook it. "This will be the last time they put their grubby paws on either of you," I promised.

Zeke stopped, tail pluming. *"Do you want to hear what happened to Bella?"*

I bent, buried a hand in his neck ruff, and waited. It would be painful, but I had to know. Thoughtful of Zeke to tell me out here, so Sita didn't have to relive the horror of losing a close friend.

"One moment, they were perched on a high beam in the great room talking," Zeke began. *"The next, Bella cried out and pitched to the floor. Sita flew to her aid..."*

CHAPTER 14

DAMIEN

Logan must have summoned our two generals because they trotted into the council chamber a few minutes after he left. Without being pushy, they quietly began drawing various battle formations on the magical equivalent of a whiteboard.

"What are you doing?" Rolf asked.

Roark straightened and shoved a riot of braids over his shoulders. He tapped the drawing nearest him. "Logan said we were going to confront several guild houses with about a half dozen warriors for each skirmish. This is one possibility for how we might deploy our forces."

"These are others," Tomas said.

He and Roark looked like twins. For all I knew, they were. Copper curls, tall, rangy builds, deep-green eyes. They wore their characteristic battle leathers. Formfitting brown leather trousers and matching tunics over white woolen shirts.

The white had never made sense to me. Bloodstains are hell on light colors.

"Best not get locked into a given strategy until we arrive at our assigned locations," a Dark Fae observed.

"True," Roark replied. "We're merely providing a few blueprints to hasten your response in the field." He rolled his shoulders back. "We will require fifty-four warriors from the Unseelie. Can you provide them? How long since they've trained?"

"Same question back at you," Rolf muttered.

Tomas nodded. "We have more than sufficient numbers, but we are rusty. Tough to maintain momentum when centuries have slid past since those same skills were needed."

Breath rattled from me. We were being honest. I'd harbored a concern we'd end up in a macho pissing contest and be woefully unprepared.

"Memorize these formations," Roark instructed. "We will meet you in the arena on Faery's lowest level. Our people can form groups and start figuring things out."

"When will we be ready to field a team?" I asked.

Many sets of eyes swiveled to me. Who was I to have the temerity to speak? I'd never been a warrior. Hell, I was a spy. Totally different skillset.

"Is there a need for haste?" Alexander asked.

I nodded. "The guild house where Morgan used to live has turned to shit. A gateway formed there. We need to close it before more sorcerers find their way through."

"What will we do with the witches?" someone asked.

I gritted my teeth. Morgan might not agree with my

answer, but she wasn't here. "We tried imprisoning the corrupt ones. It didn't work. They escaped, and now things are far worse than when they were flying beneath the radar."

"Can we kill them?" Rolf asked.

"Nay, they're immortal," Tomas tossed out.

"Morgan didn't have any trouble killing five of them," I said.

"So send her," Alexander suggested. "With maybe a few of us for backup. I still think we should coordinate with attacking the other guild houses, though."

"I like it," Roark said. "It maintains the element of surprise."

"How long will it take to ready a hundred warriors?" I asked.

Tomas and Roark exchanged a glance. "Perhaps a few days," Roark ventured.

"Hard to tell until we see what we have to work with," Tomas agreed.

"You will work with our generals," Alexander said. His tone invited anyone to defy him.

"Of course," Roark agreed. "Are they still Bron and Balthazar?"

"Bron still holds that role," Rolf said.

"What happened to Balthazar?"

I didn't exactly have a dog in this fight, but I took a chance. "If I can convince him to return, will your people quit hounding him? Beyond that, you exiled him. Why not leave him be?" I asked Alexander.

"He was exiled to a specific spot. Roaming free wasn't

part of the prince's orders. What makes you think you can find him?" the Dark Fae countered.

I shrugged. "I'm the best tracker the Fae ever spawned. If I can't find him, no one can. Plus, he trusts me."

He used to, but I didn't add that part, nor him snarling at me for ratting him out to his kinsmen.

Rolf and Alexander stood close. Power swirled around them as they debated my proposal. Finally, Alexander said. "You have a deal, Fae. But only if you locate him in time to take part in the battle preparations."

"He has to earn his way back into our good graces," Rolf added.

It meant I wouldn't be practicing with the rest of them, but I'd stay by Morgan's side when our group returned to the guild house. We'd do our best to blend in with whatever plans the warriors assigned to it had hatched.

Everyone left the council chamber, some heading for the arena, others to their quarters. I needed to return to the boardinghouse, but first, I'd find Morgan and let her know what I was doing.

As I made my way toward the infirmary, I replayed most of the conversation between us and our Dark Fae kinsmen. It had actually been more productive than I expected. There'd be hiccups in the road, and we'd have to get over our bad habit of belittling our formerly estranged kin.

I suspected they'd have to do the same. Surely, we weren't the only ones who'd coined many sayings that disparaged the other half of Faery.

Morgan sat on the edge of a bed with Sita cradled in her arms. Zeke lay at her feet.

"Don't get up," I said and joined her.

"How are you?" I asked the hawk.

"Much better, thank you."

"The witches embedded a tracking device," Morgan explained. "Your healers removed it. Her magic can flow freely now."

I mapped out what had transpired in the council chamber.

"That's incredible," she murmured. "Charles, er Balthazar was one of their generals?"

"Yes. There's a full pardon in the offing if I can find him," I said.

"Assuming he wants to return to the kinsmen who exiled him."

I laced my fingers with hers and murmured, "You share common history."

"We do, indeed. Do you want us to come with you?" she asked.

I did, but for all the wrong reasons. I never wanted to be separated from her ever again. "Yes, but it might serve us better if you join the warriors in the arena. That way, you'll be assigned to the proper group, and you'll get to know who we'll be fighting alongside."

"I want to kill them all," Sita shrieked and struggled to extricate herself from Morgan's hold.

Once she was free, she flew circles around the room.

I needed to get moving. Trails grow cold with time.

Morgan stood after I did and wrapped her arms around me. The hump of her belly pressed into mine, and I felt Niall move within her.

"Be careful," she cautioned. "You're still a wanted man. Aw crap."

"What?"

"I should go back too. I promised Smythe I'd work for two weeks only a few hours ago, and then we left."

"Morgan. You're not thinking." I rubbed knots out of her shoulders.

"I know. I know. Can't dance on two floors, and this one is far more pressing."

My lips touched hers, brief and sweet, before I kindled a spell to drop me in her room at the boardinghouse. It was the last place I'd talked with Charles, and the logical spot to track him from.

In the midst of my transport spell, I switched locations to the back of the park a few blocks away. I did not want to pop into Morgan's room and run into Smythe. For all I knew, he was sifting through her few belongings seeking clues as to her whereabouts.

It was early evening, just getting dark, when I gathered shadows from a few large trees to mask my arrival. Once there, I shrouded myself in invisibility and made my way to the boardinghouse. The street in front of the place was crawling with officers. I caught a glimpse of PDA logos on some uniforms.

What in the hell had happened?

Smythe might be pissed, but what had spurred him to call out the paranormal cops? Thank all the gods for my instincts, the ones that had switched destinations mid-spell.

After deepening my ward, I crept behind the building,

giving the gaggle of cops a wide berth. This wasn't quite as good as being inside, but it would have to do. If the PDA caught me again, I'd have hell's own time escaping.

Voices reached me.

"You have to find her, officer. I tell you, she's a witch, and she stole my child."

"Calm down, ma'am. We're working as fast as we can. We've covered the whole building. No witches in there."

"There has to be," she insisted, her voice shrilling.

Damn it. I recognized that high-pitched note. Christine was on the loose. Poisoning me hadn't slowed her down one whit. I assumed the rest of the gang were out front sowing hex bags and mayhem.

Curios as I was to spy a bit, it wasn't why I was here.

I set up shop in a root cellar attached to the next building over. It was damp and smelled of rodents but offered protection from discovery. My next move was risky, but necessary. The PDA are like fucking bloodhounds when it comes to magic. I hoped to hell they were so preoccupied with the witches masquerading as mortals that my spell would go unnoticed.

I sent a thread of tracking enchantment, fanning it wide until I caught a faint whiff of Dark Fae. Had to be Charles, and it gave me a starting point. I honed my casting and committed to following it.

Once I jumped into my combination travel and tracking spell, I breathed a little easier. Perhaps the witches' magic and hex bags had diverted the PDA, blunted their usual spot-on ability.

My channel split and split again. Each time I stopped

and assessed which way to go. Charles hadn't taken any unnecessary chances. His route was circuitous.

Hard to blame him. I wouldn't trust anyone, either.

Time passed. Tough to assess how much. Eventually, I came out on a windswept beach. A chill wind bore down on me, and the shore was caked with ice. Earth, but near one of the poles.

Gathering the edges of my tracking spell, I sought clarity. My casting ricocheted back and smacked me in the chest.

Great.

Had I come all this way to find a dry hole?

I walked away from waves crashing against ice until I hunkered in the lee of two large boulders to get out of the wind and consider my next steps.

Ha. What next steps? I'd run out of options, but I wasn't willing to concede defeat.

On a hunch, I raised my mind voice. *"Charles. Your kin have extended a pardon."*

After a long moment, *"It's a hoax,"* bounced back at me.

"No. I offer my word. We have established détente with the Unseelie. We're planning several offensives against the Coven guild houses to scour them of evil. You were one of the Unseelie generals. They've offered a full pardon if you return to your role and guide our joint forces along with Bron, Roark, and Tomas."

The crunch of footsteps on ice-crusted sand brought me to my feet. Charles walked toward me, hunched against the wind. He'd tossed a thick brown coat over his garments, presumably so he didn't have to waste magic keeping warm. His long, dark hair had been braided into two thick plaits.

When he saw me, he beckoned and turned back the way he'd come.

I followed him through a break in a rocky cliff and into a small underground grotto.

"What makes you think I want to return?" he growled.

"Morgan suspected you might feel that way."

"No one knows like someone who's lived it."

"She wanted to come with me, but battle plans are unfolding. One of us needed to establish a presence in the group that will take on her old guild house."

He drew his brows together, creating furrows between them. "Is it safe for her? The child can't be too far from being born?"

I'd worried about the same thing but hadn't said anything. "Morgan has a few months to go, yet. She'd pitch a fit if I told her to sit this one out."

He grinned. "I just bet she would."

"None of our healers have suggested she was too fragile."

"Mmph. Did either of you pose the question?"

I shook my head.

Balthazar leaned against a wall. "Not sure how I feel about this. The pardon is convenient and only because they need my skills. What happens once this offensive is over?"

"I assume they'll welcome you back into the fold."

"Big assumption."

"Actually, I didn't have to twist anyone's arm."

"Is the prince on board?"

I snorted. "Logan and Maeve were sweet taking him. He tried his high-and-mighty routine with Morgan—"

Charles burst into laughter. "Christ, I'd like to have been there to see it."

"It was pretty funny. And no contest. She ran rings around him."

"Anyone can. Xavier's not the brightest bulb in the chandelier. Is there a plan for the war against the Covens?"

I nodded. "A coordinated approach. Hit all eighteen sites in North America at the same time. Six warriors at each location. Half us, half you."

Charles blew out a breath. "How'd you get them to agree?"

"Didn't have to try very hard. The synchronized approach was Alexander's suggestion. I guess your people miss war?"

"They did," he agreed.

"How about it?" I pressed. "Will you return?"

He grinned. It transformed his craggy face. "If you speak true, and there are no hidden strings, I will."

"If your kinsmen go sideways on their offer, you would be welcome to join with us."

More laughter. "What? And become the first Dark Fae on record to change his stripes? Wouldn't that be one for the books."

I chuckled. "It would, indeed. Not sure how things are in your portion of Faery, but I'm damn near the only one who ever researches anything in our library."

"I felt the same way—before Xavier kicked me out. How'd you manage to wrangle any of my kinsmen into the same room with you?"

That's right. I hadn't told him that part. "They came to

us," I began. "Seems your seer believes my son will draw us together once more."

He whistled long and low. "Fascinating. Never would have guessed."

"Me, either. Furthermore, the Greeks and witches approached your kin with a variety of proposals painting us as the enemy. Guess it was a wakeup call to heal the rift splitting Faery."

"Probably past time," he agreed. "Ready when you are. Nothing to hold me here." Balthazar moved to the center of the grotto next to me.

"This is a solid hideout," I murmured. "If I hadn't been so motivated, I'd have given up long before I got here. Oh, by the way, the boardinghouse was crawling with PDA again."

"That's odd. Why?"

"Hard to say, but witches were behind it. I recognized at least one voice."

"I don't get it." He shook his head. "Why don't the paranormal detectives see right through them?"

"Good question. If I could stand to touch hex bags, maybe I'd be well-served to borrow a few. Seems to mask their true selves."

"Have Morgan make you one."

I clapped him across the back. "Grand idea. Never occurred to me. Not positive it's their hex bags, but what else could it be?"

He arched a dark brow. "Sex?"

"Nope. They're supposed to be celibate."

"I did not know that."

I wound a transport spell around us, aiming for the

arena beneath Faery. Once, we'd all used it. When we'd split Faery, it had ended up in our half.

Mock battles were in full swing. The air hummed with expended magic as troops resurrected rusty skillsets. Everyone was so preoccupied, no one noticed our arrival.

Enraged voices bellowed from a spot off to my right. At first, I assumed they were aiming for authenticity. Shouts escalated, followed by curses.

Goddammit. So much for our delicate truce.

I turned to tell Charles—except I needed to regroup on his name—to keep a positive attitude, but he was already striding toward another Dark Fae. The mage spun before Balthazar reached him. The tight line of his jaw relaxed into a smile, and he clapped a fist to his breast.

Balthazar did the same.

My guess was the other mage had to be Bron. They had history, and, from the looks of their reunion, they'd missed one another.

The two Dark Fae generals converged on the melee issuing staunch orders in the ancient language of our people. I sidled closer, interested in who was trashing whom. Three Dark Fae I hadn't seen before struggled beneath a holding spell. Tomas stood close, manipulating his working.

"Who's weak now?" he taunted.

"Stop that. Release them," Balthazar thundered.

"I will once they apologize." Tomas held his ground.

"Since you've stilled their tongues, you'll be waiting a long while," Bron noted dryly.

"All right. Fine." Tomas shook the casting loose from his

hands. Balancing on the balls of his feet, he faced the mages he'd trapped.

The Dark Fae started for him. Balthazar stepped between. "This stops here," he said firmly.

"Get back to work," Bron ordered. "If apologies are in order, let's hear them."

The situation was well in hand, so I turned away. Balthazar had stepped in as if he'd never left.

Morgan and Zeke ran to me. Sita landed on my shoulder. "You found him," Morgan exclaimed.

"Yes. A passel of sisters were at the boardinghouse raising Cain." I gave her a quick hug.

"Not good news. I can't wait until we put them in their place." She wriggled out of my arms. "Come on," she invited. "Meet the rest of our group. We're seven rather than six because of me." A roll of her mismatched eyes was followed by. "For some reason, everyone wants to play the pregnancy card. They're trying to talk me into staying behind."

"I am not staying anywhere," Sita cawed. "I will avenge Bella. And Zoelle."

"*As will I,*" Zeke woofed.

I walked the perimeter of the arena until Morgan and the animals stopped at a group containing Maeve and Alexander.

"Thank you for accomplishing what I could not." Alexander bowed.

I stood in front of him. "You will keep your word about that pardon. I gave him mine that you would."

"I cannot speak for Xavier, but the rest of us will honor it."

"What if your prince issues different orders?"

Alexander shrugged. "If none of us jump to carry them out, it won't matter."

Maeve clapped her hands together. "Back at it, folks. We were practicing mingling our power. It needs far more work."

"Did we determine a launch time?"

"Not yet," she replied.

"We're not ready," Alexander explained.

"Who determines when we are?" Morgan asked. My guess was she wanted to be gone yesterday.

"Our generals. We march on their orders, none other," he replied.

I flanked Morgan on one side; Zeke stood on the other. The Dark Fae faced off across from us. When Alexander gave the signal, we engaged.

Rusty was a kind word for what was left of my warrior skills—if I'd ever truly possessed any. Not the place for qualms. I filled in my gaps with magic and soldiered forward.

CHAPTER 15

MORGAN

Damien was gone so long, I'd begun to worry about him. Meanwhile, everyone from Maeve to Logan had begun making noises about how a battle zone wasn't any place for a pregnant woman. If I wasn't the only one who could actually kill witches, they'd have sidelined me.

Or tried to.

If they'd left us behind, we'd have joined the battle on our own. This conflict was intensely personal for me.

Maybe too personal. Could I kill a witch I'd thought was my friend?

None of them are my friends, I reminded myself. At least Rebecca had apologized *ex post facto*. No one had stuck up for me when they'd voted to kick me out.

"I am in my right mind, child. Finally. Forgive me for what I did," rolled through my head.

Crap. *"Go away. Every time I let my guard down, you fuck me over."*

"Do. Not. Listen. To. Her," Zeke woofed.

"Don't worry. I have no intention of it."

Talking with her had given her an edge to take over. I wasn't about to make *that* mistake again, so I spun protections around my mind. I expected she'd scratch at the edges, but she didn't.

A fight broke out—we'd had a few since this practice session began. Damien returned, Charles in tow. He and the other Unseelie general made short work of the conflict.

Hours passed, broken by occasional halts for food and drink.

We went over the same series of moves until I could do them in my sleep. But what did I know about war? Witches aren't warriors. We win by cunning, subterfuge. I considered pointing out that all our disciplined maneuvers might not matter a damn in the face of the sisterhood's tactics.

They'd never played fair.

Maeve touched my shoulder. "Get some rest. We move out in six hours."

I wasn't tired, but she was being kind, so I didn't argue.

Damien hooked an arm through mine; we walked out of the arena with Zeke trotting next to me and Sita on my shoulder.

"Can we hunt?" Zeke asked hopefully.

"Of course," Damien told him and turned to me. "I can leave you in my rooms and stay with the animals while they feed."

"What? You too?"

"Me too, what?"

"Everyone's treating me like I'm made of glass. I'm happy to sit near the veils while they scare up dinner."

He draped an arm around my shoulders. "Fine. We'll both watch over them. Love to have the company."

Niall made cooing noises deep in my mind as we made our way to Faery's border. Damien and I sat on the ground leaning against the veils. For all my protestations about not being tired, I may have dozed leaning against him.

"In the interest of full disclosure," I murmured sleepily.

"Aye, I'm listening."

"Hecate came calling again, but when I told her to get lost, she did."

"Interesting." He frowned. "We'll have to be careful inside the guild house. All that witchy enchantment could give her just the boost she needs."

"Not sure I can fight warded."

"We'll figure something out. I'm not seeing how she could defeat the spell I wrapped her in when I shipped her back to Fort William."

I relaxed against him. "We have enough to worry about. Let's back-burner that one."

Zeke had settled in with something fat and furry. Sita was perched in a tree eating something. The six hours Maeve had allotted were down to something slightly over one. A shiver crept down my spine.

"How are you doing?" Damien tightened the arm he had around me.

"Eh. Hard to say. For all my big talk about revenge, mostly I want to get this over with."

He pulled me closer. "What makes you think this will end anything?"

"If we take on all the Covens, why wouldn't it?"

"Wars don't work that way. There are always survivors who bide their time, plotting and planning and—"

"Never mind. I get the picture." A sense of desolation scoured me, leaving a bitter taste in my mouth.

Zeke trotted over licking gore from his snout. *"We can join our group."*

I motioned to Sita and untangled myself from Damien's arm. Damn I was tired. Maybe the pregnancy was sapping me. Or maybe it was finally sinking in that this was my life —from now until the moon fell out of the sky. Every time I convinced myself being ousted by the sisterhood didn't bother me any longer, the sense of peace never lasted.

Because it was a lie. Being ripped from the Coven left scars. They might fade, but they'd never completely go away.

Before I sank deeper into a funk, Maeve slid past the veils. I lumbered to my feet feeling like a beached whale. The seer eyed me oddly and then moved close enough to place a hand over my belly. Niall leaned toward her touch.

"Won't be long now," she announced.

"You're mistaken," I stammered. "By my count, I have at least four more months, maybe closer to five."

"Aye, child, if you were mortal."

"Witch pregnancies seemed to last ten months." Despite my efforts, defensiveness added prickles to my words.

"You're not exactly like them."

If she'd thrown a bucket of ice water over my head, it

wouldn't have been more jarring. The unpleasant truth was she was right. I wasn't like the others, having been crafted, not born.

My eyes burned. What in the unholy fuck was wrong with me. I refused to turn maudlin. "Let's get moving," I gritted determined to bury my hyper-emotional state deep. Witch killer or not, if Maeve—or anyone—decided I was unstable, I'd be benched.

Damien was gazing at me, a combination of worry and protectiveness stamped into his striking features. To short circuit overly solicitous commentary from him, I started through the veils.

Of course, they turned to concrete since I needed one of the Fae to pronounce abracadabra and part them. It wasn't a rejection, not really, but as raw as I felt, any reminder about how I didn't belong anywhere stung.

Fuck. I had to get hold of myself and damned quick. In minutes, I'd be in the thick of a battle—probably one where I'd be called upon to inflict grave injuries on witches I'd known for centuries.

I needed a cooler head than the one currently sitting atop my shoulders.

Someone must have done something because the veil in front of me swung to the side. I strode through, head high. Zeke's snout brushed my thigh.

"Sure you want to do this?" he woofed.

"Not sure about much of anything, but I'm doing it anyway."

"But we must avenge Zoelle, and Bella," Sita reminded me. Since Zeke and I were sticking with telepathy, she used it too. Silly of us since the Fae could listen in if they chose.

My ambivalence was a solid wakeup call. This was bigger than me. It had its roots in the antiquity of my making. Fussing because the old normal was gone wasted energy.

Damien caught up with me. "This way. Maeve said our group is in one of the small dining rooms."

I expected him to question me or cluck over me. He didn't do either.

Maeve must have engaged a mini jump spell because she was waiting in a room I'd never been in before. Food—bread, cheese, cold cuts—were laid out on a table, but I wasn't hungry. Alexander and the two other Dark Fae were garbed in leather trousers and vests.

Damien wore his usual work clothes: khaki pants and a plaid cotton shirt. "This is Naomi," he said by way of introduction. "She's my third cousin once removed, but then everyone in Faery is loosely related."

I extended a hand. "Nice to meet you."

"Same." She clasped it. Dark brown hair had been braided. Like the men, she wore leather garments. In her case, a long, slit skirt and a shirt that closed with snaps. "I admit I had my doubts about including a non-Fae in our ranks, but they tell me you can actually kill witches."

I winced. "True, but this Coven engaged evil that killed my mother."

Dark brows edged upward. "Hadn't heard that part." She eyed my belly.

Before she got any words out, I shook my head. "I'm pregnant, not infirm."

Full lips split into a grin. "I like you. When the babe is here, I'd be delighted to be her official auntie."

"His," I corrected.

"How could I have made that kind of mistake?" she murmured.

"Easily. Niall is precocious. Perhaps he cast a spell to mask his identity."

Maeve clapped her hands smartly. "Enough. Get your hair out of the way," she instructed me.

Normally, I don't appreciate being ordered about, but it was sound advice. Everyone else was eating, so I slapped cheese on a hunk of bread. It may as well have been cardboard, but I choked it down and gathered my unruly tresses into a pony tail.

"We leave in five minutes," Maeve announced. "I lead the Fae, Alexander the Dark Fae. But you will obey orders from either of us."

"Having studied the layout of the guild house," Alexander tossed out, "we will enter the basement and sweep upward. Any witch deemed to have fallen will be ended."

"Who exactly will make that determination?" I asked, rattled. From the sounds of things, I could be knee deep in blood.

"Why, each of us," he replied. "It's where your skill will shine. We identify them. You take care of them."

"What if you're wrong? No, scratch that." I blew out an unsteady breath. "What about clemency? Maybe some were coerced and are willing to mend their ways."

Christ, I sounded like a Pollyanna, but the specter of murdering scores of sisters didn't sit well."

Sita landed on my shoulder, talons digging deep. "Not the time to be kind," she cawed.

"Remember how they treated us." Zeke whined to punctuate his words.

"A witch named Rebecca offered to help me," I said. "Well before all this."

"I never intimated we'd annihilate them all." Alexander sounded miffed. Big surprise. He'd only recently come to embrace his Fae cousins. Whether I carried a half-Fae child or not, I was like a redheaded stepchild many degrees removed from Faery.

Damien sidled next to me. *"What's wrong?"*

"Eh, everything. Nothing. Don't mind me. I'll be fine." The Fae could certainly hear us if they chose. No one said anything.

Maeve's magic built around us employing a twist I wasn't familiar with. Must be Alexander. To drag myself out of my subpar mood, I tested their joined power. Interesting. It tapped much more deeply into Earth magic. For the hell of it, I wove a few strands into their casting. It earned me a sour look from Maeve.

"I don't recall requesting assistance, Witch," Alexander muttered.

I could have withdrawn my contribution. I didn't. "We have to learn how to work together." I stood tall, unapologetic.

Zeke growled, eager to defend.me.

Our joint travel spell deepened, developing terminal velocity. Next stop, the guild house.

The malaise that had gripped me dropped away. It was showtime. I was more than ready. Determination swooshed through me. Being a ninny isn't my style.

"I've got your back," Damien murmured.

We emerged in the same hallway I'd recently traversed to rescue Sita. It smelled of ozone and expended witch spells, rich with sulfur and salt. They'd been a day late and a dollar short hanging on to the hawk. Not an error they were likely to repeat.

I extended magic in a wide net, seeking beacons, otherwise known as witch early warning systems. Sure enough, three flared to life.

"What are those?" Naomi hissed.

"They know we're here," I shouted. No more reason to waste magic on stealth.

I spun, power crackling between my fingertips. Within me, Niall tensed, curling into a ball. Poor little mite. Not even born yet, and his whole existence had turned into one catastrophe followed by another even worse one.

Witches poured into the basement, down stairwells and through portals. Of course, we'd be outnumbered. Alexander's neat little system where they'd test individual witches for evil frittered to fairy dust.

A dart sliced into my shoulder. Pain stole my breath. Zeke's paws crashed down on me. He snatched the end of the dart and spat it onto the concrete floor. Even that short exposure pumped poison into me. I walled it off with magic. The flesh would slough away, but the wound wasn't deep.

Sita cawed, ducking and weaving as she drove her beak into eyes and ears, leaving trails of blood in her wake.

"Watch for poison darts," I yelled and danced this way and that. Fighting through warding is damned difficult. My best bet was to move erratically so no one else got a bead on me.

The Fae had teamed up: Seelie and Unseelie. Power flickered around each of the three dyads as they stood back-to-back. Naomi had paired with Alexander. I'd never gotten names for the Dark Fae working with Damien and Maeve. I had Zeke and Sita. I scarcely required more mage power than my familiars.

Banshees had joined the witches.

Miscalculation on the part of the sisterhood.

Maeve wove her hands in a complicated pattern that stopped them in their tracks. Alexander spoke a few words in the Fae's original language, one I'd failed to learn more than couple words of. As a unit, the Banshees turned and barreled into witches they'd obeyed mere seconds ago.

Poisoned darts still targeted me. After the first, I'd been smart enough to sidestep them. It took all my concentration and a goodly portion of my magic.

"You!" a voice shrilled from behind me. "I will end this now. You're a disgrace to your heritage."

"Over here," Alexander bellowed. Images cascaded through my head. He'd cornered three of the seven witches I'd imprisoned.

No deep thought required. I didn't even have to be close. Ensuring I had line-of-sight, I loosed a volley that should have done the trick.

"More," he shouted. "Get over here, Morgan. You can't do this from fifty paces."

I should have been able to.

Whoever had yelled from behind me about being a disgrace had yet to show themselves.

A quick check of my reservoir was reassuring. Plenty of power. The night I'd killed five witches, I'd done it from the second story of my boardinghouse. But I'd had the element of surprise—on both sides. No one had been more stunned than me those witches were dead.

The current crop knew about me. They'd taken precautions.

Could I drill through them?

Goddess only knew, but I was about to find out. If I couldn't kill them, then what?

Whoa. Getting way ahead of the curve.

Damien and his Dark Fae partner were surrounded by at least ten witches. Despite the mismatch in numbers, they were holding their own. After crafting a quick invisibility spell, I skirted them and hustled to Alexander.

The witches he'd corralled writhed on the ground, incapacitated but very much alive.

"Get to it," he snapped.

Defenses rose from my throat; I swallowed them and bent to assess what was impeding my magic. Certainly not the Fae webbing that had snared the women. The moment my fingertips grazed the nearest witch, a shock ran up my arm as if I'd been burned. Chanting furiously, I shook the arm to dispel insidious power creeping toward my core.

They weren't just warded. Their protections were specifically aimed at me and my magic.

How in the hell had they managed that?

Darts whizzed over my head. Better to stay low, where I had bodies for cover.

A triumphant howl told me Zeke had ripped out a throat or done something where magic couldn't replenish the damage. Sita zipped past, an eyeball clutched in her beak.

"What's wrong?" Alexander had spun the same golden ropes I'd seen Damien conjure, but they were loosening by the moment.

"I can't drill through their warding," I hissed.

"Why before and not now?" he demanded.

Good question. "They prepared better," I gritted.

"Then what good are you?" he muttered.

Damien didn't hear, but Zeke had. He sashayed over, a chewed-off forearm gripped in his jaws. Dropping it, he barreled into Alexander. *"You will not disparage my mistress. She's been through enough."*

"Fine," he growled. "We have to do something. My spell won't hold them much longer."

I threw power at them. It hovered, burning brightly but not touching the three.

A Kelpie pranced into the hall, snorting and stamping. His presence revived the fallen sisters. The Fae ropes glistened and faded.

Crap. I'd have to try harder, whatever that meant. I was still at eye level with them. Digging deep, I focused on the nearest witch, probing, assessing. When an answer rose, it wasn't what I expected.

Not only had they specifically crafted witchcraft against me, but anti-Fae enchantment oozed from them. Alexander was lucky his bonds had held. They'd only done so because the sisterhood wasn't anticipating Unseelie magic.

Raising my mind voice, I called, *"Rebecca. Where are you?"*

"Sub-basement. In a cell."

I sent power zinging her way and ran into a wall. Christ on a fucking crutch. They'd set traps to stymie me no matter which way I turned.

Zeke was still snarling at Alexander.

"Stop that and go find Rebecca," I instructed. *"The floor beneath this one. Free her if you can."*

The wolf faded to invisibility. I layered power atop Alexander's. If I didn't touch the witches' magic directly, mine actually worked to some extent. Deep in ensuring they didn't regain consciousness—and shuck the remaining bonds—I didn't notice Rebecca until she touched my shoulder.

"How can I help?"

A sidelong glance showed me a bruised face and shaved head. Sorrow for what she'd endured on my account married with fury.

"Are you good with killing them?"

"Would that I could. I hate what the sisterhood has turned into."

Bending near her ear, I murmured instructions. The three sprawled in front of us were specifically warded against my magic, my energy.

When I opened my magical center, Rebecca drew from

it. Following my instructions, she focused enchantment to close throats and stop hearts.

"More like it," Alexander crowed. Convinced we had the current situation well in hand, He moved to the next problem where Naomi was holding down the fort.

Zeke didn't wait for us to end the third witch. On top of her, he ripped out her entire throat. Blood geysered, coating his white fur.

I wanted to take Rebecca aside, tell her how sorry I was she'd suffered on my account, but there wasn't time.

Damien and Maeve—and their Unseelie partners—were losing ground.

Rebecca wore a shell-shocked look, but she straightened and asked, "What's next?"

Maybe she didn't need me to coo over her after all.

"Excellent, Daughter," blasted me. *"You're doing this."*

I clapped my hands over my ears, knowing it was pointless.

Fucking Hecate. Of all the times for her to show up. *"Go away,"* I hissed. *"I have enough troubles."*

"Which is exactly why you need me. Do. Not. Fight. This."

Like hell I wouldn't. No more takeovers. My body was mine, and only mine. I refused to play host to the witch goddess.

Zeke was oblivious, rolling in the carcass he'd bloodied.

Sita was nowhere in sight.

Damien shouted power words.

A glowing white portal formed in front of me. Hecate stepped through. Not part of me, but her own person.

How had she broken free?

Did it even matter? Now that she was here, what mayhem would she sow?

Damien was by my side in a trice, an arm wrapped protectively around my shoulders. "Leave her alone," he growled.

Laughter rolled from her. "Just like a Fae to miss the point."

Spinning away from us, she began to sing. It reminded me of one of her attempts to ensorcel me, except this time, the magic didn't bear my name. Much like I assumed the Pied Piper of Hamblin drew children after him, witches flocked to her side, glazed expressions on their faces as they gazed expectantly at their goddess.

DAMIEN

We were holding our own, barely. I hadn't expected we'd end up fighting the whole Coven. Either we'd badly underestimated the numbers turned to evil, or they'd been mesmerized to obey. Or they'd imported witches to swell their ranks.

I kept half an eye on Morgan, while fighting my own battles. The Dark Fae I'd been paired with, Carre, was fearless. We'd practiced enough in the arena to make a decent team.

Shorter than me, and slightly built like most of our kind, his fair hair was braided close to his skull. Untanned leather trousers were cinched around his waist. A blue woolen tunic covered his chest. His arms were tattooed with archaic runes. Despite none of us using much in the way of weaponry, a wicked looking dirk with a serrated edge sat in a sheath strapped around his waist. Knee-high boots graced his feet.

It might have been my imagination, but the more we worked together, the more robust our combined efforts. Earth magic has always been my strong suit. Dark Fae also leverage it, but in a different fashion. The net effect is additive.

We started out fighting fair, but after foul energy stabbed me in the back, I was done with the rules of engagement. Back. Front. Nothing mattered but meting out pain. I should have guessed these witches would fight dirty.

"What the fuck is that?" Carre kicked a hex bag toward the far end of the hallway. It left a noxious trail of skunk scent.

"Hex bag," I rasped and did a quick search for more. Three rolled out of goddess only knew where. I sealed them with magic. No time to disable them—if I even could without a trip back to Faery.

"I figured that out, but what do they do?"

I was so not the right one to ask. "Create chaos. Look left, mate."

Carre pivoted. Like all our race, he's light on his feet, graceful. A barrage of darts barely missed his shoulder and neck. A witch I didn't recognize glided toward us. Naked from the waist up, she wore a seductive smile and little else.

"Fancy a break from the ruckus, boys?" Blonde curls fluffed around her shapely head. Green eyes held an Asian cast. Full breasts tipped with strawberry nipples bounced alluringly.

Carre gazed her way, a speculative expression on his face. Pheromones thickened in the air. Son of a bitch, he was actually considering her offer. Didn't take much to weed out compulsion directed dead center to his groin. She knew better than to target Morgan's mate even though her invitation had been plural.

I stepped between them and sent enchanted cords to bind her thighs. They stopped her in her tracks. She raised her upper lip and snarled, "Stay out of it. Your friend is interested."

"The hell I am," Carre spat and added rope to my efforts. "Tell your woman to neutralize this one."

Morgan would have taken umbrage at his terminology, but I didn't point it out. Neither did I call her over.

She appeared to be having difficulty, or she had before another witch showed up a few minutes before. Together, they were kicking some serious ass. Ms. Seduction wasn't going anywhere. Not tangled in Fae bonds.

"Damien. Carre. Over here." Alexander thundered.

The witch who'd thought to remove us from play with sex glared.

"Now would be good," Alexander shouted.

I focused on the witch's third eye and hit her with a sleeping spell. It wouldn't last more than an hour or so, but she'd be groggy when she woke. Without waiting for her to crumple to the floor, I sprinted toward the Dark Fae with Carre protecting my flank.

Naomi crouched in front of Alexander. He'd encompassed her in a protective bubble. Blood seeped from her side, staining the concrete and her garment. Power danced around her as she frantically worked to heal her injury. Spent darts littered the floor.

"Don't fuss over me," she panted. "This is under

control." To underscore her words, she rose and shook herself. Power arced from her hands. The bloodstains vanished. This wasn't her first rodeo. Blood gives the enemy power over us—if they can get hold of it.

"Are you certain?" Alexander hovered.

I deflected still more darts. Lightning flew from Carre's fingertips as he targeted the nearest group of witches.

"Of course, I'm certain," Naomi growled. "Stop treating me like I'm delicate."

"Our women adopt auxiliary roles in battles—" Alexander began.

"We don't." She spoke over him, whirled, and in an admirable mixed-martial-arts move, kicked a witch rushing her from behind. The two went down in a flurry of hissing, spitting, and sparks.

Carre and I got back to it even before Alexander's brusque, "Dismissed," reached us. Between magic and brute force, we mowed through lines of witches. Still more materialized. Where were they coming from? We'd been fighting for hours. Winning seemed more and more unlikely, but we weren't losing ground.

For now.

At some point, our power would wane, but I couldn't worry about it.

My vision hazed. I shook my head. And then shook it again. What the hell? I switched to my third eye. Curses rained from me in Gaelic. A chamber with mirrors on every surface surrounded me. One of the oldest urban myths is you pass through mirrors to enter Faery.

It's a crock, but mages outside of our ranks don't know that.

"Show yourself," I shouted. My words echoed back at me.

Who'd nabbed me? For what purpose? Was the plan to use me as a bargaining chip to get Morgan to stand down? For all her antipathy during our training session, witch bodies had been piling up around her.

I reached outward. Something sharp jabbed me in the right kidney. Twirling to get away from it, I ran into another pikestaff aimed at the middle of my opposite thigh. I felt it but couldn't see it.

Alrighty. First order of business would be a ward. Then I'd activate a teleport spell. Divide and conquer seemed to be the message of the day, but I'd be damned if I'd end up a sacrificial sheep. Our force was small. If whoever was successful separating me from the pack, they'd do the same until none of us were left.

Except Morgan. They'd wanted to annihilate her for months.

My place was by her side, fighting with my people.

Wards are simple affairs. They bind a mage's magic with environmental protections. My power was there but separated from my command by the thinnest of spells. Digging deep, I pushed against it. Once, and then again.

My chest was tight with effort as I grunted and strained against the barrier. Earth wasn't the ticket. I added air and then fire. It was counterintuitive, but water was the only element left.

A metaphorical deluge crashed through. Panting as

sweat rolled down my body, I made a wholesale grab for my magic. It clicked into place as if it had never left.

The mirrored place exploded, leaving me precisely where I'd been: by Carre's side.

Had he even noticed I was gone? Or had the whole thing been illusion. I'd have to ask him but not just now. After a quick visual to reassure myself the rest of us were all present and accounted for, I leapt back into the fray.

"Fucking endless," Carre muttered. Dirk in hand, he'd taken to stabbing eyes. "If they can't see, they can't fight," he repeated over and over like an incantation.

All of us were running down. Would we have to retreat and return with reinforcements?

What was happening at the other Covens? Had every group run into the same roadblocks plaguing ours?

"Duck," Carre shouted.

I did him one better and executed a sideways leap.

When Hecate blasted through a portal, shock poured through me along with fear for Morgan and our son. How in the fuck had she broken loose? The casting I'd used to ship her back to Fort William should have held. Maybe not forever, but for far longer than it had.

"Gotta take care of this," I told Carre. Skirting piles of the dead, I loped to Morgan where I wrapped an arm around her shoulders and faced Hecate.

"Leave her alone," I growled.

The witch goddess laughed uproariously. "Just like a Fae to miss the point."

Out of nowhere, she began to sing. I girded myself, warding Morgan and me against ensorcellment. Could have saved my magic. Her spell wasn't directed our way. Witches raced toward her wearing vacant expressions.

"What's she up to?" I bent close to Morgan's ear.

"No idea."

"Do you suppose we're next?"

She shrugged. Zeke joined us, his pelt more red than white. Sita landed on my shoulders, cawing triumphantly as she munched on an ear.

Maeve sidled close. "Not in any of my visions. Who freed her?"

My guess was she'd finessed it on her own, but I kept my thoughts to myself.

Hecate was separating the witches into two groups.

The one who'd been helping Morgan shouted, "More of us are still in cells below."

"Good to know, dearie," Hecate said. "How about if you and Morgan free them."

"Like hell," I said.

The witch goddess rounded on me, her dark eyes burning with an inner fire. "Not your show. Take your kin and go home. I've got this."

"I don't think so." Maeve was by my side.

Hecate eyed her. "We'll have to learn how to share the child, but it's a lesson for another day. Right now, your magic is in the way."

"If we go, Morgan goes with us," Maeve said.

"She is mine. Mine!" Hecate's voice rose, her tone menacing.

"Bullshit. Back off. I'm no one's," Morgan said in a clear ringing voice.

"We will take this up later." Hecate could have tacked "young lady" onto the end with about the same meaning.

"You can, but nothing will change on my end," Morgan said.

"What about the sisters imprisoned below?" Rebecca pressed.

"I'll go with you," Zeke howled.

"Me too," Sita offered.

Morgan crouched next to Zeke, probably telling him to take care.

"I'll watch out for them," Rebecca said and herded the wolf toward a stairwell leading off the central hall. Sita landed on Zeke's back.

Since Hecate had quit singing, the groups of witches were growing restive.

"Oh for crap's sake," she muttered. Hands raised, she spoke words in a language I've never heard. A cage dropped over one group. The others fell to the ground, dead to the world.

Possibly permanently.

Damn, what I wouldn't give for that level of talent.

"What's that?" Maeve's hands came up. She twirled until she faced away from me.

"I'd like to know too," Morgan muttered. Power arced as she tested the air.

I'd had enough for one day, so I circled us with a ward. Morgan batted at it. "Leave it be until we figure this out," I murmured, adding, "Please," as an afterthought, so she didn't simply bore holes through it.

The air flickered and took on a luminous aspect. A

golden gateway disgorged two women. The one with disheveled black hair and blood runes on her forehead and cheeks had to be Medea. The gods had marked her after she'd murdered the two sons from her union with Jason. Meant the other was likely Circe. It explained how Hecate had broken free from the Greeks and my puny efforts.

She'd finally summoned aid, although why she'd waited this long was a mystery. Maybe the Greeks' attention had wavered, and she jumped on the opportunity. Her trysts with Morgan may have strengthened her too.

Equally possible she'd reached out to her minions before, and they'd ignored her until they deemed her strong enough to remain free.

"What took you so long?" Hecate motioned to her fellow sorceresses.

"Eh, this and that." Blood runes ebbing and flowing with a life of their own, Medea stalked to Hecate. Medium height, she wore golden robes the same shade as her portal. Her eyes were dark, bottomless, and rimmed in the same red as her runic markings.

I'd read about her, but nothing prepared me for those morphing runes.

Golden hair fell to Circe's feet. About the same height as Medea, she was garbed in a white robe, sashed in green. After surveying the hallway, she glided toward the cage of evil witches. Burnished golden eyes matched her hair. The effect was overwhelming, and I'm used to magic.

Visible beams of power shot through the barred enclosure. The fifteen witches within moaned piteously.

"Didn't mean to."

"Didn't want to."

"They made me."

"Why didn't you come sooner?"

"Shut up," Circe bellowed. "Bunch of whiny bitches."

Medea sidled to Circe rubbing her hands together. Blood dripped onto the concrete marking her path. "Oooh, let's drag this out, shall we? Pain feeds my magic."

Morgan punched through my warding and stalked to Circe and Medea. "Some of them are telling the truth about being coerced. Test them."

The goddesses twirled. Morgan towered over them. "I do not take orders from inferiors." Circe bit off the words.

Morgan shrugged. "Order. Suggestion. Take your pick. My point is you're about to permanently destroy those women. Do some of them deserve it? Sure. I've been killing ever since Rebecca heeded my summons and shored up my skill with pure witch magic. Look."

Swinging an arm to the side, she pointed at bodies sprawled every which way. "I made certain each witch was beyond salvage. You will do the same."

"Given your tender sensibilities, step aside. We'll finish the job," Medea snarked.

"My witches. My choice." Hecate joined her acolytes.

"She made her own choices." Medea angled a pointed look at Morgan.

"Before I arrived." Hecate's bitten off words could have marred granite.

I waited for her to play the "I made her" card, but she didn't. Surely the other two knew about her plans and how Morgan slotted into them.

Scurrying feet dragged my attention away from the squabbling goddesses. Rebecca led about twenty witches who looked like someone had rode them hard and put them away wet. Zeke and Sita brought up the rear.

"Here we are," Rebecca announced. "Some require healing. All of us are…" She stared at Circe and Medea and fell to her knees. The ragtag group with her did likewise, some sobbing softly.

"Get up." Morgan trotted to Rebecca and hauled her to her feet. "The rest of you too. We bow to no one." Without missing a beat—and before Hecate could jump in and demand allegiance—she went on. "Tell us what happened here. How'd you end up in the local dungeon?"

Rebecca wrapped her arms around herself. "They told us we had to fight if you showed up, that you were the enemy and had to be disabled. Christine said your magic was stronger than any of ours, not to take chances but to ensorcel you and keep you out of commission until the Greeks showed up to claim you.

"Some refused to go along with it. We were separated from our familiars and imprisoned."

"What about them?" Morgan pointed at the group of witches who'd fallen into a dead sleep.

"They were on the fence. Guess they decided going with the flow would buy them the most. They don't hate you, but they were scared for themselves."

"See?" Morgan faced Circe and Medea. "They've not all fallen to darkness."

Hecate hustled between Morgan and her minions. "I've

already sorted who's who. The ones in the cage need to go. The others will have to prove their loyalty."

"To whom?" Morgan inquired.

Pride for her spirit swelled through me.

"Perhaps we've done enough for one day," Maeve suggested.

"Maybe you have, but I'm not finished," Morgan announced.

"Is she this snippy with everyone?" Hecate arched a dark brow.

"'Fraid so." A corner of the seer's mouth twitched. Subtle waves of enchantment burbled around her.

"Witches answer to me," Hecate said. "They chose me as their goddess."

"A long while back." Morgan looked her dead in the eye. "The world has changed. A lot. You might want to take another look. Ruling over what modern witches have become may not be appealing."

Hecate moved so fast, all I saw was a blur. One moment, she was a few feet away from Morgan, the next her hands gripped Morgan's shoulders.

"I made you. Show some respect."

"Respect has to be earned."

Maeve's casting curved around Morgan's back. She'd built a journey spell, something I should have had the presence of mind to do.

Tension sat like a rod between my shoulder blades.

Zeke stood next to Morgan, hackles at half mast growling. Pressure and weight told me Sita was back on my shoulders.

"The other Greeks were onto something," Medea said.

"Aye, we do not need the mouthy one whether you made her or not." Circe set her mouth in a tense line.

Morgan had dealt with plenty of rejection from the day her Coven dumped her. For all her brave words, she had a tender side. I tried out and discarded conciliatory words, but I couldn't do this for her.

Alexander had moved next to Maeve. The other Fae—Seelie and Unseelie—casually joined them.

"We're leaving," flashed across my mind in the ancient language of our people.

"I'm not going anywhere without Morgan."

Hecate sent a pointed look spiraling toward Maeve. We weren't hiding a thing from her. Her words clinched it. "Your precious Fae are leaving," she spat in Morgan's face. "Choice time. It's us or them."

"This is a load of crap." Morgan jerked free of Hecate's hold. "No one issues ultimatums to me."

The air around her and Zeke burst outward, splintering into a prism of color. When the lightshow cleared, they were gone.

"Follow them," Sita cawed into my ear.

"Good riddance," Medea cried.

"I second that," Circe said.

Hecate's silence spoke volumes. Turning to the cage of witches, she extended her arms. The bars of the cage glowed red-hot. Shrieking, raving, Hecate rained destruction. One by one, the witches turned into fat black vipers.

A fitting end.

"Creative," Medea murmured.

"Our turn." Circe eyed the prostrate group with anticipation.

Rebecca had herded the witches from the dungeon into a tight circle. Leaving them here didn't sit right. I had to go after Morgan, right now while her trail was fresh.

Alexander was nearest me. I spoke into his ear. "Take the witches with you."

"Where will you be?"

"I'll catch up."

Maeve was one step ahead of me. Fae power surged. Clean and pure, it was a palate cleanser after Hecate's serpent trick. When it subsided, all the Fae as well as Rebecca and her cadre of witches were gone.

"The pretty one stayed," Circe crooned and tugged her robes open.

"Hussy," Sita crowed.

"You can play too, little hawk." Circe glided our way.

"Flattered but taken," I told her and latched onto Morgan's essence.

Hands clutched at me, but she couldn't defeat my enchantment.

Next stop, Morgan.

When I found her—and I would—we were staying put until Niall entered the world. No more battles. No more chances. My first choice was Faery, but Morgan had a say too.

"Is she out for good?" Sita cawed.

"Hecate?"

The hawk chirped.

"Looks that way."

"Will she take Morgan?"

"Kicking and screaming. Today may have convinced her the minion she crafted so long ago didn't turn out quite like she'd hoped."

Hecate might not want Morgan any longer, but her comment to Maeve about duking it out over Niall concerned me. Sharing my son was off the table.

One step at a time. First, I had to locate Morgan. Then convince her to go to ground until she gave birth.

"If anyone can find her, it's you." Sita brushed her beak over my cheek.

Encouraged by the hawk's simple faith in me, I rode out my transport spell. The edges were beginning to lighten. Since I had no idea where we'd come out, I crafted a hasty ward and held defensive magic at the ready.

CHAPTER 17

MORGAN

My temper has always been my worst enemy, but I was sick to death of people dictating to me. And rejecting me. Or imposing conditions for acceptance. Medea was downright spooky with bloody tracks forming patterns that changed, presumably with her mood. Or maybe she had no control over them, which was even more disconcerting.

I couldn't conceive what kind of magic could even do that. Had she conjured it? Or had someone else slapped a curse on her.

Circe was an imperious bitch, and Hecate still carried a streak of madness. I sensed a lack of reality contact in her. I'd been cautiously relieved when she showed up and hadn't instantly slung chaos in her wake. When she'd begun to sing, I panicked and warded the whole lot of us—until it was clear the song wasn't directed at me or the Fae. If she'd noticed, she hadn't commented, but my bet was it had flown right by her.

This time, I'd been spared. What about next time, though?

She'd used the same musical tactic to establish control over me. I still had the occasional nightmare about it.

My take-home message from today was she'd never, never accept me as an equal. Nope. Hell, Circe and Medea were acolytes. Why had I been so stupid? All those months when I'd searched for my maker, a pathetic juvenile part of me hoped she'd welcome me like a long-lost daughter, albeit a grownup one.

With agency, autonomy.

On the verge of either losing it and screaming at Hecate to eat shit or dissolving into sobs, I had to leave.

With Zeke.

I'd have rounded up Sita too, but she was firmly attached to Damien's shoulder. He loved her and would care for her.

Besides, I wasn't leaving forever. Just long enough to pull the tatters of composure around me. Niall thrashed. He didn't like it when Damien and I were separated.

Of course, he didn't. Not after my ignominious egress from Faery and the months Damien and I had been apart.

I'm not proud of this next piece, but my first stop was my old room on the third floor of the guild house. Every witch in the place was in the basement, so I was safe enough. In contrast to my conjecture about another witch moving in, the chamber hadn't changed since I left.

"Why are we still here?" Zeke demanded, followed by, *"Why'd we leave in the first place?"*

"I need breathing room to collect my thoughts."

"What about Rebecca?"

Guilt stabbed me. I focused power downward and eavesdropped. "The Fae will take care of her and her band of witches."

"It should have been you." Zeke's accusation stung.

Instead of protesting I couldn't be all things to everyone, I took in my old bed tucked into a corner. And my desk with its laptop computer. On a whim, I tugged open the closet. My clothes hadn't been disturbed.

Why kick me out and turn my room into a shrine? Were they afraid to touch my things? None of it mattered. This Coven would never be the same. I doubted it would recover from witches turning into snakes, others being imprisoned, and a third set having to prove themselves.

Whatever that meant.

"They need you," Zeke woofed softly.

Damn it. He'd been inside my head as he often was.

I crouched next to him and buried a hand in his thick, bloodstained ruff. "I have to come to terms with, well with everything." Breath stuttered from me. Some things are tough to admit. "I'm not whole. Not yet, but I'm getting closer."

He pressed into my touch, turned, and licked my face.

Once I'd thought finding Hecate would complete me. Yeah, right. Nice try, but no cigar.

I kept an eye on the basement. The Fae were leaving.

Soon Damien would too. Knowing him, he'd track me. May as well make this simple for him after all the pain I'd caused.

I bid farewell to the guild house—and my chamber. I'd never return. The place held too many painful memories.

Power jumped to my summons. My room dissolved, giving way to Faery's veils. I hadn't been there five minutes when a cheery, "Last place I expected to find you," filled my ears.

Sita cooed a greeting and traded Damien's shoulders for mine.

His arms closed around me from behind. I leaned against him, grateful for his solid presence and unwavering devotion. He'd forgiven the unthinkable. And he never tossed it in my face. The tense ball in my belly relaxed as our son's worries eased.

Zeke pushed his snout into Damien's side. *"Let me inside. I want to find the river and get cleaned up."*

"I'm going with you," Sita cawed.

Without letting go of me, Damien spoke a few words. The veils parted. Zeke and the hawk passed through.

"Been quite a day," Damien observed. "How are you holding up?"

I turned in his arms until we faced each other. "Better than when I left the basement. You did bring Rebecca and her witches out, right?"

His fair brows shot up. "Yes, but how did you—? Scratch that. Where'd you go first?"

"My old room. Needed to regroup. I didn't want to get too far away in case my magic was required."

He cupped the side of my face in a calloused hand.

Mages don't usually get calluses, but he's spent a lot of his life doing manual labor. "I want to talk with you about Hecate—and the other two. But I need to get inside, check in with the other groups and see how their efforts went."

They hadn't been front and center in my mind, but his words reminded me other guild houses were in play. My off-the-cuff guess was their assigned groups hadn't had nearly as tough a time as us.

"I want to know too."

He swung an arm to the side. The veils parted for us.

"Is everyone else back?" I asked.

"Long since."

Either a very good sign. Or a very bad one.

"Do you have news?" I reached for his hand; he clasped it.

"Not from every team, but the ones I know about were successful."

"Define successful." I laced my fingers with his as we walked one of Faery's endless corridors.

"Let's wait to hear from the others directly," he suggested.

Fae of both persuasions milled about the council chamber. Muddy footprints marred its thick rugs, but they vanished quickly, courtesy of self-cleaning enchantment.

The magical equivalent of a white board was suspended in the air at the front of the room. Each team checked in and delineated the status of their assigned guild house. I walked close and studied it.

Rebecca and the witches from my guild house stood in a tight group off to one side. When she spied me, she ran to me and threw her arms around my body, holding me close. I hugged her back.

"When you vanished, I didn't know what to think. I was afraid—" She stopped abruptly. "Better not give voice to what I feared. Might jinx things."

"This will be okay."

"How?" She screwed her mouth into a moue, looking like she'd been sucking on lemons.

"Nothing will be the same, but at least you won't live in the shadow of evil."

A shudder racked her; she let go of me and wrapped her arms around herself. Her hazel eyes narrowed to slits. "I never want to go back there."

"Know what you mean. I had the same reaction when I stopped by my chamber on the upper floor."

"Why'd you do that?"

"I had to get away from Hecate, but I wanted to remain close. In case I was needed."

"We could start over."

"Huh? Start over, how?"

She shrugged. "Find another place, make it our own. We'd be small, but at least we'd trust each other."

The import of her words sank in. "Why would you want to include me?"

"Why not? You were always a part of us before that craziness around your eyes spurred all those rumors."

"What about Hecate?"

Another shrug. "None of us have worshipped her for time out of mind. Hard to see how her returning from wherever would alter any of that."

"Probably not how she views it."

"She can't force us to revere her."

I closed my teeth over my lower lip. "One of many things I'm still conflicted about is exactly what I owe her."

Rebecca locked gazes with me. "Given the turn of events, I'd say nothing. Now, if she'd shown up and claimed you early on, things might have been different. She's why Zoelle is dead."

True, but not. So much was shading to gray.

The specter of returning to "business as usual" was appealing. Damned appealing. And then I caught myself and folded both hands over my belly. "What about my son?"

Spots of color formed on her cheeks. Looking away, she murmured, "Not sure. Now, if the babe were female..."

"Big if since he's not."

"I just don't know, Morgan. It's a brave new world out there. Maybe we can recraft our rules."

"Everyone would have to agree. Plus, there's also Damien."

Rebecca's full mouth curved into a soft smile. "I always thought the celibacy requirement was stupid. No other mages do that. Why should we? Besides, it was a joke. The majority of us had a bit of side action going."

I stared at her. Damn it. I'd been woefully out of touch, treading water in my own little world.

Logan strode into the room and clapped his hands for silence. Myriad side conversations died away. Everyone turned to face him.

"Today was a success on many fronts," he began. "First, we fielded troops with our Unseelie cousins and began healing the schism between us. Second, we met or exceeded our goals and sustained no casualties. Witches who refused to relinquish their ties with evil were detained."

My ears pricked. Logan would probably shush me, but I still asked, "By whom."

"Initially by us, but Arianrhod volunteered to ensure they didn't cause any more trouble. She tapped a few Celts, and they closed the gateway beneath Morgan's old guild house. The Banshees resurrected their allegiance to Faery. Not that they had a choice."

"Kelpies are still an unknown," Maeve offered. "For now, I don't believe they'll launch another offensive. Hecate is loose for good this time. Her power appears mostly restored. Enough that the Greeks won't recapture her. Hopefully, they've moved on."

Everything seemed too "tied up with a bow." Happy endings happen to other people. Besides, they've always been overrated. When you live forever, nothing stays the same—good or bad. The Greeks may have given up on Hecate, but they'd voiced strong feelings about my son.

We'd addressed the Covens in North America, but others were scattered throughout the world. Hecate wouldn't quietly walk away from me, no matter how snarky I was to her. Even if she counted me out, I could see her plotting to start over with Niall.

It would never happen.

A damp, fluffy Zeke bounded into the room. Sita flew after him. *"What'd I miss?"* he woofed.

"We're about to find out," I told him.

One by one, Logan invited team leaders to provide brief

encapsulations of their efforts. A few Covens were now missing significant numbers of witches. As I listened, a plan took shape. It might pit me against Hecate—something I wanted to avoid if possible—but the more I turned it this way and that, the more it held a certain appeal.

Once the reports were complete, Logan said, "Well done, everyone. Now that this project is over, what are our next steps mending Faery?"

"So, that's where all of you are," someone screeched from the hallway.

Oh-oh. I remembered who owned that voice.

Xavier pelted into the council chamber. "I specifically instructed you to return to our side of Faery. Why are you still here? Leave. Immediately."

Logan strode toward him. Xavier extended his hands palms outward. "Last time, you plied me with mead. Not falling for that again. Whatever you've done to tempt my people, undo it."

The Unseelie in the room moved toward their regent like a wave. It flowed around Logan, parting and then reforming as the Dark Fae surrounded their leader and moved him into the hall.

Maeve wrapped a hand around Logan's upper arm. I couldn't hear what she said, but it was probably along the lines of *let them manage their own problems.*

"Why is he even their leader?" Zeke's tail plumed.

"Because he always has been," Damien replied. "In much the same way that Logan heads our council, his role is usually more ceremonial than actual. Until recently. The last time he got this involved was during a war in the 1500s."

The buzz of magic from outside the council chamber suggested a spirited conversation was in process. I leaned closer to Damien. "What would you think if I did a bit of cleanup work for the more broken of the Covens."

He spun one hand in a need-more-information signal.

I looked for Rebecca, but she'd rejoined the witches from my Coven.

"The Covens who lost significant numbers of witches will require assistance to get back on track. I was thinking I could provide guidance, leadership. Maybe even set things up so they formed a network rather than operating independently."

"It could work." Damien nodded thoughtfully. "If they were willing to listen."

"All I can do is try. Some may chase me off, but once they recognize the other guild houses have formed a cadre, I bet they'll want to be part of it too."

I stopped long enough to blow out a breath. Now I'd begun talking about this, it was taking shape for me. "I'd start with the Coven I used to be part of. The witches know me. Might make it simpler."

"What happens once Niall is born?" Damien took hold of my hands. "And what about me? Where would I fit in an all-woman culture?"

"That's just it," I hurried on. "Nowhere is it written things can't change. According to Rebecca, I was about the only one who kept the celibacy requirement."

"Some witches won't accept that level of transformation," he warned. "Hecate probably won't, either."

"Of course, Hecate is an unknown. She could derail the best of plans. Absent her intervention, some witches will welcome the changes I have in mind. It's kind of like the Unseelie. They're in the hallway basically telling Xavier to get with the program or go home."

Damien grinned. It made him look about sixteen and heartbreakingly gorgeous. "Were you eavesdropping?"

"I don't have to. Are you all right with my plan? I ran it past you for your blessing."

"What have you done with Morgan?" he teased.

I leaned into him and wrapped my arms around his broad back. "She's learning how to be part of a couple."

"I like the sound of that." His lips brushed my forehead and hovered over my lips. Anticipation shot through me like a jolt of high-voltage electricity.

"Let's get out of here," I murmured about the time the Dark Fae trooped back into the chamber minus Xavier.

Balthazar and Bron approached Logan. "Our liege extends his apologies," Balthazar said.

"He will return once he's feeling more himself," Bron added smoothly.

"Remain and celebrate with us," Logan invited.

"Of course." Balthazar motioned to the Unseelie.

Tankards of mead floated into the room, followed by trays laden with food.

"We should stay for a while." Damien held me close. "Do you mind?"

"Not at all. We'll have the rest of our lives together."

"Will we? Once you refused the Fae mating ceremony." His greener-than-green eyes bored into mine.

"That was the old me. If you ask again, you'll receive a different answer."

Zeke must have been listening. Enthusiastic woofs filled the air along with chirps and caws from Sita.

Damien leapt onto a table and whistled loudly. Everyone looked at him as if he'd lost his mind. "The lady said yes," he crowed.

"Which lady and yes to what?" a Dark Fae cried.

A swoosh of power lifted me to the table next to Damien. "This lady agreed to join her life with mine," he exclaimed.

Logan loped near, a warm smile illuminating his usually austere features. "Let's add it to the festivities," he boomed. "Before she changes her mind."

"Not much fear of that," I said. My face was so warm, it was probably nine shades of crimson.

Maeve motioned me back to the floor. Once I jumped down, she looped an arm through mine. "Come with me, child. It's not every day one of us marries. Let me find you something special to wear."

I looked at my garments, blood and sweat stained from the battle. What had I been thinking? Maybe that the ceremony wouldn't be imminent.

"That would be lovely," I murmured.

Within the protective folds of my womb, Niall cooed and gurgled like a normal baby. Maybe he'd have a childhood after all, rather than a blood-stained tapestry of epic disasters.

"Come on then." Maeve tugged on my arm, and I followed.

Zeke started after us, but the seer said, "No. Bad luck to see a bride while she's preparing. We'll be back soon."

"Come on, you two." Damien gathered Zeke and Sita. "You can help me get ready."

"Do you want maids of honor?" Rebecca called from across the room.

"More the merrier," I told her.

Our troupe grew as the witches joined us, all of us en route to the Fae wardrobe room.

CHAPTER 18

DAMIEN

Zeke yipped with excitement. Sita flew in circles between the council chamber and my rooms. When I'd floated the Fae mating ceremony, I'd expected Morgan to smile pretty and refuse again.

Her acquiescence was more than a pleasant surprise. Joy cascaded through me filling every nuance of my being with delight. A part of me had withered from the moment I'd discovered she'd been secretly communing with Hecate.

I'd overreacted, but once anger took over it made me stupid. I'd also been hurt she hadn't trusted me enough to tell me, not a combination that leant itself to a clear head.

No reason to rehash old news. I felt whole again, and I savored the sensation.

"Tell us what to expect from the ceremony," Sita cawed.

"Please," Zeke seconded. *"Witches never mated."*

No wonder Rebecca was so enthusiastic about being part of the festivities. This had to be the first joining of mages she'd seen. For whatever reason, electronics had worked perfectly well in the guild house, which was interesting since they didn't work at all in Faery. Access to the Internet and television must have given the Coven working knowledge about mortals and their rituals.

Most mages lack that. I was an anomaly since I'd chosen to live amongst humans. Or, more accurately, I'd decided to live apart from Faery. I could have settled on a borderworld, but most aren't inhabited.

"We're waiting." Sita swooped around my bedroom.

"Sorry. My mind was wandering. I still can't believe Morgan will be part of my life from now on."

"Us too," Sita chirped.

"Yes, dear one. All of us," I murmured.

"She would have been anyway," Zeke woofed in response to my statement about Morgan being part of my life. *"She was miserable when you were apart, but she was too proud to beg forgiveness."*

The innate wisdom of wolves touched me. He'd never doubted. Why had I?

"She was frightened for her pup," he added.

I winced. "It was wrong of me to weave a geas."

"Yes, it was." The wolf's mismatched gaze skewered me.

I'd never apologized, and I vowed to do so.

"The ceremony," Sita cooed as a reminder.

"I've only attended a couple of Fae mating ceremonies. I'll describe them once I've cleaned up," I told them as I searched in a cedar chest for my ceremonial robes. Once I had them in hand, I hung them and tossed magic about to remove the wrinkles.

After a thorough rinse in the shower, I wrapped myself in a towel and continued while I brushed out my hair.

"The ceremony is twofold. Logan will bind us first with blood and then with magic."

"Can our blood be part of it?" Zeke gazed expectantly at me.

"It should be," Sita cawed. "It's an element in the familiar bond."

"I'll ask Logan," I promised and swung the heavy folds of a cream-colored silken robe over my shoulders. It was richly embroidered with runes in every color of the rainbow. I couldn't remember the last time I'd worn it.

I had to dig a bit to locate a deep-green sash. Once it was cinched in place, I herded the animals out of my rooms and back toward the council chamber. It was empty.

"Where are we doing this?" I directed my mind voice at Logan.

"Good question. The council chamber seemed too political. All the Dark Fae are coming—except Xavier—and that group of witches."

Faery didn't have any really large rooms. No need for them. But that was on our side.

"Is there space in the Unseelie Court?" I asked. Anyone's guess what they'd done with it in the years since we'd gone our separate ways.

"Brilliant. Let me ask."

While he was tackling a venue, I detoured back to my rooms.

"What are we doing?" Zeke woofed.

"Does Morgan ever wear jewelry?" I asked her familiar.

I'd never seen any on her, but the Coven had ejected her with only the clothes on her back.

"Not often, but she had a diamond pendant and ring Zoelle gave her."

Morgan had just visited her room in the guild house. If she'd retrieved anything, I hadn't seen it.

I opened a teak case inlaid with jade that sat atop a shelf in my bedroom. Since I didn't have to make this choice alone, I selected a square cut emerald ring, a fire opal, a spray of pearls, and an unusual pear-shaped violet sapphire, laying them side by side.

"Which do you think she'd prefer?" I asked.

"That one." Zeke touched the sapphire with a paw.

"This is pretty too." Sita touched her beak to the fire opal.

"No reason I can't gift her both," I said. The opal already had a spot to thread a fine filigree chain through. Turning the sapphire into a ring required magic. I guessed at size and settled for a slender golden band and plain setting. The stone was so lovely, I didn't want to detract from its splendor.

Hawk and wolf waited patiently, although Zeke did mention he was hungry.

"If you leave to hunt, you might miss the wedding," I told him.

He shook his shaggy head. *"She'd never do this without me there."*

"If you're sure, return to that place just beyond the veils, but be quick about it."

Apparently, he wasn't because he stayed put.

I pocketed the jewelry and set out once again. I was about to call Logan when he zipped around a corner and stopped in front of us.

"*Where is Morgan?*" Zeke demanded.

Logan scratched between his ears. "Still getting dressed. No worries. She'll be along soon."

"Do we have a spot yet?" I asked.

"Balthazar tells me they have a perfect room. It opens into gardens." The golden dirk Logan reserved for special occasions was tucked into a waist sheath. Sky-blue robes swirled around him.

"Did you tell Maeve and Morgan?"

"Of course. And the others as well. Everyone is nearly ready."

I fell into step next to him. We traversed ground I hadn't trod in hundreds of years. The place a barrier had stood was open.

A few twists and turns brought us to an expansive open area with a bevy of plants so exotic I'd have been hard-pressed to name half of them. The floor was grainy marble with deep veins of green in several shades. Rows of Unseelie already lined two walls.

The delectable scents of lilies and lilacs tickled my nostrils.

We lost a lot when we split Faery; so did our Unseelie cousins. They're the artists, the dreamers, the creative force while we espoused logic and learning. When we used to fight together, we were the tacticians. Through long years apart, both sides had filled in the gaps. It had been

Alexander who'd suggested a coordinated attack on the guild houses.

Baltazar strode toward me. He'd traded battle leathers for a deep red robe trimmed in silvery fur. "I will stand with Morgan."

"I'm sure she'd appreciate it," I murmured. Who knew how the witches would react. So far, acceptance was the byword of the day, so perhaps it would be fine.

Distant flute music was followed by Fae carrying decorative sprays rich with the blossoms I'd smelled. They created an archway of blooms. Other instruments joined the flutes, making me long for my mandolin.

Witch enchantment, spicy and exotic, drew near.

Morgan and Maeve walked at the head of a line of witches with Zeke between them. Sita rode on Morgan's right shoulder. Breath caught in my throat. My chest tightened. Tall, regal, her dark hair woven with gemstones, Morgan looked every inch a queen.

A simple gown of shimmery white silk clung to her lush curves. Pregnancy had softened the lines of her face and augmented her breasts. After withdrawing the opal from a pocket, I motioned for her to stop long enough for me to fasten the chain's clasp around her neck. The unusual stone nestled in the vee between her breasts, its color reflecting light like a prism.

"Thank you," she murmured. "It's lovely."

"Nothing can compare with your beauty." I brushed my lips over her forehead.

The room was rapidly filling with Fae of both persuasions.

Logan guided Morgan beneath the archway of blooms. I stood next to her. Balthazar took up a position on her other side, displacing Maeve. The seer joined Rebecca behind us. The other witches formed a protective semi-circle behind them.

"What role would you play?" Logan asked Balthazar so softly I wouldn't have heard if I weren't close.

"Have you forgotten?" Balthazar asked. "I am her protector."

I started to tell him it was scarcely needed. I'd guard Morgan with every bone in my body, but he meant well, and that tradition dated back millennia. It was where the human practice of giving the bride away rose from.

Standing next to Morgan with our shoulders and hips touching felt right in a way very little else has in my long life. Joy, pure, bright, and blinding shot through me. Soon, our souls would be joined.

In my mind, the ceremony was a formality. I couldn't be any more in love than I already was.

Logan glanced at the growing crowd. "If everyone is here, please close the doors."

He blew on tall, white tapers—half a dozen of them— lighting them with magic. From behind me, the soft thud of double doors shutting suggested we were all assembled.

"'Tisn't often I'm called upon to invoke the mate bond," he began. "This particular journey was set in motion months ago. It is the most auspicious route for Morgan and Damien, the one that will ensure their future as mages from different persuasions."

"I am in favor," Balthazar intoned.

"Well, I most certainly am not," a disembodied voice shouted.

Fuck. I knew that voice. Before I could draw another breath, Hecate plummeted into the room wearing the same battle-stained garments from our recent fight.

"State your reasons." Balthazar planted his bulk between the witch goddess and us. Had he known Hecate would show up? Was that why he'd adopted the ancient role as Morgan's defender?

A staff that glowed with an inner light materialized in Hecate's right hand. She banged it on the marble floor. "The witch is mine," she bellowed. "I made her for a specific purpose. No one else has a claim to her."

Zeke's hackles rose. He growled, showing plenty of fang.

"You never helped Zoelle," Sita cawed. "She did everything you asked, yet you didn't lift a charm to save her life. You do not deserve Morgan. Or any witch."

Zeke's growls escalated.

"This is ridiculous," Morgan sputtered. Swinging around, she faced Hecate. "I don't care what kind of epiphany you've had. You gave up any claim to me when you tried to kill Damien. Hell, when you vanished after forcing Mother to hold silence—a silence that cost her life—you forfeited any loyalty from me and mine."

The witch goddess's features twisted into a snarl. She raised her hands in front of her. "Fine. I can unmake you."

Morgan burst out laughing. "Yeah? Try it."

"Your reasons are insufficient," Balthazar gritted. "You will leave Faery with all due haste."

His words sounded scripted. Perhaps they were. Ritual has never been my strong suit.

Jets of power flowed from Hecate's extended hands, circling the witches. Since Maeve stood next to Rebecca, she was snared as well.

"I am not leaving without Morgan," Hecate thundered.

"We'll see about that," Morgan shot back.

Maeve punched through Hecate's casting. It glowed red and reformed. She tried again. On the third effort, Hecate's power circle sputtered and winked out. Before she could cast it again, make it stronger, the witches scattered slotting in with the many Fae.

"Your time has passed," Rebecca shouted.

"We haven't worshipped you in centuries," another witch tossed out.

"Morgan will lead us," someone else cried.

Out of everything that had been said, that last had an impact. Hecate's imperious demeanor developed a fragile aspect. Or maybe I only imagined it because power sheeted from her, taking on shades of gray and black.

Morgan twirled, slid past Balthazar and hurled power of her own at the witch goddess. Zeke ran behind Hecate, darting in to bite and retreat. Sita screeched like a Banshee and divebombed the witch goddess only to be rebuffed by what had to be partial warding. The wolf was drawing blood, but he aimed low and angled his attack from her rear.

Rebecca and the other witches formed an honor guard behind Morgan, adding power of their own. I'd never seen witches join enchantment. Colors merged like an out-of-control kaleidoscope.

The air sizzled with expended power. The scents of cinnamon, ginger, and cloves thickened until my nostrils stung. The opal I'd gifted Morgan turned red and glowed hotly.

Stones hold power; that one had transformed to mirror Morgan's innate talent. I started toward her, intent on adding my magic to the mix.

Maeve gripped my upper arm. "Not your battle. Not this time."

I shook her off, but she fastened her fingers around my wrist. "Morgan must end this once and for all, or Hecate will keep on popping up. Especially after the child is born. In her mind, she's already staked a claim to him, views him as a second chance to make up for the one she missed raising Morgan."

Balthazar pushed through the wall of witches, his Fae magic visible. Green arrows joined the rush of witch power crashing between Hecate and the Coven witches. Where the two collided, sparks rose.

Hecate's blood flowed freely, courtesy of Zeke's indefatigable efforts. His snout was streaked with red. He seemed to be tiring. Odd. I'd never known the wolf to require breaks.

"Look at Zeke," I told Maeve.

Her sharp blue gaze focused on the wolf. She muttered, "Aw, crap," and rushed toward him. A blue bubble, the color of many of our workings, surrounded the wolf, lifting him away from his position. He wasn't fighting Maeve's casting, which spoke volumes.

The moment the bubble closed around him, he collapsed.

Sita made a beeline for them, but Maeve vanished along with her protective bubble. "Where's she taking him?" the hawk screeched.

"Our healers."

"I'm going too." She flew toward double doors sealing the chamber. I ordered them to open.

"One down," Hecate screeched.

Daggers appeared in Morgan's hands. Lethal little numbers with wickedly serrated blades. She must have powered them with magic as she leapt toward Hecate and sliced through her warding. The other witches surged after her. Darts flew from their hands, pinning Hecate to the ground.

Morgan impaled her throat with one dagger and ran the other one from collarbones to pelvis. Snakes glided from her body cavity. Balthazar was ready. Bron stood next to him.

The two Unseelie generals lopped off viper heads the moment they came into view. The acrid stench of poison displaced the floral scent from the arched sprays of blossoms.

Maeve wasn't here to hold me back. I catapulted to Morgan's side in time to watch the ruins of Hecate's body turn to black smoke. Once she was gone, the remains of the serpents followed suit.

Morgan turned to me, blood dripping from the daggers still clutched in her hands. "Where's Zeke? I can't feel my bond with him."

Fear gripped me. I'd been certain Maeve could save the wolf.

"Where is he?"

"Infirmary with our healers."

My words weren't even out before Morgan disappeared. The expression on her face, fury mingled with desolation, ripped me to shreds. Logan called my name. So did Balthazar.

I followed Morgan. Plenty of Fae left to mop up the mess. No one here would miss me.

CHAPTER 19

MORGAN

I'm not the praying type, but I begged divine intervention. Hecate was gone. Permanently gone, but if the cost was my wolf, my heart, I couldn't bear it.

My trip to the Fae infirmary, a place where I'd spent entirely too much time, was over in the blink of an eye. Zeke lay on a low cot. At first, I was afraid he was gone, but a tortured breath ripped through him.

I fell to the ground by his side and gathered him into my arms. He made a pathetic, mewling sound that cracked my heart wide open.

"What's wrong with him?" I asked a healer who'd moved nearby.

"Too much black blood from that abomination. Unfortunately, he inhaled some. We're working on an antidote, but that type of magic takes time."

She didn't add it was time Zeke might not have. She didn't have to.

Sita flew through the door squawking mournfully.

Damien rolled out of a jump spell and crouched by my side, laying a hand on the wolf's flank. "Thank Danu, he's still with us," he murmured.

Maeve hustled in carrying a bubbling glass flask smelling of marigolds and roses.

"It's not ready yet," another healer protested. "It needs time to cure."

"I tried something to hurry it along," Maeve said tightlipped and joined us on the floor. "This is your call, Morgan. It might make things worse."

"How much longer would it need to...to be right?" Torment slashed down my spine.

"At least a day," the nearest healer said.

I swallowed hard. Zeke didn't have a day. If I was any judge, he didn't have more than a handful of hours, if that. The space between his struggling breaths was increasing.

"Do something," Sita cawed.

Maeve chanted over her concoction. Some of it spewed over the beaker's edge.

I stretched full length behind Zeke with my arms around his shoulders. Reaching within him, I found our connection and fortified it one strand at a time. When it was stronger, though nowhere near its original configuration, I met Maeve's eyes and said, "I'll tell you when."

Damien lay on Zeke's other side between his front legs. I reached for his magic and wove it in with my familiar bond to Zeke. Ready as we'd ever be, I told Maeve, "Now."

Power words streamed from her, words that hurt my ears and my soul, as she poured the decoction the length of

Zeke's body beginning with his head. The place my magic touched our familiar bond caught fire. I tightened my grasp on my wolf.

And prayed.

To Danu. To Gaia. To Arianrhod. To Ceridwen. To Anubis.

Begging them to save my wolf.

Once Maeve finished pouring, she settled into a chant in the ancient language of the Fae. Last time she'd done that, it had pushed Damien into the Fae death coma. Was she doing the same to my wolf?

Time passed. Healers came and went, clucking over us. Damien stayed the course, never moving as he held onto my magic, augmenting it with his own.

Sita perched on Zeke's head, wings beating slowly.

The familiar bond pulsed. Once. Twice.

Silence.

"Nooooo," I screamed. "Nooooo. Don't leave me."

I clung tighter. Pushed more magic into my link with Zeke.

Within me, the babe wailed.

And then, the bond pulsed again. This time, it beat steadily like the heartbeat it was. Zeke thrashed weakly against me.

"You're holding him too tight," Maeve said.

More than anything, her words drove home that we'd pulled off the impossible. I rolled to a sit, stroking his rough outer guard hairs. Damien sat too and reached for my hands across the wolf's body.

Zeke whined and flopped onto his belly. Someone placed

a bowl of water fragrant with healing herbs in front of him. He lapped noisily. Sita planted herself on his shoulders.

Cheers erupted. When I glanced around, the infirmary was full of witches and Fae. Everyone had gathered to protect and honor Zeke. To aid in his healing.

There'd been a time when the Fae barely tolerated me.

Now I felt included, like family. The empty place within me—the one created after the Coven exiled me—filled to overflowing.

Rebecca came close and bent to kiss the top of Zeke's head. "We must rescue our familiars," she told me.

I felt stupid. Until she said that, it hadn't occurred to me they were still missing. "Where are they?"

"The other witches returned them to the animals' world when they imprisoned us. We will travel there and reclaim them." A soft smile illuminated her face. "But first, we would see you mated."

"Rescue your familiars," I told her. "The ceremony will hold until all of you return. If my animals are part of the festivities, yours should be too."

"Are you certain?" Rebecca asked.

"Yes, very. Come back as soon as you can."

"Do not get married without us." Rebecca hugged me.

"No worries on that front."

She herded the witches out of the infirmary.

"*Let me up,*" Zeke woofed.

I let go of Damien's hands and rose. Zeke got his feet under him and shook himself from nose to tail tip. The healers had cleaned all the blood off him before I arrived. The blood that had nearly killed him.

"Why was Hecate's blood poison? Would it have had the same effect on me?" I asked.

One of the healers stepped forward. "Not sure about your second question. In terms of the first, best we can tell, that wasn't exactly Hecate."

"What do you mean?"

"Parts of the apparition were her. Most of her mind was her own, but her body had been absorbed by something wicked."

"How did you determine that?" Damien stood.

"By the composition of the blood we scraped off Zeke," Maeve replied. "Some of it was what we expected, but there were other elements."

It explained why her presentation had been all over the map. For the barest of moments, I felt sorry for her. She'd paid a price for her folly creating me, a witch in her image.

But she'd made the rest of us suffer along with her.

Logan joined Maeve. "Nice work."

She shrugged. "Glad it succeeded. Nip and tuck there for a while."

She always did have a talent for understatement.

Logan tapped Damien's shoulder. "Shall we regroup in a few hours?"

Zeke yipped hoarsely. I took it as a yes.

"We have to wait till the witches and their familiars return," I told him.

"When will that be?"

"Not long."

"Let me know as soon as they're back. If we'd had the mate bond in place, some of this could have been avoided." Logan ruffled Zeke's fur before walking out of the room.

Balthazar came close and scratched between Zeke's ears. "I am grateful for a decent ending."

Maeve wasn't the only one prone to understatements.

"Thank you for protecting me." I bowed.

"My pleasure." He inclined his head and strode from the room. The other Fae wished us well, stopped to stroke Zeke's fur, and left too.

After a final look at Zeke, the healers withdrew, leaving the four of us in the infirmary.

"Do you feel well enough to walk to our rooms?" I asked Zeke.

He padded toward the door. Moving slowly, we covered the distance from the infirmary to Damien's chamber.

I filled a glass bowl with water from the bathroom and placed it within easy reach. Zeke sighed and stretched out, lying on his tummy, paws extended.

"Can I hunt for you?" Sita chirped.

"*Mice,*" he woofed just before his eyes closed.

The hawk flew out of the room. Faery had plenty of mice. No need to accompany her beyond the veils. Damien left the door open for her to come and go.

Still worried, I wrapped Zeke in a restorative cocoon. When I did a quick scan, no poison remained. He was just tired, as well he would be after Hecate's bid to end him.

Damien motioned me to follow him into the bedroom where he held me close. Words would have been superfluous. He smoothed hair back from where it had fallen into my face. We stood like that for a long while taking comfort from one another's presence.

Finally, we moved to a small sofa across from the bed. My eyes were heavy, but I was too keyed up to sleep. I'd run a shit ton of power through me, and it left me full of nervous energy. Maeve's power words had taken a toll too.

Damien left. When he returned, he pressed a goblet of mead into my hand. "Drink. You'll feel better."

"Quite an eventful wedding day," I murmured before draining half the glass. The liquid burned a trail down my gullet before setting my empty stomach on fire.

"It's not over yet." Damien clinked his goblet against mine. "To weddings."

I smiled. "Yeah, here's to hoping the next attempt actually happens."

"It will. We're destined for one another. I told you that almost the day we met."

"So you did."

Everyone believed it. I should give up and go with the flow, but happiness belonged to other people. And then I remembered the sense of family when I'd stood next to Damien beneath the bower. Somewhere along the line, the Fae had moved from tolerance to acceptance.

Still decked out in my wedding finery, I took stock of the ruins of what had been a striking gown. "Too bad about the dress."

"Plenty more in the wardrobe room. It's not the dress I'm marrying, sweetheart." He tightened the arm he'd placed around my shoulders. "How are you feeling?"

"Conflicted. Guilty. Maeve's quick thinking pulled Zeke

through." I closed my teeth over my lower lip hard enough to hurt. "I should have paid better attention."

"How could you have? Hecate was a brutal adversary."

"Not sure, but if Maeve hadn't realized Zeke was fading, we'd have lost him." The tears I hadn't shed stung my eyes.

"It was both of us," Damien explained. "I thought something was wrong and asked Maeve for her opinion. When she sprang into action, I kicked myself for not doing the same."

Gratitude carved a path through me, cutting deep. "Thank you. My wolf has many guardians."

"I love him too," Damien murmured. "Sita as well."

"When we stood beneath all those fragrant blooms, I realized I have a family again. It's something I never expected. Maybe not anything I deserve after, well, after some of my actions."

"Look forward, Morgan." He nuzzled my neck, his breath warm, enticing. "Infinite years lie ahead."

"I used to take my immortality for granted. Never thought much about it one way or the other. Having you to share those years puts a whole different spin on things."

A smile made him even more gorgeous than usual. "You're not given to compliments. I'll treasure that one."

I winced and vowed to do better. Witches didn't toss compliments about, but then we hadn't done a whole lot of things. With Hecate's era behind us, we could create something better, stronger, more realistic.

Damien ran his tongue down the side of my neck. I shivered and angled my face for a kiss. His lips were firm, demanding, sweet.

Sita flew into the room cawing, "Zeke is up. I brought him mice. Off to catch a few more."

The hawk didn't require a response, so I kept on kissing Damien, but not for long.

A staunch knock was followed by, "Save that for after the ceremony, you two."

I untangled my arms from Damien's broad back and smiled at Maeve.

"It's time to start over with a new gown." She crooked a finger my way. "The witches are on their way back. If you'd been on top of things, you'd have known."

I wasn't about to apologize for a well-deserved break, so I changed the subject. "Zeke will be happy to be reunited with all those animals. He was friends with everyone."

"He is special," Maeve agreed.

Damien got to his feet. "I'll rustle up Logan and get everyone into position on the Unseelie side of Faery."

"We need an attitude adjustment," Maeve murmured. "From here on in, it's just Faery. No this half or that half."

Damien walked out of the bedroom. I heard the low murmur of his voice as he stopped to talk with Zeke.

A sudden lump formed in my throat. "Zeke never complained, but leaving the guild house must have been hard for him."

"It's behind you."

"Damien said much the same. He told me to look forward."

"Solid advice. Now, let's get moving so you'll be ready for your wedding."

"I was ready before," I reminded her.

"So you were. I'll breathe easier once the ceremony is over—and its protections are in place."

Something chilly slithered down my spine. "What have you seen?"

"Nothing, child. Truly. But being prepared is important."

Seers are famous for withholding information. Still, asking her a second time wouldn't yield different results. I followed her out of the bedroom and knelt next to Zeke. He stopped crunching through rodents long enough to rub his head against my side.

Sita swooped in and dropped two more mice in front of the wolf.

"Keep them coming," he woofed.

"This makes ten," the hawk retorted. "You're strong enough to do your own hunting now."

He howled merriment. *"It was worth a try."*

I chuckled. If Zeke was joking, he truly was on the road to recovery.

"You're quiet," Maeve observed as we wended our way through Faery's corridors.

"I was thinking about Mother, wondering how she'd feel about me marrying. It's not very witchlike."

"What the Coven turned into wasn't very witchlike, either," Maeve reminded me.

Touché.

One more place to focus on the future since I couldn't do squat about the past.

～

HALF AN HOUR LATER, I was garbed in a different gown, this one a deep teal with long sleeves and a rounded neckline. Woven from fine wool, it clung to me like a second skin once Maeve made a few adjustments.

She tilted her head as if she were listening and said, "They're ready for us."

"I have to get Zeke and Sita."

"Damien already did."

"Nothing for me to do but show up?"

Maeve focused a rare smile my way. "After that last mess, no one's taking any chances."

Went for her as well. I'd assumed we'd walk, but the familiar feel of her magic surrounded me. When it dissipated, we were next to the bower. Rebecca, the other witches, and a bevy of familiars were sandwiched between iterations of Fae.

Zeke trotted to my side looking none the worse for wear. Sita fluttered to a shoulder. Damien extended a hand. I grasped it and walked to his side. Balthazar took up his post on my other side and slightly behind me.

Logan got right to it. No philosophical commentary on mate bonds or cross-mage pairings. Golden dirk in hand, he chanted in his language. Before I could request a translation, he offered it freely.

"Morgan, do you willingly pledge yourself to Damien?"

I nodded and he said, "Hold out your right hand."

Once I did, he made a short cut in the ball of my thumb before asking Damien much the same question except, obviously, in reverse. Another slice, and he pressed our cut places together.

"Us too." Zeke pushed forward.

After a brief hesitation, Logan nicked the wolf's extended paw and one of Sita's talons. He inserted the blade, shiny with familiar blood, between Damien's hand and my own.

A sparkly sensation flowed up my arm where our blood mingled. Within me, Niall cooed with delight. We would raise him together. All of us. Me. Damien. Zeke. Sita.

Logan had reverted to the Fae language. Words flowed as his voice rose and fell. I didn't know all of them, but I got the gist. We were bound, would be together through this life and all lives to come. Not only was I bound to Damien, but also to the Fae.

Loyalty. Devotion. Allegiance. Their enemies would become mine. I would lend my magic as needed to support my new family.

When I glanced at my hand, the cut was gone, absorbed by the enchantment binding me to Damien, my familiars, and Faery.

Zeke tossed his head back and howled. Sita chirped merrily.

Logan swept a hand to the side. A second room opened. Tables laden with all manner of food and drinks beckoned.

"These are for us," Zeke yipped and led the familiars to special platters lined against a back wall.

Rebecca and the witches mobbed me. I hugged and kissed them all. Once they moved on to the food, Fae and Dark Fae wished us well.

Someone pushed mead into my hand. An assortment of meats, cheeses, and crusty bread materialized.

Finally, the crowd was all in the room with food, leaving us alone.

"What would you like to do?" Damien asked.

I laced my fingers with his. "Would it be rude for us to leave?"

"Music to my ears. No, not rude at all."

For the second time in the past couple of hours, Fae enchantment swept me away. This time, it spit me out on a moonlit tropical beach.

"Where are we?" I murmured.

"A special place, just for us. If we remained in Faery, we might have been disturbed. This way, no one can find us for a while."

Laughter bubbled from me. "Especially since the Fae's main tracker is right here."

"There is that. I have another gift for you. Didn't seem to be a way to work it into Logan's ceremony." Reaching into a pocket in his robes, Damien withdrew a stunning violet sapphire ring and slipped it onto my finger.

The stone warmed, pulsing with an inner light. "It's beautiful, but I don't have anything for you."

"The best gift of all was when you agreed to the mate bond, darling."

He circled me with his arms. The kiss we'd begun in his rooms developed new life, and my body caught fire beneath his touch.

For once, I was entirely caught in the moment. Tomorrow would show up, but Damien would be part of it. Part of all my tomorrows. I hadn't fully appreciated the mate bond until I felt it thrumming through my veins.

He lifted his lips from mine long enough to murmur, "You damn betcha."

"You were in my mind."

"Better get used to it. From here on in, I'm never leaving."

Once, I'd have considered it an intrusion. Today, I welcomed his presence. "I love you."

"Good because you're stuck with me." Fingers danced down my spine as he worked the million tiny buttons out of their buttonholes.

My gown slithered to the sand in a flurry of soft wool.

Chest tight, throat dry, I undid his sash and tugged his robe out of the way.

Him. Me. A full moon, the sand, and a thousand stars. Such a fitting spot for our first lovemaking as mates.

And then, I stopped thinking about anything but the wonder of the mage in my arms and the feel of his body pressed against mine.

EPILOGUE, MORGAN

A *month later*
Once we returned from our honeymoon—and we stayed on that beach for a solid week, longer than I'd ever been separated from Zeke before—I got busy with Coven business.

I'd been worried Damien might not want me to adopt any role in the new, improved Coven structure, but he's told me over and over how proud he is of me.

It's ironic. I'm living the role Hecate envisioned for me, but she's not here to orchestrate anything. It's better this way. Aside from her swan dive into evil, she wasn't part of the modern world.

She'd have fought most of the changes we instituted.

No more celibacy.

No more separation. Covens needed to work together, so I instituted a council structure not unlike what the Fae have.

Speaking of which, they've been busy too, healing the

schism between them and their Dark cousins. It hasn't been without hiccups, but the same could be said about drawing the Covens, which had always operated independently, into a cohesive whole.

Plenty of work remained on both fronts.

When Damien and I lay in bed at night, we'd sometimes compare notes. Hard to say who'd had a rougher go of it. At least the Fae had history to fall back on, a history when they'd been one.

I had no idea how Coven structure had evolved, but there was plenty of resistance to ceding any power to a central council. What we finally settled on was a larger council than I'd envisioned since every one of North America's Covens insisted on representation.

Meant eighteen members. Not the most wieldy number, it made crafting decisions challenging. But at least we achieved consensus regarding having a council at all.

Rebecca and the witches we'd rescued from my original Coven had proven invaluable. Traveling from Coven to Coven, they'd pitched the concept of unification. On the heels of our coordinated attack against them, the Covens hadn't exactly welcomed us with open arms. In the end, getting them out from under black magic added credibility to our current efforts.

Despite saying I'd never return, I was in my old room in the guild house, mostly because I had a computer there and was working up articles of incorporation. I could have written them out longhand in Faery, but this was so much simpler.

A twinge in my lower back drove me to my feet.

More accurately, I lumbered upright. My belly had grown unwieldy. Witches and Fae whispered about the length of my pregnancy when they didn't think I was listening.

I'd spoken with Niall. He'd staunchly told me he wasn't quite ready to make an appearance. My womb was his for as long as he heeded it, so I endured escalating back pain and thrashing about like a walrus whenever I tried to stand.

I rubbed the small of my back and sent a sprinkling of magic to ease the discomfort.

"Ready now." The child's voice didn't sound sure.

I folded my hands over my belly. "Are you certain?"

He didn't answer. I started to sit back in my chair, but a long, rippling pain tore through me.

Oh-oh.

Maybe it really was time.

I gathered my magic and engaged a jump spell that landed me in Damien's rooms. Probably should have aimed for the infirmary, but I was pregnant, not sick.

Zeke woofed a greeting, took one look at me, and shot out of Damien's apartment. Sita left her perch and flew a few transits of the room. "The hatchling is coming. The hatchling is coming."

Maeve burst into the room with a couple of blue-robed healers in tow. Rebecca followed.

I waved a hand. "I'm fine. I don't need—"

Words grew slippery. What exactly didn't I need?

Pain sluiced through me. I gripped a nearby chair and struggled to remain upright.

"Why is this going so fast?" I gritted.

"Because he should have been born a month ago," Maeve replied dryly.

Rebecca closed a hand around my upper arm. "Walk with me. It will go quicker."

Damien raced into the room and skidded to a stop on my other side. "What can I do? How can I help?"

"Stay out of the way," Maeve mumbled, but I heard her.

"Take her other arm," Rebecca instructed. "We're walking."

Walk we did. Up the room, down the room, and back again. Pain clawed at me. I never thought to send magic to ease it, afraid if I interrupted the process I might harm Niall.

Finally, when picking up my feet required gargantuan effort, Rebecca led me to a low cot piled with pillows at both ends. "It's time," she said firmly once I'd collapsed, writhing and panting.

A Fae healer crouched between my legs. Damien joined her. Rebecca held my hands.

"Push," Damien cried. "He's almost here."

Almost for everyone but me. It took a lot of pushes before the child slithered from my body. His cries broke the silence in the room.

Damien laid him in my arms. "He's beautiful, darling."

I'd dreamed of my babe since conception. Laying eyes on him for the first time made my soul crack open. He had Damien's fair hair and delicately pointed ears and my eyes, one dark, the other white. I hadn't seen that part in the dreamscape.

Zeke pushed close and licked Niall, cleaning afterbirth from his skin.

Sita cooed and brushed her beak against his cheek.

"One more push," Rebecca told me. "For the placenta."

Damien caught it in a pan and started out of the room.

"Where are you going?" I called.

"To bury this where no one can ever find it."

"Is that a Fae tradition?" I asked Maeve.

For once, the seer was beaming with delight. "Aye. The afterbirth is a part of Niall, so it cannot be destroyed. It would offer enemies power over him—and Damien and Faery. Safest to ensure it's well hidden."

The same chill I'd felt when she'd been insistent about hurrying up the mating ceremony intruded. I pushed it aside.

Today was cause for celebration, for joy.

If the goddess was good to us, we'd surround our son with love, peace, and joy.

He nuzzled my breast, seeking the nipple. I settled in to nurse and examined every inch of him. Every finger. Every toe.

By the time Damien returned, our son was asleep, still latched onto my breast. He lay next to me, cradling us both.

Over the next several hours, Fae, Dark Fae, and witches trooped through. Everyone wanted to wish us well.

"So this is why I lost control of my people," a voice boomed.

Alarmed, I shielded Niall and pushed to a sitting position. Damien shot to his feet and stood facing Xavier.

"It would have happened sooner or later, mate."

The Unseelie prince smiled. "Perhaps you're right. I wanted to add my congratulations to the mix. All the things

I was afraid of if our people came together haven't happened.

"Not yet, anyway."

"Nor will they." Damien clapped a fist over his breast.

Xavier mirrored his salute before leaving the room.

"That was unexpected," Maeve said.

"Overdue and welcome," Damien replied and pried the child out of my arms. "Get some rest," he told me.

"Come on." Rebecca helped me stand. "Let's get you cleaned up and back to bed."

"I'm not tired. Not in the least," I protested.

"Okay. We'll do the cleaning part, and then you can decide what's next."

"I need to finish the articles of incorporation for our council."

"Those will keep. I'll work on them. For now, concentrate on your son."

I may be driven, but I recognize good advice when it's offered.

The warm shower felt divine as sweat sluiced from my body. I washed my hair, and Rebecca braided it out of the way. She handed me a robe. From time to time, I focused magic to check in on Niall and Damien. Proud to bursting, Damien was showing his son off.

Niall loved the attention.

I didn't blame him for waiting as long as he had to make an appearance. His time within me had more than a few rocky moments.

I turned to Rebecca. "I hope I'll be a good mother."

"Of course, you will."

I shook my head. "You kind of have to say that."

"No, I don't. Besides, Niall has a lot of people who already adore him, including all our familiars."

A robust *mrowwww* seconded Rebecca's statement. Her coal-black tomcat sashayed into view.

"He's kind of the poster child for the reunification of Faery. It's a big responsibility."

"Honey." Rebecca set down the comb. "By the time he's walking, no one will even remember Faery was ever divided. Stop worrying."

"Goes with all these hormones." I grinned.

"Yes, it does."

Damien swooped into the bathroom. "You are so beautiful."

Rebecca waved merrily and left with the cat riding on her shoulders.

Zeke and Sita trooped through the door.

I held my arms out for Niall.

"Sure you don't want to rest?" Damien asked and tucked the babe into my arms.

"Yeah, I'm sure." I touched the silk of the baby's skin. "Look what we made. He's perfect."

"So are you. Come on. I have food waiting for us. All your favorite dishes."

"You're spoiling me."

"We can spoil each other." Damien tucked an arm around us both and guided me into the living room.

"*Happy,*" Zeke woofed, his tail pluming.

"Zoelle would have loved this moment," Sita cawed.

"Somehow, she knows," I said.

"Yes," Damien agreed. "I believe she does."

A knock on the door was followed by familiar energy. Balthazar bounded into the room accompanied by a beautiful woman with flame-red hair cascading down her back. Blue eyes were tilted at the edges, and faint ridges scribed her cheeks and forearms.

"I heard the wonderful news." Balthazar crouched next to Niall and me and touched the baby's fine hair. "May he have every opportunity and the best Faery has to offer."

The woman drew near. "I am Ophir. My father has told me so much about all of you. It's an honor to meet everyone."

She knelt next to Balthazar, red wings folded against her back.

Sudden tears stung my eyes. Ophir had called him father. "This must be the child you bore with your dragon lover."

He nodded. "Thanks to Damien's suggestion, I made a trip to the dragons' world and reunited with her mother. So far, everyone's been nothing but happy for us."

Damien clapped him across the back. "Excellent news, mate. We'll have to celebrate once Morgan's recovered a bit from the birth."

"I would love that." Ophir clasped long-fingered hands together. "We have so many years to make up for, so much lost time."

I extended a hand; she gripped it. I knew more than I wanted to about lost time and not letting archaic traditions get in the way of moving forward.

Balthazar rose. "We'll let you get some rest, but I didn't

want Niall's birth date to pass without adding our congratulations to the mix."

Damien saw them to the door. The low rise and fall of their voices was soothing. I must have drifted off because the next thing I remember was him lifting us into his arms and carrying us to the bedroom.

"Love you," I murmured as he tucked us into bed.

"I love you too. My heart, my life. Sleep well, darling. I'll be here if you need anything."

And he would. Now and for always. My life was so much more than I'd ever envisioned or hoped for. Waves of peace and contentment surrounded me, some from Damien, some from Niall.

I'm a fortunate witch, to be sure.

Zeke padded into the bedroom and curled up at the end of the bed. Sita took up her usual position on a nearby dresser. With my family complete, I drifted toward the dreamscape.

Tomorrow would be along all too soon. For now, I savored the joy running through me. Niall cooed, shifting in my arms, and I curled my body around him. Nothing is promised, but I wasn't cursed any longer. The future stretched before me, bright, shining, and full of possibilities.

You've reached the end of Bound by Shadows. I hope you've enjoyed this trilogy. Please leave a review for *Promised*. Do it now while it's fresh in your mind. Reviews mean so much to authors. It's an opportunity for you to tell other readers what you loved about a book or series.

Until next time, dear readers.

My next series will be *Sanctuary*, a dystopian fantasy. While you're waiting, if you enjoy Fae-based urban fantasy, you'll love my Magick and Misfits series. A sample from *Court of Rogues*, first book from that series follows.

BOOK DESCRIPTION: COURT OF ROGUES

Strange bedfellows rock worlds.

Reluctant recruit to the nines, I became Faery's regent by default. Sure, I was next in line for the throne, but I never believed Oberon and Titania were gone for good until first a decade rolled by, and then two, and then ten.

They'll never be back, and the land is mourning. Or pissed. It's hard to tell which, and I'm not sure what difference it makes. I split my time between Faery and Earth searching for a way to mend the rift that's killing my realm. I haven't made much progress. Time is running through the glass, mocking my paltry efforts.

A sultry Witch is barely a blip on the radar. So what if she counts cards in the casino I run on Earth and makes my pit boss a little nuts? Out of the blue, she spits out the unbelievable, and I discover she's not a Witch after all. A glamour hid her Fae-Sidhe blood so well, she'd fooled me.

Her mixed blood is an affront. By rights, I should haul

her before the Court to face justice. She understood the chance she took revealing herself to me, and her offer to join forces is tempting, but it could cost me my throne.

Some risks are worth the price. If I cross the line, there'll be no going back.

COURT OF ROGUES, CHAPTER ONE, CYN

The door to my cramped office slapped against its stops, rattling the frosted glass blazoned with Jedediah Rolfson, General Manager, Lady Luck Casino. The gilt lettering had faded, but everyone in the gaming house knew who I was and where to find me. Of course, Jedediah isn't my true name. Names hold immeasurable power. Even if mortals had been able to pronounce my real one, I'd never, never give them that sort of leverage over me.

My door was still vibrating. A knock would have been nice. Respectful, even, but manners had passed most mortals by. Fueled by irritation, my power simmered so close to the surface it took an effort to rein it in. No need to turn around to identify the man who'd disturbed what passed for peace in this place.

"What is it, Rudy?" I still hadn't swiveled my chair to face him.

"How'd you know it was me?" he demanded.

Because I can smell you, idiot…

I did twist then. The motion of my big body forced the ratty leather chair around almost as an afterthought. Stick-straight black hair fell across Rudy's face, and his white shirt was rolled to the elbows. His usual dark pants were rucked up over the tops of battered leather boots. He looked more like a kitchen knave than a pit boss—an underfed kitchen knave who'd stopped growing as a teenager. I made a point of hiring oddballs—freaks and losers. They weren't in a rush to use Lady Luck as a steppingstone for something better.

Angling a pointed look his way, I growled, "Never mind how I know things. What's gone wrong?" I snapped my fingers in the vain hope he might hurry things up.

He squeezed his bloodshot dark eyes shut for a count of two before opening them. "That infernal twit who counts cards is back."

Many patrons count cards, but only one had posed a challenge recently. Interest flickered as I constructed an image of the leggy red-haired Witch with an iridescent nimbus of power floating around her. "You mean the woman?"

"Of course I mean the blasted woman." A touch of his Russian accent slipped through. "She's the only one who's been able to beat our system."

"What exactly were you hoping I'd do?"

Color stained his sallow cheeks. It was such an unusual response, I delved into his mind and helped myself to his thoughts. Mortals were quite the superficial lot. Culling through their secrets saved me a lot of time.

"Well?" I snapped my fingers again, more out of frustration than actual hope it would move Rudy off the dime.

"Maybe you can tell her to leave." He drew himself up to his full five-foot-eight-inch height, but it didn't have the desired effect. He wanted me to respect him, to back his play, but I'd seen the whole sorry charade in his puny mind. He'd chased the Witch out the last time she stopped by the casino, but he'd also done his damnedest to fuck her.

She'd lured him with a fine set of tits, and then hexed him. Even though he had no concept of what she'd done, her sneaky spell had rendered him impotent. I smothered a chuckle. Witchy charms had a shelf-life. Eventually his little johnny would stand up and salute again, and—

A muted crash came through the audio on one of many screens I'd had mounted so I could see the entire gaming house. Not that I needed them, but they looked good and avoided explanations about how I knew jack concerning the brawl in the basement lounge. The patrons had no idea I spied on them—until I turned them over to the authorities for cheating the house. I've been called a lot of names since I was suckered into taking on this thankless job. So far, I've maintained my cool.

Eventually, though, some hapless mortal will find himself skewered by Fae magic. They'll beg for mercy, for the compassion of a human court, but it will be too late. Mortals never leave Faery unless we release them, not intact, anyway. Those who break free end up in institutions.

"Jed?" Rudy prodded.

"Yeah. Yeah. On my way." I flowed out of my seat. If

Rudy weren't hovering in my doorway, I'd have teleported four floors down. Meanwhile, the ruckus was escalating amid the crash of breaking glassware.

"The thieving card counter?" Rudy's gaze skittered away.

"Is that why you're still standing there?" I made shooing motions with both hands. "Christ. Strap on a set. Get moving. I have bigger problems."

The color that had stained his face turned an ugly tomato shade before he spun and pelted down a nearby stairwell mumbling in Russian. He thought I'd never hear him, but he was whining about the fight that had broken out not being on his floor. If it were, the Witch would have beat a hasty retreat.

A snarl of frustration burbled past my throat. I'd never been able to pound the whole team player concept down everyone's throats. Rudy had risen to pit boss because he was honest—and loyal. Maybe it was too much to expect him—or any human in my employ—to show any initiative beyond the basics.

He didn't like me, but then none of the staff did. They sensed I was different, couldn't put their fingers on why that was, and felt uncomfortable in my presence.

Good. I'd never lift a finger to alter their instinctive dread of me.

The day humans can lounge in front of Fae royalty—never mind how far we've fallen—is the day for me to retire to the *Dreaming* and never resurface. A quick glance at the monitor reassured me the brawl was in full swing. No one would notice an unorthodox entrance, so I hopped on an enchanted conduit and emerged in the largest of five gaming halls in a blaze of light.

Muted light, but it still would have given someone pause. Not here, though, and not now. What looked like a motorcycle gang—leather and tatts and piercings—had faced off against a bunch of Asian street hoods who fancied themselves a modern-day version of the mob.

Ha! Bugsy and Al, two of my old buddies, would have laughed until they puked at the comparison. They'd understood how to be badasses because they'd borrowed liberally from Faery. Much of their wickedness never saw the light of day; they were too smart to reveal themselves, and I'd sworn them to silence. Most mortals wouldn't honor such a bond, but they did. They had no idea what I was, but they'd absorbed my lessons like mother's milk. I crossed a few lines—eh, more than a few—by teaching them gruesome ways to inflict pain and death. Even then, my kingdom was on its way out. What were a few more broken rules?

Turned out flaunting Fae law held a price beyond measure, but I'm getting ahead of things.

No one noticed me as I crunched over broken glass, my fury growing at the senseless destruction. The acrid stench of piss merged with the coppery tang of blood. If I didn't establish control over the situation, this room wouldn't be usable for a few days.

Unacceptable. The tables in this gambling hall raked in better than $50,000 a night.

Grunts and curses rained around me as men punched and knifed one another. I sent magic spiraling out, hunting for the telltale bite of metal. Lady Luck had a no-firearms-or-knives rule, and a metal detector sat at the main entrance. It netted us an impressive array of weapons that we stashed in a safe and turned over to the cops once a week.

Yeah. That's right. Bring a gun or a shiv into my club, and you have to petition the cops to get it back. Works great if the piece is legal, but most of them weren't. Ever since I'd established that brilliant bit of policy, we hadn't seized too many of them.

I'd made it to the front of the large hall. Not a dealer or croupier in sight. Either they were hiding in the shadows, or they'd fled at the first hint of trouble. I'd deal with that later. They were supposed to alert someone like Rudy. Or me. I employed half a dozen pit bosses who rotated through the club.

I'd heard from Rudy, but not about this mess.

Someone catapulted into me from the side brandishing a knife. I punched him squarely in the neck, and he dropped like a stone. Shouts told me I'd made someone happy by knocking out one of their enemies. Another dude decked out in black leather rushed me from the back. I knew he was coming, but I let him think he was getting away with something.

I swear, mortals' intelligence has been on the wane for the past hundred years. If Shit For Brains had any at all, he'd have recognized a dead-to-the-world five-year-old would have heard him bearing down on me. Timing is everything. I turned at the precise moment to hit him with a one-two combo to the gut and heart. I might have killed him, but I didn't care.

Once he was squealing and twitching at my feet, I cupped my hands around my mouth and amplified my voice with magic laced with you'd-better-do-what-I-say-or-your-days-will-be-numbered compulsion.

"Stop. Right Now." Three little words. No need to repeat them.

A slow lazy smile formed, stretching my face into an unaccustomed configuration. Yay me. I still had it. Everyone had frozen in place.

"Excellent," I went on, smooth as melted butter. "Everyone get the fuck out of here except your top dogs. Take the fallen with you."

As the crowd cleared, shuffling toward the door, another of my pit bosses scuttled to my side and cleared her throat. "Sorry, boss," Tatiana mumbled. "I went to find you, but your office was empty."

Kind of like your head.

I'd learned to squelch comments like that long ago. Mortals were notoriously thin-skinned, and Tatiana reeked of fear. She hadn't pissed herself, but it had been nip-and-tuck. Her blonde hair was in an updo, and her skin pale under heavy makeup. She would have been pretty without all the war paint. Blue eyes, her best feature, were framed by thick lashes, and she wore Lady Luck's standard employee uniform: white shirt and black pants. Most of the shirts carried the Lady Luck logo, a phoenix sinking into a crater.

The symbolism escaped everyone except me, and I'd never

been in a sharing mood when it came to questions like, "What's that mean, boss?" Besides, even if I told them it represented Faery's decline, they'd have thought I'd had too much to drink.

Meanwhile, four men had moved closer, but not too close. Like I said, I make humans nervous.

"Yeah?" One narrowed his eyes. "What'd you want us for?"

I nailed him with my gaze. I employ a glamour. It smooths the points of my ears and makes my eyes appear blue, rather than a mix of silver and gold with coppery centers. For the slightest of moments, I let it slip a notch, just a hint of a blur.

The dude rubbed his eyes. "Shit. Drunker than I thought." His words were slurred.

It was tempting to display more of what I really was. I shrugged it off. No point in making him yearn for the impossible. He'd be drawn to my deviant beauty. More than drawn. He'd twist himself into a pretzel for one more peek. If I'd wanted a lackey, sure, but I had other plans for him and his partners in crime.

"You have two choices," I told the men who were shifting from foot to foot as they looked mostly at the floor. "Grab mops and buckets and clean up the mess you made."

"Or?" One tried for a sneer, but didn't quite manage it.

"Or I hold you here and call the cops. Property damage is a felony. Bet you've had a few of those already."

I rocked back on my heels, waiting. Tatiana had drawn closer to me, not because I was warm and fuzzy, but because the thugs made her even more nervous than I did.

"Big talk. How are you planning to keep us from leaving?" Shit For Brains Number Two asked.

I swept an arm wide. "I don't have to. You're all on camera. I give the cops the feed and voila." I dusted my hands together. "I'm sure they know you already."

"We'll clean," he gritted out.

"It would go faster with more of us," another pointed out.

"Probably so, but I don't want 'more of you' in here," I told him. "While we're on that little topic, you and your gang members are barred from Lady Luck from here on in."

The one who'd said his life would be simpler with drones to order about drew himself up. "You can't do that, man."

"The hell I can't," I retorted and turned to Tatiana. "Show these fellows where the cleaning supplies are and oversee the work. They don't leave until you're satisfied they've done a good job."

Her blue eyes widened. "Erm. Maybe the head of janitorial would be better for that."

"He might be," I agreed, trying for an amiable tone, "but I assigned this job to you."

Something in my voice told her arguing was pointless. She'd run at the first whiff of fighting. That story about coming to find me had been pure fabrication. She rolled her shoulders back, barked, "Follow me," and loped across the expanse of parquet flooring.

After a pause a shade too long for my liking, the men turned to follow her. Just so there'd be no misunderstandings later, I called after them, "Don't even think about hassling her. If you do, I'll find out."

I left it there. No need to spell out what I'd do to their sorry, shitty asses if they made a grab for Tatiana's tits or any other part of her. I retreated to one side and wrapped myself in shadows. I wouldn't remain long, only until the cleanup project was underway.

I hadn't realized I'd clenched my hands into fists, and I uncurled my fingers one by one. Damn it, anyway. Everything was broken—and I didn't mean in this gaming room. I was here, straddling worlds, to mend what I could, but I hadn't made much progress.

Or any if I were honest.

Aye, and when I start lying to myself, I'm done for, a patronizing inner voice spouted off.

I wasn't the source of the original damage. It could be traced directly to the Fae court, who'd decided it would be a grand idea to kick Faery's gates open to mortals a century ago. Not that any of us ever cared about humans. We've always held them in contempt, but we wanted their money.

They'd done a bang-up job stripping their world of everything salable and grown filthy rich in the process. My kinsmen are drawn by gold—and I'd be lying if I said it didn't sing to me as well. We all love wealth, which is strange since our creature needs are taken care of in Faery.

At first, around the end of the 1800s, everything appeared to be going smoothly. We provided something not unlike a circus attraction for the well-heeled. One element none of us had reckoned on was Faery herself. Our land is alive, and she rebelled at the presence of those without power. Not right away, but when it happened the backlash was swift, sure, and brutal...

Buckets clattered as they rolled across the faux wooden floor. Some establishments have carpet. Not mine. For just this reason. My impromptu work crew dug in. Two men looked as if they'd never seen a mop before, but after Tatiana taunted them for being inept dicks, they shaped up.

I heard cheers from the strip show one floor up. No reason for me to stay here. I'd have it out with the dealers and croupiers at the all-staff meeting tomorrow afternoon. Tucking my hands into my pockets, I strolled through a wall, angling until I intersected a stairwell. Rather than naming the deserters, perhaps I'd be better served reiterating club policies to everyone.

The more I considered it, the better I liked my idea. I'd gin up something and have everyone e-sign it. I started to head for the floor show. Getting a gander at bouncing breasts and shaved pussies always settled my mind. Or diverted it, anyway. My cock thickened where it was tucked into my trousers, and I curled my fingers around it, enjoying sensation as it skittered through me.

Sex served as a reminder of the Witch. My cock grew more distended as I remembered her striking face and generous curves. To hell with the dancers in the lounge. I wanted the Witch—up close and personal.

If she was still in Lady Luck, I'd weave a lust spell, make her see only me. My errant member twitched against my fingers. "Yes, yes," I told my sidekick. "She'll want you so much, she won't be able to contain herself."

Rudy managed the blackjack and poker tables. A magnet

for card counters, they spanned two rooms on the second floor. I couldn't do much about my erection. It would be as useless as attempting to stuff a genie back into a bottle, so I crafted a diversion spell from my waist down. It would draw eyes away from the tented-out front of my pants.

I bounded into the nearest chamber, gratified by the small noises that verified Lady Luck was making money. Chips clicking, dealers calling for bets, and cries of delight as patrons raked in cash.

Rudy sidled up to me. "How'd it go?"

"It's handled. How about your assignment."

He screwed his face into an angry mask, adding ten years to his grizzled appearance. "I tried, but I'm not getting anywhere near that bitch ever again. She did something to her blackjack dealer."

"What do you mean, did something?" I added a jot of magical coercion to my question.

"He's not right. Won't look at me. Won't answer me."

Damn my eyes, it sure sounded like a hex. "Is she still at his table?"

Rudy nodded. "I told the dealer not to authorize payout, but—"

"Never mind. I'll take it from here."

"Thanks." For once, Rudy looked cowed, and embarrassed. Like most men, admitting defeat is right up there with swallowing glass shards.

The Witch wasn't in this room, so I crossed the hall and walked into the other one. The feel of her power smacked me mid-chest. Witch magic smells delightful. Aged whiskey and wildflowers with a touch of blood to blend everything together. This witch was old. I could tell from her scent and the extent of her power. It oozed from her and had wrapped around the dealer in visible strands.

Oberon's balls. She didn't need to count cards. She had the dealer in thrall. What did she think she was? A fucking Vampire? Whatever game she was running, she could damn well take it elsewhere.

I strode across the big room with its colorful tables. Horse races played on big screen televisions lining one wall. We took a bite out of bets placed on them too. Unlike a mortal, the Witch knew I was coming. I felt her attention, even though her back was turned.

A long skirt swirled around her sandal-clad feet. Made of a pale green sheer material, it offered tantalizing glances of long legs and made it clear she hadn't bothered with underwear. An equally sheer tunic made of silver fabric embroidered with violet runes covered her from shoulder to hip. Her shapely arms were bare. She told the dealer to hold up—in Gaelic—and he complied. I knew damn good and well Hector didn't speak Gaelic. He's Native American from a local reservation.

How deep in trance did she have him, anyway, that he responded to commands in a foreign tongue?

Slowly, tantalizingly, she twisted until she faced me, upper body first, followed by a two-step motion that bought her hips around. Her eyes were a pale, clear green, her face a study in perfection with high, slanted cheekbones, a regal forehead, and a strong chin.

When she smiled and ran her tongue over her lush lower lip, I dropped a hasty ward around myself. She could dupe a mortal—snare them in her spells—but I was Fae, and my interest in fucking her had staged a dramatic retreat.

The Witch angled her head to one side, still giving me come-hither vibes. "I know what you are," she purred.

Her words tossed still more cold water on my arousal. "Aye, and I know what ye are as well, Madame Witch," I growled back in Gaelic. "Get out of my casino."

Her full lips formed a pout. "You're no fun." Her magic intensified, pummeling my warding.

My control snapped and I grabbed her upper arm, squeezing hard. "Where is your coven? I will return you, as is my duty for any renegade Witch." I'd stuck to Gaelic, and an archaic form at that. Zero chance of anyone understanding it—other than Witchy-gal.

"No need to get tetchy." She yanked her arm, but I held fast.

"Your coven?" I added a whopping heap of compulsion to my query.

Her face twisted in pain, and I had a momentary twinge of conscience for forcing her. "Don't have one," she ground out.

Her reply had been true, but it shocked me. "Covens are a requirement," I lectured. "After the Witch uprising of 1943—"

A violent twist jerked her arm out of my grasp. "Don't lecture me on my own history," she hissed. "I'm...different."

"We all are, sweetheart," I told her tartly. "Misfits attract magic."

Her lips twitched into half a smile. "Hate to admit it, but that's catchy."

Fuckity-fuck. She was still trying to con me. "Yeah. Now beat it. And don't come back."

"But I need the money." Her pouty look was back.

"Not my problem, darling. Turn tricks. Get an honest job. Before you go, release my dealer from whatever you did to him."

"If I do, will you hire me?"

The question came out of left field, leaving me dumbstruck. Luckily, a loss for words never lasts long. I started to say hell would freeze over before I'd offer her work, but something stayed my tongue.

"Show up here at five tomorrow afternoon. We'll talk about it."

She tilted her chin and ran her gaze from my toes to my head. Something about her direct stare got me going all over again, even through my warding.

"Good enough." She nodded and walked to the dealer. Reaching into his pants pocket, she withdrew a charm, breathed on it, and we both watched it disintegrate into motes of light.

I eyed the dealer. He still stood motionless, a dreamy expression in place. "Get rid of the other ones too," I told her.

Breath swooshed from her mouth. "I was getting to them. Can't hurry these things or he might turn into the village idiot."

Village idiots predated medieval times, so I asked, "How old are you?"

"Never ask a lady her age," she retorted and retrieved two more charms. By the time they were dead, the dealer was starting to look more like a man and less like a puppet.

She regarded him and spoke a few words before turning to me. "There. Give it a few and he won't remember a thing about any of this. See you tomorrow." Her hips swung enticingly as she strode away.

"What's your name?" I called after her.

"You'll find out tomorrow. When I complete the employment application," she replied in mind speech, not bothering to turn around.

I was still sorting how a Witch had mastered telepathy, not a skill native to their magic, when the dealer made a grunting noise. "Boss. What happened? I feel...off."

"Take a break," I told him. "Back to your table in fifteen."

Without waiting for more questions, I walked out of the card room. It was only an hour from closing time. I could skip the rest of tonight's never-ending drama and slip into Faery. My magic needed a boost, and my mind a rest. The mortal world dragged at me, drained my essence, and made me long for an earlier time.

One before we'd opened our doors to humankind.

KEEP right on reading Court of Rogues.

About the Author

Ann Gimpel is a USA Today bestselling author. A lifelong aficionado of the unusual, she began writing speculative fiction a few years ago. Since then her short fiction has appeared in many webzines and anthologies. Her longer books run the gamut from urban fantasy to paranormal romance. Once upon a time, she nurtured clients. Now she nurtures dark, gritty fantasy stories that push hard against reality. When she's not writing, she's in the backcountry getting down and dirty with her camera. She's published over 100 books to date, with several more planned for 2023 and beyond. A husband, grown children, grandchildren, and wolf hybrids round out her family.

Keep up with her at www.anngimpel.com or http://anngimpel.blogspot.com

If you enjoyed what you read, get in line for special offers and pre-release special reads. Newsletter Signup!

ALSO BY ANN GIMPEL

Circle of Assassins

Shira

Quinn

Rhiana

Kylian

Grigori

Coven Enforcers

Blood and Magic

Blood and Sorcery

Blood and Illusion

Demon Assassins

Witch's Bounty

Witch's Bane

Witches Rule

Dragon Heir

Dragon's Call

Dragon's Blood

Dragon's Heir

Dragon Lore

Highland Secrets

To Love a Highland Dragon

Dragon Maid

Dragon's Dare

Dragon Fury

Earth Reclaimed

Earth's Requiem

Earth's Blood

Earth's Hope

Elemental Witch

Timespell

Time's Curse

Time's Hostage

Gatekeeper

Shadow Reaper

Rebel Reaper

Untamed Reaper

GenTech Rebellion

Winning Glory

Honor Bound

Claiming Charity

Loving Hope

Keeping Faith

Ice Dragon

Feral Ice

Cursed Ice

Primal Ice

Magick and Misfits (Fall and Winter 2020)

Court of Rogues

Midnight Court

Court of the Fallen

Court of Destiny

Rubicon International

Garen

Lars

Soul Dance

Tarnished Beginnings

Tarnished Legacy

Tarnished Prophecy

Tarnished Journey

Soul Storm

Dark Prophecy

Dark Pursuit

Dark Promise

Underground Heat

Roman's Gold

Wolf Born

Blood Bond

Wayward Mage

Hands of Fate

Jinxed

Hunted

Salvaged

Tiana

Wolf Clan Shifters

Alice's Alphas

Megan's Mates

Sophie's Shifters

Wylde Magick

Gemstone

Lion's Lair

Unbalanced

STANDALONE BOOKS

Branded, That Old Black Magic Romance (paranormal romance)

Edge of Night (short story collection, paranormal and horror)

Grit is a 4-Letter Word (nonfiction)

Heart's Flame (post-apocalyptic romance)

Icy Passage (science fiction romance)

Marked by Fortune (post-apocalyptic coming of age story)

Melis's Gambit (historical paranormal romance)

Midnight Magic (paranormal romance)

Red Dawn (post-apocalyptic paranormal romance)

Shadow Play (historical paranormal romance)

Shadows in Time (Highland time travel romance)

Since We Fell (contemporary romance)

Warin's War (paranormal romance)